STORIES THAT COUNT

HOLT, RINEHART AND WINSTON, INC.
New York Chicago San Francisco Atlanta
Dallas Montreal Toronto

STORIES THAT COUNT

Edited by
William A. Roecker
University of Arizona

Library of Congress Catalog Card Number: 78-126799
SBN: 03-084146-1
Printed in the United States of America
0123 40 9 8 7 6 5 4 3 2 1

For Bob Lacy, Ralph Salisbury and my other teachers, and with thanks and respect for the authors who wrote these stories.

disbelief. He gaped, seeing nothing but the flat shelf of rock. He whirled, started toward the boys, slipped, recovered himself, fetched a complete circle, and stared at the unimaginably empty shelf. Its emptiness made him feel as if everything he had done that day so far he had dreamed. What could have happened? The tide was still nearly a foot below. There had been no sea to speak of. The skiff could hardly have slid off by itself. For the life of him, consciously careful as he inveterately was, he could not now remember hauling it up the last time. Perhaps in the heat of hunting, he had left it to the boy. Perhaps he could not remember which was the last time.

"Christ—" he exclaimed loudly, without realizing it because he was so entranced by the invisible event.

"What's wrong, Dad?" asked his son, getting to his feet.

The fisherman went blind with uncontainable rage. "Get back down there where you belong!" he screamed. He scarcely noticed the boy sink back in amazement. In a frenzy he ran along the ledge thinking the skiff might have been drawn up at another place, though he knew better. There was no other place.

He stumbled, half falling, back to the boys who were gawking at him in consternation, as though he had gone insane. "God damn it!" he yelled savagely, grabbing both of them and yanking them to their knees. "Get on your feet!"

"What's wrong?" his son repeated in a stifled voice.

"Never mind what's wrong," he snarled. "Look for the skiff—it's adrift!" When they peered around he gripped their shoulders, brutally facing them about. "Down wind—" He slammed his fist against his thigh. "Jesus!" he cried, struck to madness at their stupidity.

At last he sighted the skiff himself, magically bobbing along the grim sea like a toller, a quarter of a mile to leeward on a direct course for home. The impulse to strip himself naked was succeeded instantly by a queer calm. He simply sat down on the ledge and forgot everything except the marvellous mystery.

As his awareness partially returned he glanced toward the boys. They were still observing the skiff speechlessly. Then he was gazing into the clear young eyes of his son.

"Dad," asked the boy steadily, "what do we do now?"

That brought the fisherman upright. "The first thing we have to do," he heard himself saying with infinite tenderness as if he were making love, "is think."

"Could you swim it?" asked his son.

He shook his head and smiled at them. They smiled quickly back, too quickly. "A hundred yards maybe, in this water. I wish I could," he added. It was the most intimate and pitiful thing he had ever said. He walked in circles round them, trying to break the stall his mind was left in.

He gauged the level of the water. To the eye it was quite stationary, six inches from the shelf at this second. The fisherman did not have to mark it on the side of the rock against the passing of time to prove to his reason that it was rising, always rising. Already it was over the brink of reason, beyond the margins of thought—a senseless measurement. No sense to it.

All his life the fisherman had tried to lick the element of time, by getting up earlier and going to bed later, owning a faster boat, planning more than the day would hold, and tackling just one other job before the deadline fell. If, as on rare occasions he had the grand illusion, he ever really had beaten the game, he would need to call on all his reserves of practice and cunning now.

He sized up the scant but unforgivable three hundred yards to Brown Cow Island. Another hundred yards behind it his boat rode at anchor, where, had he been aboard, he could have cut in a fathometer to plumb the profound and occult seas, or a ship-to-shore radio on which in an interminable short time he would have heard his wife's voice talking to him over the air about homecoming.

"Couldn't we wave something so somebody would see us?" his nephew suggested.

The fisherman spun round. "Load your guns!" he ordered. They loaded as if the air had suddenly gone frantic with birds. "I'll fire once and count to five. Then you fire. Count to five. That way they won't just think it's only somebody gunning ducks. We'll keep doing that."

"We've only got just two-and-a-half boxes left," said his son.

The fisherman nodded, understanding that from beginning to end their situation was purely mathematical, like the ticking of the alarm clock in his silent bedroom. Then he fired. The dog, who had been keeping watch over the decoys, leaped forward and yelped in confusion. They all counted off, fired the first five rounds by threes, and reloaded. The fisherman scanned first the horizon, then the contracting borders of the ledge, which was the sole place the water appeared to be climbing. Soon it would be over the shelf.

They counted off and fired the second five rounds. "We'll hold off a while on the last one," the fisherman told the boys. He sat down and pondered what a trivial thing was a skiff. This one he and the boy had knocked together in a day. Was a gun, manufactured for killing.

His son tallied up the remaining shells, grouping them symmetrically in threes on the rock when the wet box fell apart. "Two short," he announced. They reloaded and laid the guns on their knees.

Behind thickening clouds they could not see the sun going down. The water, coming up, was growing blacker. The fisherman thought he might have told his wife they would be home before dark since it was Christmas day. He realized he had forgotten about its being any particular day. The tide would not be high until two hours after sunset. When they did not get in by nightfall, and could not be raised by radio, she might send somebody to hunt for them right away. He rejected this arithmetic immediately, with a sickening shock, recollecting it was a two-and-a-half hour run at best. Then it occurred to him that she might send somebody on the mainland who was nearer. She would think he had engine trouble.

He rose and searched the shoreline, barely visible. Then his glance dropped to the toy shoreline at the edges of the reef. The shrinking ledge, so sinister from a boat, grew dearer minute by minute as though the whole wide world he gazed on from horizon to horizon balanced on its contracting rim. He checked the water level and found the shelf awash.

Some of what went through his mind the fisherman told to the boys. They accepted it without comment. If he caught their eyes they looked away to spare him or because they were not yet old enough to face what they saw. Mostly they watched the rising water. The fisherman was unable to initiate a word of encouragement. He wanted one of them to ask him whether somebody would reach them ahead of the tide. He would have found it possible to say yes. But they did not inquire.

The fisherman was not sure how much, at their age, they were able to imagine. Both of them had seen from the docks drowned bodies put ashore out of boats. Sometimes they grasped things, and sometimes not. He supposed they might be longing for the comfort of their mothers, and was astonished, as much as he was capable of any astonishment except the supreme one, to discover himself wishing he had not left his wife's dark, close, naked bed that morning.

"Is it time to shoot now?" asked his nephew.

"Pretty soon," he said, as if he were putting off making good on a promise. "Not yet."

His own boy cried softly for a brief moment, like a man, his face averted in an effort neither to give or show pain.

"Before school starts," the fisherman said, wonderfully detached, "we'll go to town and I'll buy you boys anything you want."

With great difficulty, in a dull tone as though he did not in the least desire it, his son said after a pause, "I'd like one of those new thirty-horse outboards."

"All right," said the fisherman. And to his nephew, "How about you?"

The nephew shook his head desolately. "I don't want anything," he said.

After another pause the fisherman's son said, "Yes he does, Dad. He wants one too."

"All right—" the fisherman said again, and said no more.

The dog whined in uncertainty and licked the boys' faces where they sat together. Each threw an arm over his back and hugged him. Three strays flew in and sat companionably down among the stiff-necked decoys. The dog crouched, obedient to his training. The boys observed them listlessly. Presently, sensing something untoward, the ducks took off, splashing the wave tops with feet and wingtips, into the dusty waste.

The sea began to make up in the mounting wind, and the wind bore a new and deathly chill. The fisherman, scouring the somber, dwindling shadow of the mainland for a sign, hoped it would not snow. But it did. First a few flakes, then a flurry, then storming past horizontally. The fisherman took one long, bewildered look at Brown Cow Island three hundred yards dead to leeward, and got to his feet.

Then it shut in, as if what was happening on the ledge was too private even for the last wan light of the expiring day.

"Last round," the fisherman said austerely.

The boys rose and shouldered their tacit guns. The fisherman fired into the flying snow. He counted methodically to five. His son fired and counted. His nephew. All three fired and counted. Four rounds.

"You've got one left, Dad," his son said.

The fisherman hesitated another second, then he fired the final shell. Its pathetic report, like the spat of a popgun, whipped away on the wind and was instantly blanketed in falling snow.

Night fell all in a moment to meet the ascending sea. They were now barely able to make one another out through driving snowflakes, dim as ghosts in their yellow oilskins. The fisherman heard a sea break and glanced down where his feet were. They seemed to be wound in a snowy sheet. Gently he took the boys by the shoulders and pushed them in front of him, feeling with his feet along the shallow sump to the place where it triangulated into a sharp crevice at the highest point of the ledge. "Face ahead," he told them. "Put the guns down."

"I'd like to hold mine, Dad," begged his son.

"Put it down," said the fisherman. "The tide won't hurt it. Now brace your feet against both sides and stay there."

They felt the dog, who was pitch black, running up and down in perplexity between their straddled legs. "Dad," said his son, "what about the pooch?"

If he had called the dog by name it would have been too personal. The fisherman would have wept. As it was he had all he could do to keep from laughing. He bent his knees, and when he touched the dog hoisted him under one arm. The dog's belly was soaking wet.

So they waited, marooned in their consciousness, surrounded by a monstrous tidal space which was slowly, slowly closing them out. In this space the periwinkle beneath the fisherman's boots was king. While hovering airborne in his mind he had an inward glimpse of his house as curiously separate, like a June mirage.

Snow, rocks, seas, wind the fisherman had lived by all his life. Now he thought he had never comprehended what they were, and he hated them. Though they had not changed. He was deadly chilled. He set out to ask the boys if they were cold. There was no sense. He thought of the whiskey, and sidled backward, still holding the awkward dog, till he located the bottle under water with his toe. He picked it up squeamishly as though afraid of getting his sleeve wet, worked his way forward and bent over his son. "Drink it," he said, holding the bottle against the boy's ribs. The boy tipped his head back, drank, coughed hotly, then vomited.

"I can't," he told his father wretchedly.

"Try—try—" the fisherman pleaded, as if it meant the difference between life and death.

The boy obediently drank, and again he vomited hotly. He shook his head against his father's chest and passed the bottle forward to his cousin, who drank and vomited also. Passing the bottle back, the boys dropped it in the frigid water between them.

When the waves reached his knees the fisherman set the warm dog loose and said to his son. "Turn around and get up on my shoulders." The boy obeyed. The fisherman opened his oilskin jacket and twisted his hands behind him through his suspenders, clamping the boy's booted ankles with his elbows.

"What about the dog?" the boy asked.

"He'll make his own way all right," the fisherman said. "He can take the cold water." His knees were trembling. Every instinct shrieked for gymnastics. He ground his teeth and braced like a colossus against the sides of the submerged crevice.

The dog, having lived faithfully as though one of them for eleven years, swam a few minutes in and out around the fisherman's legs, not knowing what was happening, and left them without a whimper. He would swim and swim at random by himself, round and round in the blinding night, and when he had swum routinely through the paralyzing water all he could, he would simply, in one incomprehensible moment drown. Almost the fisherman, waiting out infinity, envied him his pattern.

Freezing seas swept by, flooding inexorably up and up as the earth sank away imperceptibly beneath them. The boy called out once to his cousin. There was no answer. The fisherman, marvelling on a terror without voice, was dumbly glad when the boy did not call again. His own boots were long full of water. With no sensation left in his straddling legs he dared not move them. So long as the seas came sidewise against his hips, and then sidewise against his shoulders, he might balance—no telling how long. The upper half of him was what felt frozen. His legs, disengaged from his nerves and his will, he came to regard quite scientifically. They were the absurd, precarious axis around which reeled the surged universal tumult. The waves would come on and on; he could not visualize how many tossing reinforcements lurked in the night beyond—inexhaustible numbers, and he wept in supernatural fury at each because it was higher, till he transcended hate and took them, swaying like a convert, one by one as they lunged against him and away aimlessly into their own undisputed, wild realm.

From his hips upward the fisherman stretched to his utmost as a man does whose spirit reaches out of dead sleep. The boy's head, none too high, must be at least seven feet above the ledge. Though growing larger every minute, it was a small light life. The fisherman meant to hold it there, if need be, through a thousand tides.

By and by the boy, slumped on the head of his father, asked, "Is it over your boots, Dad?"

"Not yet," the fisherman said. Then through his teeth he added, "If I fall—kick your boots off—swim for it—downwind—to the island. . . ."

"You . . . ?" the boy finally asked.

The fisherman nodded against the boy's belly. "—Won't see each other," he said.

The boy did for the fisherman the greatest thing that can be done. He may have been too young for perfect terror, but he was old enough to know there were things beyond the power of any man. All he could do he did, by trusting his father to do all he could, and asking nothing more.

The fisherman, rocked to his soul by a sea, held his eyes shut upon the interminable night.

"Is it time now?" the boy said.

The fisherman could hardly speak. "Not yet," he said. "Not just yet."

As the land mass pivoted toward sunlight the day after Christmas, a tiny fleet of small craft converged off shore like iron filings to a magnet. At daybreak they found the skiff floating unscathed off the headland, half full of ducks and snow. The shooting *had* been good, as someone hearing on the nearby mainland the previous afternoon had supposed. Two hours afterward they found the unharmed boat adrift five miles at sea. At high noon they found the fisherman at ebb tide, his right foot jammed cruelly into a glacial crevice of the ledge beside three shotguns, his hands tangled behind him in his suspenders, and under his right elbow a rubber boot with a sock and a live starfish in it. After dragging unlit depths all day for the boys, they towed the fisherman home in his own boat at sundown, and in the frost of evening, mute, laid him on his wharf for his wife to see.

She, somehow, standing on the dock as in her frequent dream, gazing at the fisherman pure as crystal on the icy boards, a small rubber boot still frozen under one clenched arm, saw him exaggerated beyond remorse or grief, absolved of his mortality.

William A. Kittredge
1932-

William Kittredge has been a football player, an aerial reconnaissance photo interpreter and a ranch foreman. He was born in Portland, Oregon, studied with Bernard Malamud at Oregon State University, and is presently completing a novel. "The Waterfowl Tree" was inspired by Hall's story "The Ledge," but it works on other, more sophisticated levels. Coming of manhood is the theme here, but the story has a nearly mystical strength that may be gained through the combination of the harsh eastern Oregon climate and powerful characters. "The Waterfowl Tree" was first published in the *Northwest Review* in 1966, and received an O. Henry honorable mention that year. This is the first time it has been anthologized.

THE WATERFOWL TREE

They ran into snow almost two hours before reaching the valley. Soon the storm and twilight and narrow road combined, and the station wagon only crept through near darkness. "Be a long haul," the man said. "Eva will be wondering."

His son, tall and seventeen, sat huddled and finally warm. He rested his hands behind his neck and watched out the glazed and crusted side windows at the indeterminate light. This mention of the woman could be a signal, some special beginning.

"Is she a pretty woman?" he asked.

"Pretty enough for me. And that's pretty enough."

"What color is her hair?"

"Kind of brown, I guess." The man laughed in the darkness and hammered at his son's knee. He was a massive, dark-faced and hulking man, a widower in his late fifties. "I've got too old for worrying about pretty," he said. "All I want is gentle. When you want that, you're getting old."

"I remember hunting when I was a kid," the man said, breaking a long silence. "It was different then, more birds and you had to kill something with every shot."

"How do you mean?" the boy asked.

"We were meat hunters. You spent money for shells, you brought

Published originally in *Northwest Review*, University of Oregon, Eugene, Oregon, 1966. Reprinted by permission of William Kittredge and *Northwest Review*.

home meat. I saw a boy die on that very account. Went off into open water chest deep, just to get some birds he shot. Cramped up and drowned. We hauled a boat down and fished him out that afternoon." The snow began to thin and the man pushed the car faster and concentrated on his driving.

"It was like this then," he said. "Snowing and ice a foot thick and below zero all day."

The boy looked at his father, shadowed and defined by the instrument lights. He wished the man would go on talking, tell these unsuspected things. But the man, long estranged from this remote and misted valley of his childhood, an early traveler, sat hunched over the wheel, absorbed in the road.

"I guess it was different in those days," the boy said.

"Quite a bit different," his father answered. "A different life altogether."

After that they drove in warm silence. It was completely dark when they came out of the storm, driving through the last drifting flakes into the light of a pure three-quarter moon and an intense and still cold that made the new snow crystallize and occasionally sparkle in the headlights.

"Freeze solid by morning," the man said. "Be some new birds coming in."

Then he stopped the car and switched off the headlights.

"Look there," he said, pointing to the west.

The boy cranked down the frozen side window and looked across the distorted landscape of snow, blue and subdued in the moonlight, and saw a high ridge of shadowed darkness.

"That's the rim," his father said. "We'll be home directly."

The boy looked again at the black fault. How could this be home, this walled place?

"All my life," the man said, "in strange places, I've caught myself looking up and expecting to see that rim. Under the rim is home."

The long attic room, unfinished, peak roofed and raftered, was filled with darkness, illuminated by blue softness where moonlight shone through windows on either end. On the floor and inward sloping east wall he could see diffuse, square-framed and reflected cold light. The boy lay in the bundled warmth of a mummy bag on an iron cot and watched the light and imagined that he could see it move, slowly climb the wall as the moon dropped. The cold in this shedlike room above the barn frosted his breath when he moved.

"You're young and tough," his father had said. "You draw the outdoor room."

They unloaded the boy's suitcase and the new gear quickly in the darkness, trying to be quiet because the house across the road was completely dark and sleeping. Then his father led with a flashlight and they carried the gear up a creaking flight of stairs on the side of the ancient barn and pushed through the hanging door that opened into this long, barren room. After unrolling the sleeping bag on the cot, his father gripped him by the shoulder and shone the light in his face.

"You'll be warm inside the bag," the man said. "Sleep in your clothes. That way they won't be frozen in the morning. Stick the boots under you. We'll get you up for breakfast."

Then he turned and took the light and left the boy standing in the cold. What warmth would greet his father in that dark house among trees across the road? The place had been come upon after rounding a curve in the gravel road that crossed the upper part of the valley. Trees and a house and barn and some fallen-over corrals, just that in the midst of unending fields of fenced snow.

The boots made a comforting hump and the boy curled around them and tried to warm himself, and wished he were back in his bed at school, enduring the vacation, guessing about tomorrow's movie.

But warmth came and with it a quiet numbness and he felt himself drift and then slept, almost surprised that he was not going to lie awake and search for a sense of how it would be in the morning.

And now, just as quickly, he was awake and watching the slow light on the far wall. Then he recognized, almost unnoticed among his thoughts, an ancient crying. Coyotes. He smiled and huddled in his warmth, secure against their night. The calls came fine and clear and he struggled to get an arm out of the warmth and looked at his watch, illuminated in the darkness. It was almost three o'clock.

The wailing stopped and there was silence.

Geese were flying. He could hear, farther away, but clear and distinct, their wandering call. He was warm and slipping again into peaceful sleep. Then the coyotes began with a long and undulating wail and small yipping. He rested his head on his arm and then slept, lulled by their noise and a small rhythm of his own.

A hand shook him, gently and firmly, and for a moment he was elsewhere and lost, then awake the remembering. He pushed up from the interior warmth of the sleeping bag and looked out at the morning, at the smile of this strange woman and at the faintly yellow, silver-frosted windows and the rough shingle and rafter roof. His breath was frozen and swirled softly in this still colder morning air and he smiled at the woman and stretched his arms into the cold. The woman stood posed at his side, leaning with one hand touching him through the layers of the sleeping bag.

"Welcome," she said. "On the coldest day in a thousand years."

Really nothing but a fuzzy-headed woman. She was bundled in hunting clothes and wore a down cap tied under her chin with fringes and curls of hair protruding. Not the expected woman. The face was heavier and older than he had imagined and he experienced the tiny revelation that his father was almost an old man, really different and much changed from the remembered man of childhood.

"You must be Eva."

"The same," she said. "The famous Eva. Come on, breakfast is almost ready."

"I can't." He grinned, surprised at her easiness, taken in spite of himself. "I haven't any pants on."

"Come on. I won't look if I can help myself." She pulled on his arm, then caught a handful of his hair, tugging him up.

It seemed a joke and he scrambled out of bed and was shocked at the cold and jumped in dismay when she grabbed one of his bare ankles with both ice cold, slender hands. He struggled and escaped and she dropped the mittens she had tucked under one arm and began rummaging in the bed, fishing in his warm darkness and finally pulling out his pants and coat while he wrapped his arms around himself and watched. "Get 'em on," she said. When he finished, the boots were standing in front of him, open and ready.

The wide space between the tree-surrounded house and the barn was ankle-deep in new snow and marked only by their tracks of the night before and her footprints of this morning. The trees in front of the house were heaped with ice and snow, molded in the morning sunlight. He had to squint against the glare.

The house was rough and worn and old, whitepainted inside, with a bare plank floor and homemade wooden chairs and a long table with benches for furniture. The boy stood in the doorway and felt with pleasure the shock of warm, moist air that softened his face. In one corner of this main room was a wood stove with chopped wood and kindling in a box beside it. His father sat on a stool beside the stove, filling shell belts. Open shell boxes were scattered around him on the floor.

"Come on in," the man said. "Close the door. Charlie will have breakfast on in a minute."

Through an open doorway on the far side of the room came the reflection of morning sunlight, out of a back room where he could see another, smaller man working over a cook stove. The woman began pulling off her cap and coat, piling them on the far end of the table. No one, not even the woman, paid attention to the water and melting ice on the floor.

"Jesus Christ," the woman said, brushing her hair back and tucking her shirt in her pants. "It's so damned cold out there he could have froze."

"Make you tough, won't it boy." His father looked up, directly at him.

"It wasn't bad," the boy said. "I was warm."

"That's the spirit." The man stood, dropping the finished shell belts from his lap to the floor. "Come on."

The boy followed into the next room where the little man was tending a frying pan full of eggs and another with bacon. "This is Charlie Anderson," his father said. "Me and Charlie are hunting partners. From the old days."

This was Charlie from the past, dark and smooth-faced in his heavy woolen shirt, looking younger, but still as old as his father. He turned and shook hands with the boy. "Glad to have you, son," he said. "Eat in a minute."

Then Charlie smiled and went back to his cooking.

"Come here." His father, huge in boots and khaki gear, walked to the far end of the kitchen and opened a door to the outside. The boy followed and the cold was at him again, hard and stiff.

"Look at that," his father said. Behind the house was a small orchard of six or seven trees. The tree nearest the house, gnarled and holding winter limbs towards the thin sky, was hung with dead birds. They were in bunches of a dozen or more, strung together on short pieces of rope and suspended from heavy nails driven into the limbs, crusted with ice and frozen and absolutely still, frosted and sparkling in the light. Most hung about eye level, some higher.

"Deep freeze," the man said. "We hung them like that when we were kids."

The boy supposed that he should say something to please his father but was not sure what that would be. He turned away from the tree and looked to the west where the winter rim he had seen in the moonlight rose high over the far edge of the valley. Through the still air he could define individual trees among the groves of juniper along its upper edge. He heard the geese calling again and looked to see them flying, distant and wavering, and remembered the night before. 'They sound so far away," he said.

"We'll get after them," his father said. "Soon as we eat."

The boy turned and looked again at the tree, hung with dead birds. He was unable to feel anything beyond his own chill.

"We hung them there when I was a kid," his father said. "A man named Basston owned this place and my old man would bring me down here to help out on the weekends. There would be a crowd all season—

city men. I guess he lost money in the crash, anyway they stopped coming. Let's eat."

The boy watched his father turn and go in and saw him new, surprised at the life that had been his father's. Maybe that's why he brought me here, he thought. To let me see what he was.

"Coming," he said, and closed the door behind himself, hungry and glad for the warmth.

The boy huddled lower in the blind of tules and reeds and wished the birds would hurry and come again. He and his father sat hidden only a few yards from a small patch of open water on a neck of land in the tule swamps of the valley. They were alone and a long way from the warmth of the station wagon.

"I'll take you with me," the man said when they first spotted the birds with field glasses. He pointed far off from where they were parked above the frozen swamp, and the boy saw them, milling and keeping a stirred bit of water open and free of ice. A fantastic sight through the glasses—thousands of ducks crowding in the water and great bunches of Honkers and lesser Canadians walking the ice around them.

"Eva and Charlie can go over and wait at the decoys," his father said. "Give us two shots at them."

No one said anything, and after straightening the tangled gear in the back of the station wagon, the four of them walked off, two in each direction. He and his father walked in a long arc around the birds, to come up on them from the sheltered land side and get as close as possible before they flushed. "Lots of time," his father said, after they walked a half mile or so. He was panting and sweating in the heavy gear. "Give Eva and Charlie time to get over to the decoys."

And their stalk was a good one. They had five green head Mallard drakes and two hens between them. "Pick the green heads," his father whispered before they came up shooting. "Pick one each time before you shoot."

The geese had been too wise and flushed early, taking a few ducks with them, but the main flock of ducks were almost too easy, standing nearly still in the air during the long and suddenly clamorous second as they flushed, rising in waves and giving time to reload and shoot again before the total mass was gone. His first two shots had simply been pulled off into the rising mass. Then he remembered his father's words and aimed carefully and selectively.

After the first flush, the man and the boy dropped into tules near the water's edge, leaving the dead birds on the ice, and the thousands of ducks grouped and then turned in the distance and came back at them in long whirring masses, always sensing something and veering off before getting into shooting range, but filling the air with the coming and mounting rush of their wings. The boy, awed nearly to tears by the sight above him and the sound of flight, sat concealed by his father and was unable and unready to shoot again.

"Charlie and I used to hunt here when we were kids," the man said. "This is the real coming back. I remember waking in the spring when the birds were flying north. I could hear them from my bed and then I would go out and stand on the knoll behind the house and watch them leave and hear them calling and smell the corrals and just look at the valley where it had turned green and then over at the rim with a little snow near the top. I guess those were the best days I ever lived." The man talked softly all the time the birds were in the air and the boy half-listened to him and sucked in his breath waiting for the birds to come wheeling at them again, thinking the sound of their flight the most simply beautiful thing he had ever heard.

Then the birds stopped coming back and he and his father went out on the ice and gathered the dead ones, five green heads and the two hens, and carried them back to the hiding place. "The dead ones scared them off," his father said. "Now we'll have to wait awhile on the Honkers."

And so they waited, the boy trying to be comfortable in the heavy clothing and the man talking, remembering.

"We used to haul the birds back to the house in a wagon. There was ten times as many in those days and lots of Canvas Backs and Redheads. You don't see them any more." The man moved quietly around their nest, pulling reeds together over them until they were completely hidden.

"I remember one afternoon when the wind was blowing and the clouds were below the rim and we sat in one place, just Charlie and me, fourteen years old, and shot up over a case of old man Basston's 12 gauge shells. The birds kept coming and settling their wings into the wind and we just kept on shooting. We killed over a hundred and fifty birds that one afternoon. It was almost night when we got back to camp and we hung those birds in the dark and old man Basston came out and we stood under that tree and he gave each of us a couple of drinks of the best bourbon whiskey on earth and sent us to bed like men. I guess that was the best day, the tops in my life."

Had everything been downhill since? The boy understood, or hoped that he did, why he was here, that his father was trying to make up, to present a sight of life before the time had completely passed. Was this only for himself he wondered and listened to his father talking and thought of this woman and the others and the different man his father had become in this place.

Eventually the geese came back, very high and veed out in their great formations, then dropped and started to wheel when they saw the water.

They seemed endless, long flights coming one before the next, circling and wheeling and dropping. "I'll tell you when," the man said. "Just lay quiet."

The first flight had landed and was calming itself in the water and on the edge of the ice when the next, under a larger flight of ducks, came directly over them, settling on stiff wings, falling directly towards the water, unconscious and intent. "Now," the man said, and they rose, waist deep in the tules, and shot three times each and dropped six birds easily, the huge black and white geese dropping dead and broken with an inert thud to the ice.

"That's it," his father said. "Beautiful shooting. Enough for this day. They'll be back."

The birds scattered and wheeled above them while they went out on the ice and began to pick up the dead. They were heavy and warm birds and the boy twisted their necks the way his father did and felt sorry that they could not have lived and yet was glad that they were dead. They were trophies of this world, soft and heavy and damp dead birds.

"We'll sit around this afternoon and play some four-handed gin," his father said, after they had gathered the birds. "You ever play gin?"

"Sure," the boy said. "For pennies and buttons." They strung the ducks together on a short piece of rope and the geese together on another. "You carry the ducks," his father said. "I'll bring the geese. We'll go back on the ice."

It was a mile directly across to where the station wagon sat on a knoll, and the going was slick and tricky with the new snow sliding on the ice. The boy walked gingerly at first, then faster. Soon he was well out ahead of the man. His father came slowly and solidly, breathing heavily and sliding back with each step.

Far away the rim was a sharply defined upper edge on reality and between them and that high point the boy watched the ever increasing, now incessantly flying and clamorous birds, some clear in the flat sky and others almost indistinguishable against the snow and rock patterned slope of the rim.

Behind him a distant, muffled cry.

He turned and the man was gone, only to reappear far behind, floundering and chest deep. The boy dropped the shotgun and birds and ran towards his father.

While running he saw the man raise himself violently and wave, shout soundlessly, then fall away.

The cry, whatever it was, he heard distantly, some command to stay back, more intuited than understood, and he ran on, slipping and falling, towards the now visible hole in the ice. The water steamed and the ice, incredibly, was soft and only inches thick, and the geese, on their little rope, floated beside the man.

The man waved him back and the boy stopped, yards short of the edge, watched his father for some sign of what had happened, what to do.

The man stood quietly in the steaming and putrid water, gasping and dripping. He had been completely submerged and now the water was under his armpits. "Stay there," the man said finally, as he began to shake. "There's a hot spring and the ice is rotten." He slowly regained his breath.

"Let me rest a little," he said. "Then I'll try to work my way over to the solid ice."

The boy stood helpless, saw that the edges of this broken and jagged water had begun to freeze again, solidifying as he watched. "The cold," he said. "Can you stand it?"

"It's not so bad here," the man said, composed now and shaking less and speaking quietly. "But it'll be cold out there."

Then the man began to move again, working slowly, pulling each leg out of the deep bottom mud and then going forward another step. He made it almost to the edge of the ice and then stopped. "God Almighty," he said. "It's so Gaddamned cold."

And then the boy stood and watched his father mutter again, something subdued and private, saw his face begin to collapse, the rough and dark, always-remembered face drawing into itself and growing distant. The man began to thrash and move forward in lunges, finally reaching towards the edge of the ice, then hesitating as though suspended with the floating geese, fighting and gasping towards the boy.

Clutching, watching the boy, he simply rolled backwards, eyes turning finally sightless, inwards and blank, and then sank, clasping and flailing at himself and the entangled birds and then bubbling and thrashing out of sight and then nothing but the water bubbling.

And then no bubbles, nothing but the dead geese floating quietly, their heads pulled under the surface by the rope that still encircled his own father's body.

The boy heard again the distant honking of the flying geese and the beautiful whirring flight as a lonesome trio of ducks came directly at him and suddenly swung away.

He turned and began to rush erratically, scrambled and slipped across the open ice between himself and the station wagon, left the shotgun and the string of ducks on the ice.

Back in the station wagon with the heater turned on, he began to shake and curled before the warmth and dissolved into it, uncomprehending.

This time he awoke in the soft and warm shadowed darkness of an unknown room and wondered what place this was. And then, with final swiftness, he was again in the moment of the inexplicable thing that had happened, his father's eyes rolling backwards. He knew that it had happened and was then himself, understood that this was one of the bedrooms in the strange house. He rolled his feet onto the floor and was surprised to find himself only in his underwear. A door slammed in another part of the house and he heard a voice, the woman.

"I wonder if he's still sleeping?"

She appeared in the dim doorway.

"He's awake," she said over her shoulder, speaking to some unseen person.

She came into the room and turned on the light. Her hair was brushed smooth and away from her face, fell in new waves to her shoulders. She looked younger, he thought, out of place. He pulled the sheets over his bare legs.

"I'm all right now," he said, then hesitated. "Did they fish him out?"

"He is out." The woman spoke formally and slowly, showing, he thought, that they were still really strangers. "And now it is night. You slept a long time."

"How could that have happened? Just gone that quick?"

"It was the hot spring," she said. "He knew it was there and must have forgotten."

"Yes, he must've." And so he too could forget. The boy turned and collapsed on the bed, face down and fighting to keep from crying and dissolving into the terror of what can happen.

The woman turned off the light and came across the room to him. "Try to rest," she said. "I'm going to bed now."

The boy rolled face up. "What a stupid thing," he said.

"Your father loved this place. He told me it was the only surely happy place in his life. I'll be back." She walked out of the room, leaving the boy stranded in the middle of the unfamiliar bed.

The only happy place. And what of all the other places? A home somewhere and all the others? He turned to the pillow and this time wept and did not understand why, if for his loss or his father's.

Eventually the woman returned, wearing a brocade robe that reached the floor and with her hair pulled back and knotted behind her head. He turned and looked at her in the dim light and saw her drop the robe and pull back the covers on the other side of the bed and get beneath, flinching when she touched the sheets.

"It'll get cold," she said.

"I can't stay here like this."

"No. Stay and we'll talk." She reached out and took him by the arm and pulled him towards her and he was again surprised at the coldness of her hands.

"Why?" he said. "Why did it happen?"

"His heart," she said. "He had been having trouble."

"But why should it end like that?"

The woman moved closer to him and put her arm around his shoulders. "I'm sorry you don't understand," she said. "But neither do I."

And then he saw that it had not been understanding that his father had come home for and then tried to pass forward, but something more immediate and important.

He slept again, exhausted and calmed, slowly moving to huddle against the warmth of the woman. In the middle of the night he woke and felt the woman shuddering and crying beside him and tried silently to comfort her.

Morning. He woke to warmth and sunlight coming through the open doorway of the room. He was alone in the bed.

In the outer room the woman and his father's friend Charlie Anderson were sitting quietly at breakfast. "Sit down," Charlie said. "I'll get you some food."

"Charlie doesn't trust my cooking," the woman said. She smiled at the boy and went into the kitchen, returning with a mug of coffee for him. She seemed self-conscious and almost shy. She was simply dressed and completely without makeup.

His father's friend came from the kitchen with eggs and a thick slice of fried ham. "Eat good," he said. "Like a man."

"He will." The woman smiled directly at him, bright and almost flirtatious.

He wondered where the grief had gone, if his father had been so easily dismissed, if there had been grief.

"We seen the end of a fine man," Charlie Anderson said, then began to remove the dishes.

So he ate and watched them, these strangers. And then walked through the house uneasily and went out through the kitchen door and stood beneath the laden tree and shuffled in the snow and fingered the frozen bark while looking again to the far off rim.

She followed him. He was conscious of her standing behind him, silent and plain. He blinked in the radiance and watched the flying birds, geese moving to feed and water.

"I was foolish to cry last night." From behind him the woman spoke softly. He turned and saw her braced and rigid, her face forced into stillness and nearly in tears.

And then she gasped slightly and came to him and pressed herself against him while she shook and wept. He stood with arms hanging and empty and felt the softness of her breasts and then nothing but the cold in her hair which was loose and open against his face.

Then she was quiet.

"Take me in," she said. "I'm cold."

She moved away and he followed her, oblivious and completely drawn into himself.

"It will make you tough," his father had said.

He slammed the door and went to stand before the fire. The woman stood at the window with her hands folded behind her and the other man was busy with the dishes. The house seemed full of the warm fecundity and musk of the dead birds. The fire pained his numb fingers and was radiant in the cold.

THE REAL WEST

H. L. Davis
1896-1960

Born near the small town of Yoncalla, Oregon, Davis began writing as a poet, publishing often in the magazine *Poetry: A Magazine Of Verse.* His first novel, however, won him both the Harper Novel Prize and the Pulitzer Prize. Most of his work is about Oregon and the northwest, and is impressive for its accurate and feeling description of that country and its people. "Open Winter" is a fine example of his writing, and offers in rich detail and Davis' own warm brand of understated humor what it was like to become a man in the early days of eastern Oregon. Suggested readings: *Team Bells Woke Me and Other Stories* and *Honey In The Horn,* the novel for which Davis won the Pulitzer Prize.

OPEN WINTER

The drying east wind, which always brought hard luck to Eastern Oregon at whatever season it blew, had combed down the plateau grasslands through so much of the winter that it was hard to see any sign of grass ever having grown on them. Even though March had come, it still blew, drying the ground deep, shrinking the watercourses, beating back the clouds that might have delivered rain, and grinding coarse dust against the fifty-odd head of work horses that Pop Apling, with young Beech Cartwright helping, had brought down from his homestead to turn back into their home pasture while there was still something left of them.

The two men, one past sixty and the other around sixteen, shouldered the horses through the gate of the home pasture about dark, with lights beginning to shine out from the little freighting town across Three Notch Valley, and then they rode for the ranch house, knowing even before they drew up outside the yard that they had picked the wrong time to come. The house was too dark and, the corrals and outbuildings too still, for a place that anybody lived in.

There were sounds, but they were of shingles flapping in the wind, a windmill running loose and sucking noisily at a well that it had already pumped empty, a door that kept banging shut and dragging open again. The haystacks were gone, the stackyard fence had dwindled to a few naked posts, and the entire pasture was as bare and as hard as a floor all the way down into the valley.

The prospect looked so hopeless that the herd horses refused even to explore it, and merely stood with their tails turned to the wind, waiting to see what was to happen to them next.

Old Apling went poking inside the house, thinking somebody might have left a note or that the men might have run down to the saloon in town for an hour or two. He came back, having used up all his matches and stopped the door from banging, and said the place appeared to have been handed back to the Government, or maybe the mortgage company.

"You can trust old Ream Gervais not to be any place where anybody wants him," Beech said. He had hired out to herd for Ream Gervais over the winter. That entitled him to be more critical than old Apling, who had merely contracted to supply the horse herd with feed and pasture for the season at so much per head. "Well, my job was to help herd these steeds while you had 'em, and to help deliver 'em back when you got through with 'em, and here they are. I've put in a week on 'em that I won't ever git paid for, and it won't help anything to set around and watch 'em try to live on fence pickets. Let's git out."

Old Apling looked at the huddle of horses, at the naked slope with a glimmer of light still on it, and at the lights of the town twinkling in the wind. He said it wasn't his place to tell any man what to do, but that he wouldn't feel quite right to dump the horses and leave.

"I agreed to see that they got delivered back here, and I'd feel better about it if I could locate somebody to deliver 'em to," he said. "I'd like to ride across to town yonder, and see if there ain't somebody that knows something about 'em. You could hold 'em together here till I git back. We ought to look the fences over before we pull out, and you can wait here as well as anywhere else."

"I can't, but go ahead," Beech said. "I don't like to have 'em stand around and look at me when I can't do anything to help 'em out. They'd have been better off if we'd turned 'em out of your homestead and let 'em run loose on the country. There was more grass up there than there is here."

"There wasn't enough to feed 'em, and I'd have had all my neighbors down on me for it," old Apling said. "You'll find out one of these days that if a man aims to live in this world he's got to git along with the people in it. I'd start a fire and thaw out a little and git that pack horse unloaded, if I was you."

He rode down the slope, leaning low and forward to ease the drag of the wind on his tired horse. Beech heard the sound of the road gate being let down and put up again, the beat of hoofs in the hard road, and then nothing but the noises around him as the wind went through its usual process of easing down for the night to make room for the frost. Loose boards settled into place, the windmill clacked to a stop and began to drip water into a puddle, and the herd horses shifted around facing Beech, as if anxious not to miss anything he did.

He pulled off some fence pickets and built a fire, unsaddled his pony and unloaded the pack horse, and got out what was left of a sack of grain and fed them both, standing the herd horses off with a fence picket until they had finished eating.

That was strictly fair, for the pack horse and the saddle pony had worked harder and carried more weight than any of the herd animals, and the grain was little enough to even them up for it. Nevertheless, he felt mean at having to club animals away from food when they were hungry, and they crowded back and eyed the grain sack so wistfully that he carried it inside the yard and stored it down in the root cellar behind the house, so it wouldn't prey on their minds. Then he dumped another armload of fence pickets onto the fire and sat down to wait for old Apling.

The original mistake, he reflected, had been when old Apling took the Gervais horses to feed at the beginning of winter. Contracting to feed them had been well enough, for he had nursed up a stand of bunch grass on his homestead that would have carried an ordinary pack of horses with only a little extra feeding to help out in the roughest weather. But the Gervais horses were all big harness stock, they had pulled in half starved, and they had taken not much over three weeks to clean off the pasture that old Apling had expected would last them at least two months. Nobody would have blamed him for backing out on his agreement then, since he had only undertaken to feed the horses, not to treat them for malnutrition.

Beech wanted him to back out of it, but he refused to, said the stockmen had enough troubles without having that added to them, and started feeding out his hay and insisting that the dry wind couldn't possibly keep up much longer, because it wasn't in Nature.

By the time it became clear that Nature had decided to take in a little extra territory, the hay was all fed out, and, since there couldn't be any accommodation about letting the horses starve to death, he consented to throw the contract over and bring them back where they belonged.

The trouble with most of old Apling's efforts to be accommodating was that they did nobody any good. His neighbors would have been spared all their uneasiness if he had never brought in the horses to begin with. Gervais wouldn't have been any worse off, since he stood to lose them anyway; the horses could have starved to death as gracefully in November as in March, and old Apling would have been ahead a great deal of carefully accumulated bunch grass and two big stacks of extortionately valuable hay. Nobody had gained by his chivalrousness; he had lost by it, and yet he liked it so well that he couldn't stand to leave the horses until he had raked the country for somebody to hand the worthless brutes over to.

Beech fed sticks into the fire and felt out of patience with a man who could stick to his mistakes even after he had been cleaned out by them. He heard the road gate open and shut, and he knew by the draggy-sounding plod of old Apling's horse that the news from town was going to be bad.

Old Apling rode past the fire and over to the picket fence, got off as if he was trying to make it last, tied his horse carefully as if he expected the knot to last a month, and unsaddled and did up his latigo and folded his saddle blanket as if he was fixing them to put in a show window. He remarked that his horse had been given a bait of grain in town and wouldn't need feeding again, and then he began to work down to what he had found out.

"If you think things look bad along this road, you ought to see that town," he said. "All the sheep gone and all the ranches deserted and no trade to run on and their water threatenin' to give out. They've got a little herd of milk cows that they keep up for their children, and to hear 'em talk you'd think it was an ammunition supply that they expected to stand off hostile Indians with. They said Gervais pulled out of here around a month ago. All his men quit him, so he bunched his sheep and took 'em down to the railroad, where he could ship in hay for 'em. Sheep will be a price this year, and you won't be able to buy a lamb for under twelve dollars except at a fire sale. Horses ain't in much demand. There's been a lot of 'em turned out wild, and everybody wants to git rid of 'em."

"I didn't drive this bunch of pelters any eighty miles against the wind to git a market report," Beech said. "You didn't find anybody to turn 'em over to, and Gervais didn't leave any word about what he wanted done with 'em. You've probably got it figured out that you ought to trail 'em a hundred and eighty miles to the railroad, so his feelings won't be hurt, and you're probably tryin' to study how you can work me in on it, and you might as well save your time. I've helped you with your accommodation jobs long enough. I've quit, and it would have been a whole lot better for you if I'd quit sooner."

Old Apling said he could understand that state of feeling, which didn't mean that he shared it.

"It wouldn't be as much of a trick to trail down to the railroad as a man might think," he said, merely to settle a question of fact. "We couldn't make it by the road in a starve-out year like this, but there's old Indian trails back on the ridge where any man has got a right to take livestock whenever he feels like it. Still, as long as you're set against it, I'll meet you halfway. We'll trail these horses down the ridge to a grass patch where I used to corral cattle when I was in the business, and we'll leave 'em there. It'll be enough so they won't starve, and I'll ride on down and notify Gervais where they are, and you can go where you please. It wouldn't be fair to do less than that, to my notion."

"Ream Gervais triggered me out of a week's pay," Beech said. "It ain't much, but he swindled you on that pasture contract too. If you expect me to trail his broken-down horses ninety miles down this ridge when they ain't worth anything, you've turned in a poor guess. You'll have to think of a better argument than that if you aim to gain any ground with me."

"Ream Gervais don't count in this," old Apling said. "What does he care about these horses, when he ain't even left word what he wants done with 'em? What counts is you, and I don't have to think up any better argument, because I've already got one. You may not realize it, but you and me are responsible for these horses till they're delivered to their owner, and if we turn 'em loose here to bust fences and overrun that town and starve to death in the middle of it, we'll land in the pen. It's against the law to let horses starve to death, did you know that? If you pull out of here I'll pull out right along with you, and I'll have every man in that town after you before the week's out. You'll have a chance to git some action on that pistol of yours, if you're careful."

Beech said he wasn't intimidated by that kind of talk, and threw a couple of handfuls of dirt on the fire, so it wouldn't look so conspicuous. His pistol was an old single-action relic with its grips tied on with fish line and no trigger, so that it had to be operated by flipping the hammer. The spring was weak, so that sometimes it took several flips to get off one shot. Suggesting that he might use such a thing to stand off any pack of grim-faced pursuers was about the same as saying that he was simple-minded. As far as he could see, his stand was entirely sensible, and even humane.

"It ain't that I don't feel sorry for these horses, but they ain't fit to travel," he said. "They wouldn't last twenty miles. I don't see how it's any worse to let 'em stay here than to walk 'em to death down that ridge."

"They make less trouble for people if you keep 'em on the move," old Apling said. "It's something you can't be cinched for in court, and it makes you feel better afterwards to know that you tried everything you could. Suit yourself about it, though. I ain't beggin' you to do it. If you'd sooner pull out and stand the consequences, it's you for it. Before you go, what did you do with that sack of grain?"

Beech had half a notion to leave, just to see how much of that dark threatening would come to pass. He decided that it wouldn't be worth it. "I'll help you trail the blamed skates as far as they'll last, if you've got to be childish about it," he said. "I put the grain in a root cellar behind the house, so the rats wouldn't git into it. It looked like the only safe place around here. There was about a half a ton of old sprouted potatoes riched up in it that didn't look like they'd been bothered for twenty years. They had sprouts on 'em—" He stopped, noticing that old Apling kept staring at him as if something was wrong. "Good Lord, potatoes ain't good for horse feed, are they? They had sprouts on 'em a foot long!"

Old Apling shook his head resignedly and got up. "We wouldn't ever find anything if it wasn't for you," he said. "We wouldn't ever git any good out of it if it wasn't for me, so maybe we make a team. Show me where that root cellar is, and we'll pack them spuds out and spread 'em around so the horses can git started on 'em. We'll git this herd through to grassland yet, and it'll be something you'll never be ashamed of. It ain't everybody your age gits a chance to do a thing like this, and you'll thank me for holdin' you to it before you're through."

II

They climbed up by an Indian trail onto a high stretch of tableland, so stony and scored with rock breaks that nobody had ever tried to cultivate it but so high that it sometimes caught moisture from the atmosphere that the lower elevations missed. Part of it had been doled out among the Indians as allotment lands, which none of them ever bothered to lay claim to, but the main spread of it belonged to the nation, which was too busy to notice it.

The pasture was thin, though reliable, and it was so scantily watered and so rough and broken that in ordinary years nobody bothered to bring stock onto it. The open winter had spoiled most of that seclusion. There was no part of the trail that didn't have at least a dozen new bed grounds for lambed ewes in plain view, easily picked out of the landscape because of the little white flags stuck up around them to keep sheep from straying out and coyotes from straying in during the night. The sheep were pasturing down the draws out of the wind, where they couldn't be seen. There were no herders visible, not any startling amount of grass, and no water except a mud tank thrown up to catch a little spring for one of the camps.

They tried to water the horses in it, but it had taken up the flavor of sheep, so that not a horse in the herd would touch it. It was too near dark to waste time reasoning with them about it, so old Apling headed them down into a long rock break and across it to a tangle of wild cherry and mountain mahogany that lasted for several miles and ended in a grass clearing among some dwarf cottonwoods with a mud puddle in the center of it.

The grass had been grazed over, though not closely, and there were sheep tracks around the puddle that seemed to be fresh, for the horses, after sniffing the water, decided that they could wait a while longer. They spread out to graze, and Beech remarked that he couldn't see where it was any improvement over the tickle-grass homesteads.

"The grass may be better, but there ain't as much of it, and the water ain't any good if they won't drink it," he said. "Well, do you intend to leave 'em here, or have you got some wrinkle figured out to make me help trail 'em on down to the railroad?"

Old Apling stood the sarcasm unresistingly. "It would be better to trail 'em to the railroad, now that we've got this far," he said. "I won't ask you to do that much, because it's outside of what you agreed to. This place has changed since I was here last, but we'll make it do, and that water ought to clear up fit to drink before long. You can settle down here for a few days while I ride around and fix it up with the sheep camps to let the horses stay here. We've got to do that, or they're liable to think it's some wild bunch and start shootin' 'em. Somebody's got to stay with 'em, and I can git along with these herders better than you can."

"If you've got any sense, you'll let them sheep outfits alone," Beech said. "They don't like tame horses on this grass any better than they do wild ones, and they won't make any more bones about shootin' 'em if they find out they're in here. It's a hard place to find, and they'll stay close on account of the water, and you'd better pull out and let 'em have it to themselves. That's what I aim to do."

"You've done what you agreed to, and I ain't got any right to hold you any longer," old Apling said. "I wish I could. You're wrong about them sheep outfits. I've got as much right to pasture this ridge as they have, and they know it, and nobody ever lost anything by actin' sociable with people."

"Somebody will before very long," Beech said. "I've got relatives in the sheep business, and I know what they're like. You'll land yourself in trouble, and I don't want to be around when you do it. I'm pullin' out of here in the morning, and if you had any sense you'd pull out along with me."

There were several things that kept Beech from getting much sleep during the night. One was the attachment that the horses showed for his sleeping place; they stuck so close that he could almost feel their breath on him, could hear the soft breaking sound that the grass made as they pulled it, the sound of their swallowing, the jar of the ground under him when one of the horses changed ground, the peaceful regularity of their eating, as if they didn't have to bother about anything so long as they kept old Apling in sight.

Another irritating thing was old Apling's complete freedom from uneasiness. He ought by rights to have felt more worried about the future than Beech did, but he slept, with the hard ground for a bed and his hard saddle for a pillow and the horses almost stepping on him every minute or two, as soundly as if the entire trip had come out exactly to suit him and there was nothing ahead but plain sailing.

His restfulness was so hearty and so unjustifiable that Beech couldn't sleep for feeling indignant about it, and got up and left about daylight to keep from being exposed to any more of it. He left without waking old Apling, because he saw no sense in a leave-taking that would consist merely in repeating his common-sense warnings and having them ignored, and he was so anxious to get clear of the whole layout that he didn't even take along anything to eat. The only thing he took from the pack was his ramshackle old pistol; there was no holster for it, and, in the hope that he might get a chance to use it on a loose quail or prairie chicken, he stowed it in an empty flour sack and hung it on his saddle horn, a good deal like an old squaw heading for the far blue distances with a bundle of diapers.

III

There was never anything recreational about traveling a rock desert at any season of the year, and the combination of spring gales, winter chilliness and summer drought all striking at once brought it fairly close to hard punishment. Beech's saddle pony, being jaded at the start with overwork and underfeeding and no water, broke down in the first couple of miles, and got so feeble and tottery that Beech had to climb off and lead him, searching likely-looking thickets all the way down the gully in the hope of finding some little trickle that he wouldn't be too finicky to drink.

The nearest he came to it was a fair-sized rock sink under some big half-budded cottonwoods that looked, by its dampness and the abundance of fresh animal tracks around it, as if it might have held water recently, but of water there was none, and even digging a hole in the center of the basin failed to fetch a drop.

The work of digging, hill climbing and scrambling through brush piles raised Beech's appetite so powerfully that he could scarcely hold up, and, a little above where the gully opened into the flat sagebrush plateau, he threw away his pride, pistoled himself a jack rabbit, and took it down into the sagebrush to cook, where his fire wouldn't give away which gully old Apling was camped in.

Jack rabbit didn't stand high as a food. It was considered an excellent thing to give men in the last stages of famine, because they weren't likely to injure themselves by eating too much of it, but for ordinary occasions it was looked down on, and Beech covered his trail out of the gully and built his cooking fire in the middle of a high stand of sagebrush, so as not to be embarrassed by inquisitive visitors.

The meat cooked up strong, as it always did, but he ate what he needed of it, and he was wrapping the remainder in his flour sack to take along with him when a couple of men rode past, saw his pony, and turned in to look him over.

They looked him over so closely and with so little concern for his privacy that he felt insulted before they even spoke.

He studied them less openly, judging by their big gallon canteens that they were out on some long scout.

One of them was some sort of hired hand, by his looks; he was broad-faced and gloomy-looking, with a fine white horse, a flower-stamped saddle, an expensive rifle scabbarded under his knee, and a fifteen-dollar saddle blanket, while his own manly form was set off by a yellow hotel blanket and a ninety-cent pair of overalls.

The other man had on a store suit, a plain black hat, fancy stitched boots, and a white shirt and necktie, and rode a burr-tailed Indian pony and an old wrangling saddle with a loose horn. He carried no weapons in sight, but there was a narrow strap across the lower spread of his necktie which indicated the presence of a shoulder holster somewhere within reach.

He opened the conversation by inquiring where Beech had come from, what his business was, where he was going and why he hadn't taken the county road to go there, and why he had to eat jack rabbit when the country was littered with sheep camps where he could get a decent meal by asking for it?

"I come from the upper country," Beech said, being purposely vague about it. "I'm travelin', and I stopped here because my horse give out. He won't drink out of any place that's had sheep in it, and he's gone short of water till he breaks down easy."

"There's a place corralled in for horses to drink at down at my lower camp," the man said, and studied Beech's pony. "There's no reason for you to bum through the country on jack rabbit in a time like this. My herder can take you down to our water hole and see that you get fed and put to work till you can make a stake for yourself. I'll give you a note. That pony looks like he had Ream Gervais' brand on him. Do you know anything about that herd of old work horses he's been pasturing around?"

"I don't know anything about him," Beech said, side-stepping the actual question while he thought over the offer of employment. He could have used a stake, but the location didn't strike him favorably. It was too close to old Apling's camp, he could see trouble ahead over the horse herd, and he didn't want to be around when it started. "If you'll direct me how to find your water, I'll ride on down there, but I don't need anybody to go with me, and I don't need any stake. I'm travelin'."

The man said there wasn't anybody so well off that he couldn't use a stake, and that it would be hardly any trouble at all for Beech to get one. "I want you to understand how we're situated around here, so you won't think we're any bunch of stranglers," he said. "You can see what kind of a year this has been, when we have to run lambed ewes in a rock patch like this. We've got five thousand lambs in here that we're trying to bring through, and we've had to fight the blamed wild horses for this pasture since the day we moved in. A horse that ain't worth hell room will eat as much as two dozen sheep worth twenty dollars, with the lambs, so you can see how it figures out. We've got 'em pretty well thinned out, but one of my packers found a trail of a new bunch that came up from around Three Notch within the last day or two, and we don't want them to feel as if we'd neglected them. We'd like to find out where they lit. You wouldn't have any information about 'em?"

"None that would do you any good to know," Beech said. "I know the man with that horse herd, and it ain't any use to let on that I don't, but it wouldn't be any use to try to deal with him. He don't sell out on a man he works for."

"He might be induced to," the man said. "We'll find him anyhow, but I don't like to take too much time to it. Just for instance, now, suppose you knew that pony of yours would have to go thirsty till you gave us a few directions about that horse herd? You'd be stuck here for quite a spell, wouldn't you?"

He was so pleasant about it that it took Beech a full minute to realize that he was being threatened. The heavy-set herder brought that home to him by edging out into a flank position and hoisting his rifle scabbard so it could be reached in a hurry. Beech removed the cooked jack rabbit from his flour sack carefully, a piece at a time, and, with the same mechanical thoughtfulness, brought out his triggerless old pistol, cut down on the pleasant-spoken man, and hauled back on the hammer and held it poised.

"That herder of yours had better go easy on his rifle," he said, trying to keep his voice from trembling. "This pistol shoots if I don't hold back the hammer, and if he knocks me out I'll have to let go of it. You'd better watch him, if you don't want your tack drove. I won't give you no directions about that horse herd, and this pony of mine won't go thirsty for it, either. Loosen them canteens of yours and let 'em drop on the ground. Drop that rifle scabbard back where it belongs, and unbuckle the straps and let go of it. If either of you tries any funny business, there'll be one of you to pack home, heels first."

The quaver in his voice sounded childish and undignified to him, but it had a more businesslike ring to them than any amount of manly gruffness. The herder unbuckled his rifle scabbard, and they both cast loose their canteen straps, making it last as long as they could while they argued with him, not angrily, but as if he was a dull stripling whom they wanted to save from some foolishness that he was sure to regret. They argued ethics, justice, common sense, his future prospects, and the fact that what he was doing amounted to robbery by force and arms and that it was his first fatal step into a probably unsuccessful career of crime. They worried over him, they explained themselves to him, and they ridiculed him.

They managed to make him feel like several kinds of a fool, and they were so pleasant and concerned about it that they came close to breaking him down. What held him steady was the thought of old Apling waiting up the gully.

"That herder with the horses never sold out on any man, and I won't sell out on him," he said. "You've said your say and I'm tired of holdin' this pistol on cock for you, so move along out of here. Keep to open ground, so I can be sure you're gone, and don't be in too much of a hurry to come back. I've got a lot of things I want to think over, and I want to be let alone while I do it."

IV

He did have some thinking that needed tending to, but he didn't take time for it. When the men were well out of range, he emptied their canteens into his hat and let his pony drink. Then he hung the canteens and the scabbarded rifle on a bush and rode back up the gully where the horse camp was, keeping to shaly ground so as not to leave any tracks. It was harder going up than it had been coming down.

He had turned back from the scene of his run-in with the two sheepmen about noon, and he was still a good two miles from the camp when the sun went down, the wind lulled and the night frost began to bite at him so hard that he dismounted and walked to get warm. That raised his appetite again, and, as if by some special considerateness of Nature, the cottonwoods around him seemed to be alive with jack rabbits heading down into the pitch-dark gully where he had fooled away valuable time trying to find water that morning.

They didn't stimulate his hunger much; for a time they even made him feel less like eating anything. Then his pony gave out and had to rest, and, noticing that the cottonwoods around him were beginning to bud out, he remembered that peeling the bark off in the budding season would fetch out a foamy, sweet-tasting sap which, among children of the plateau country, was considered something of a delicacy.

He cut a blaze on a fair-sized sapling, waited ten minutes or so, and touched his finger to it to see how much sap had accumulated. None had; the blaze was moist to his touch, but scarcely more so than when he had whittled it.

It wasn't important enough to do any bothering about, and yet a whole set of observed things began to draw together in his mind and form themselves into an explanation of something he had puzzled over: the fresh animal tracks he had seen around the rock sink when there wasn't any water; the rabbits going down into the gully; the cottonwoods in which the sap rose enough during the day to produce buds and got driven back at night when the frost set in. During the day, the cottonwoods had drawn the water out of the ground for themselves; at night they stopped drawing it, and it drained out into the rock sink for the rabbits.

It all worked out so simply that he led his pony down into the gully to see how much there was in it, and, losing his footing on the steep slope, coasted down into the rock sink in the dark and landed in water and thin mud up to his knees. He led his pony down into it to drink, which seemed little enough to get back for the time he had fooled away on it, and then he headed for the horse camp, which was all too easily discernible by the plume of smoke rising, white and ostentatious, against the dark sky from old Apling's campfire.

He made the same kind of entrance that old Apling usually affected when bringing some important item of news. He rode past the campfire and pulled up at a tree, got off deliberately, knocked an accumulation of dead twigs from his hat, took off his saddle and bridle and balanced them painstakingly in the tree fork, and said it was affecting to see how widespread the shortage of pasture was.

"It generally is," old Apling said. "I had a kind of a notion you'd be back after you'd had time to study things over. I suppose you got into some kind of a rumpus with some of them sheep outfits. What was it? Couldn't you git along with them, or couldn't they hit it off with you?"

"There wasn't any trouble between them and me," Beech said. "The only point we had words over was you. They wanted to know where you was camped, so they could shoot you up, and I didn't think it was right to tell 'em. I had to put a gun on a couple of 'em before they'd believe I meant business, and that was all there was to it. They're out after you now, and they can see the smoke of this fire of yours for twenty miles, so they ought to be along almost any time now. I thought I'd come back and see you work your sociability on 'em."

"You probably kicked up a squabble with 'em yourself," old Apling said. He looked a little uneasy. "You talked right up to 'em, I'll bet, and slapped their noses with your hat to show 'em that they couldn't run over you. Well, what's done is done. You did come back, and maybe they'd have jumped us anyway. There ain't much that we can do. The horses have got to have water before they can travel, and they won't touch that seep. It ain't cleared up a particle."

"You can put that fire out, not but what the whole country has probably seen the smoke from it already," Beech said. "If you've got to tag after these horses, you can run 'em off down the draw and keep 'em to the brush where they won't leave a trail. There's some young cottonwood bark that they can eat if they have to, and there's water in a rock sink under some big cottonwood trees. I'll stay here and hold off anybody that shows up, so you'll have time to git your tracks covered."

Old Apling went over and untied the flour-sacked pistol from Beech's saddle, rolled it into his blankets, and sat down on it. "If there's any holdin' off to be done, I'll do it," he said. "You're a little too high-spirited to suit me, and a little too hasty about your conclusions. I looked over that rock sink down the draw today, and there wasn't anything in it but mud, and blamed little of that. Somebody had dug for water, and there wasn't none."

"There is now," Beech said. He tugged off one of his wet boots and poured about a pint of the disputed fluid on the ground. "There wasn't any in the daytime because the cottonwoods took it all. They let up when it turns cold, and it runs back in. I waded in it."

He started to put his boot back on. Old Apling reached out and took it, felt of it inside and out, and handed it over as if performing some ceremonial presentation.

"I'd never have figured out a thing like that in this world," he said. "If we git them horses out of here, it'll be you that done it. We'll bunch 'em and work 'em down there. It won't be no picnic, but we'll make out to handle it somehow. We've got to, after a thing like this."

Beech remembered what had occasioned the discovery, and said he would have to have something to eat first. "I want you to keep in mind that it's you I'm doin' this for," he said. "I don't owe that old groundhog of a Ream Gervais anything. The only thing I hate about this is that it'll look like I'd done him a favor."

"He won't take it for one, I guess," old Apling said. "We've got to git these horses out because it'll be a favor to you. You wouldn't want to have it told around that you'd done a thing like findin' that water, and then have to admit that we'd lost all the horses anyhow. We can't lose 'em. You've acted like a man tonight, and I'll be blamed if I'll let you spoil it for any childish spite."

They got the horses out none too soon. Watering them took a long time, and when they finally did consent to call it enough and climb back up the side hill, Beech and old Apling heard a couple of signal shots from the direction of their old camping place, and saw a big glare mount up into the sky from it as the visitors built up their campfire to look the locality over. The sight was almost comforting; if they had to keep away from a pursuit, it was at least something to know where it was.

V

From then on they followed a grab-and-run policy, scouting ahead before they moved, holding to the draws by day and crossing open ground only after dark, never pasturing over a couple of hours in any one place, and discovering food value in outlandish substances—rock lichens, the sprouts of wild plum and serviceberry, the moss of old trees and the bark of some young ones—that neither they nor the horses had ever considered fit to eat before. When they struck Boulder River Canyon they dropped down and toenailed their way along one side of it where they could find grass and water with less likelihood of having trouble about it.

The breaks of the canyon were too rough to run new-lambed sheep in, and they met with so few signs of occupancy that old Apling got overconfident, neglected his scouting to tie back a break they had been obliged to make in a line fence, and ran the horse herd right over the top of a camp where some men were branding calves, tearing down a cook tent and part of a corral and scattering cattle and bedding from the river all the way to the top of the canyon.

By rights, they should have sustained some damage for that piece of carelessness, but they drove through fast, and they were out of sight around a shoulder of rimrock before any of the men could get themselves picked up. Somebody did throw a couple of shots after them as they were pulling into a thicket of mock orange and chokecherry, but it was only with a pistol, and he probably did it more to relieve his feelings than with any hope of hitting anything.

They were so far out of range that they couldn't even hear where the bullets landed.

Neither of them mentioned that unlucky run-in all the rest of that day. They drove hard, punished the horses savagely when they lagged, and kept them at it until, a long time after dark, they struck an old rope ferry that crossed Boulder River at a place called, in memory of its original founders, Robbers' Roost.

The ferry wasn't a public carrier, and there was not even any main road down to it. It was used by the ranches in the neighborhod as the only means of crossing the river for fifty miles in either direction, and it was tied in to a log with a good solid chain and padlock. It was a way to cross, and neither of them could see anything else but to take it.

Beech favored waiting for daylight for it, pointing out that there was a ranch light half a mile up the slope, and that if anybody caught them hustling a private ferry in the dead of night they would probably be taken for ciminals on the dodge. Old Apling said it was altogether likely, and drew Beech's pistol and shot the padlock apart with it.

"They could hear that up at that ranch house," Beech said. "What if they come pokin' down here to see what we're up to?"

Old Apling tossed the fragments of padlock into the river and hung the pistol in the waistband of his trousers. "Let 'em come," he said. "They'll go back again with their fingers in their mouths. This is your trip, and you put in good work on it, and I like to ruined the whole thing stoppin' to patch an eighty-cent fence so some scissorbill wouldn't have his feelings hurt, and that's the last accommodation anybody gits out of me till this is over with. I can take about six horses at a trip, it looks like. Help me to bunch 'em."

Six horses at a trip proved to be an overestimate. The best they could do was five, and the boat rode so deep with them that Beech refused to risk handling it. He stayed with the herd, and old Apling cut it loose, let the current sweep it across into slack water, and hauled it in to the far bank by winding in its cable on an old homemade capstan. Then he turned the horses into a counting pen and came back for another load.

He worked at it fiercely, as if he had a bet up that he could wear the whole ferry rig out, but it went with infernal slowness, and when the wind began to move for daylight there were a dozen horses still to cross and no place to hide them in case the ferry had other customers.

Beech waited and fidgeted over small noises until, hearing voices and the clatter of hoofs on shale far up the canyon behind him, he gave way, drove the remaining horses into the river, and swam them across, letting himself be towed along by his saddle horn and floating his clothes ahead of him on a board.

He paid for that flurry of nervousness before he got out. The water was so cold it paralyzed him, and so swift it whisked him a mile downstream before he could get his pony turned to breast it. He grounded on a gravel bar in a thicket of dwarf willows, with numbness striking clear to the center of his diaphragm and deadening his arms so he couldn't pick his clothes loose from the bundle to put on. He managed it, by using his teeth and elbows, and warmed himself a little by driving the horses afoot through the brush till he struck the ferry landing.

It had got light enough to see things in outline, and old Apling was getting ready to shove off for another crossing when the procession came lumbering at him out of the shadows. He came ashore, counted the horses into the corral to make sure none had drowned, and laid Beech under all the blankets and built up a fire to limber him out by. He got breakfast and got packed to leave, and he did some rapid expounding about the iniquity of risking the whole trip on such a wild piece of foolhardiness.

"That was the reason I wanted you to work this boat," he said. "I could have stood up to anybody that come projectin' around, and if they wanted trouble I could have filled their order for 'em. They won't bother us now, anyhow; it don't matter how bad they want to."

"I could have stood up to 'em if I'd had anything to do it with," Beech said. "You've got that pistol of mine, and I couldn't see to throw rocks. What makes you think they won't bother us? You know it was that brandin' crew comin' after us, don't you?"

"I expect that's who it was," old Apling agreed. "They ought to be out after the cattle we scattered, but you can trust a bunch of cowboys to pick out the most useless things to tend to first. I've got that pistol of yours because I don't aim for you to git in trouble with it while this trip is on. There won't anybody bother us because I've cut all the cables on the ferry, and it's lodged downstream on a gravel spit. If anybody crosses after us within fifty miles of here, he'll swim, and the people around here ain't as reckless around cold water as you are."

Beech sat up. "We got to git out of here," he said. "There's people on this side of the river that use that ferry, you old fool, and they'll have us up before every grand jury in the country from now on. The horses ain't worth it."

"What the horses is worth ain't everything," old Apling said. "There's a part of this trip ahead that you'll be glad you went through. You're entitled to that much out of it, after the work you've put in, and I aim to see that you git it. It ain't any use tryin' to explain to you what it is. You'll notice it when the time comes."

VI

They worked north, following the breaks of the river canyon, finding the rock breaks hard to travel, but easy to avoid observation in, and the grass fair in stand, but so poor and washy in body that the horses had to spend most of their time eating enough to keep up their strength so they could move.

They struck a series of gorges, too deep and precipitous to be crossed at all, and had to edge back into milder country where there were patches of plowed ground, some being harrowed over for summer fallow and others venturing out with a bright new stand of dark-green wheat.

The pasture was patchy and scoured by the wind, and all the best parts of it were under fence, which they didn't dare cut for fear of getting in trouble with the natives. Visibility was high in that section; the ground lay open to the north as far as they could see, the wind kept the air so clear that it hurt to look at the sky, and they were never out of sight of wheat ranchers harrowing down summer fallow.

A good many of the ranchers pulled up and stared after the horse herd as it went past, and two or three times they waved and rode down toward the road, as if they wanted to make it an excuse for stopping work. Old Apling surmised that they had some warning they wanted to deliver against trespassing, and he drove on without waiting to hear it.

They were unable to find a camping place anywhere among those wheat fields, so they drove clear through to open country and spread down for the night alongside a shallow pond in the middle of some new grass not far enough along to be pastured, though the horses made what they could out of it. There were no trees or shrubs anywhere around, not even sagebrush. Lacking fuel for a fire, they camped without one, and since there was no grass anywhere except around the pond, they left the horses unguarded, rolled in to catch up sleep, and were awakened about daylight by the whole herd stampeding past them at a gallop.

They both got up and moved fast. Beech ran for his pony, which was trying to pull loose from its picket rope to go with the bunch. Old Apling ran out into the dust afoot, waggling the triggerless old pistol and trying to make out objects in the half-light by hard squinting. The herd horses fetched a long circle and came back past him, with a couple of riders clouting along behind trying to turn them back into open country. One of the riders opened up a rope and swung it, the other turned in and slapped the inside flankers with his hat, and old Apling hauled up the old pistol, flipped the hammer a couple of rounds to get it warmed up, and let go at them twice.

The half darkness held noise as if it had been a cellar. The two shots banged monstrously, Beech yelled to old Apling to be careful who he shot at, and the two men shied off sideways and rode away into the open country. One of them yelled something that sounded threatening in tone as they went out of sight, but neither of them seemed in the least inclined to bring on any general engagement. The dust blew clear, the herd horses came back to grass, old Apling looked at the pistol and punched the two exploded shells out of it, and Beech ordered him to hand it over before he got in trouble with it.

"How do you know but what them men had a right here?" he demanded sternly. "We'd be in a fine jack pot if you'd shot one of 'em and it turned out he owned this land we're on, wouldn't we?"

Old Apling looked at him, holding the old pistol poised as if he was getting ready to lead a band with it. The light strengthened and shed a rose-colored radiance over him, so he looked flushed and joyous and lifted up. With some of the dust knocked off him, he could have filled in easily as a day star and son of the morning, whiskers and all.

"I wouldn't have shot them men for anything you could buy me!" he said, and faced north to a blue line of bluffs that came up out of the shadows, a blue gleam of water that moved under them, a white steamboat that moved upstream, glittering as the first light struck it. "Them men wasn't here because we was trespassers. Them was horse thieves, boy! We've brought these horses to a place where they're worth stealin', and we've brought 'em through! The railroad is under them bluffs, and that water down there is the old Columbia River!"

They might have made it down to the river that day, but having it in sight and knowing that nothing could stop them from reaching it, there no longer seemed any object in driving so unsparingly. They ate breakfast and talked about starting, and they even got partly packed up for it. Then they got occupied with talking to a couple of wheat ranchers who pulled in to inquire about buying some of the horse herd; the drought had run up wheat prices at a time when the country's livestock had been allowed to run down, and so many horses had been shot and starved out that they were having to take pretty much anything they could get.

Old Apling swapped them a couple of the most jaded herd horses for part of a haystack, referred other applicants to Gervais down at the railroad, and spent the remainder of the day washing, patching clothes and saddlery, and watching the horses get acquainted once more with a conventional diet.

The next morning a rancher dropped off a note from Gervais urging them to come right on down, and adding a kind but firm admonition against running up any feed bills without his express permission. He made it sound as if there might be some hurry about catching the horse market on the rise, so they got ready to leave, and Beech looked back over the road they had come, thinking of all that had happened on it.

"I'd like it better if old Gervais didn't have to work himself in on the end of it," he said. "I'd like to step out on the whole business right now."

"You'd be a fool to do that," old Apling said. "This is outside your work contract, so we can make the old gopher pay you what it's worth. I'll want to go in ahead and see about that and about the money that he owes me and about corral space and feed and one thing and another, so I'll want you to bring 'em in alone. You ain't seen everything there is to a trip like this, and you won't unless you stay with it."

VII

There would be no ending to this story without an understanding of what that little river town looked like at the hour, a little before sundown of a windy spring day, when Beech brought the desert horse herd down into it. On the wharf below town, some men were unloading baled hay from a steamboat, with some passengers watching from the saloon deck, and the river beyond them hoisting into white-capped peaks that shone and shed dazzling spray over the darkening water.

A switch engine was handling stock cars on a spur track, and the brakeman flagged it to a stop and stood watching the horses, leaning into the wind to keep his balance while the engineer climbed out on the tender to see what was going on.

The street of the town was lined with big leafless poplars that looked as if they hadn't gone short of moisture a day of their lives; the grass under them was bright green, and there were women working around flower beds and pulling up weeds, enough of them so that a horse could have lived on them for two days.

There was a Chinaman clipping grass with a pair of sheep shears to keep it from growing too tall, and there were lawn sprinklers running clean water on the ground in streams. There were stores with windows full of new clothes, and stores with bright hardware, and stores with strings of bananas and piles of oranges, bread and crackers and candy and rows of hams, and there were groups of anxious-faced men sitting around stoves inside who came out to watch Beech pass and told one another hopefully that the back country might make a good year out of it yet, if a youngster could bring that herd of horses through it.

There were women who hauled back their children and cautioned them not to get in the man's way, and there were boys and girls, some near Beech's own age, who watched him and stood looking after him, knowing that he had been through more than they had ever seen and not suspecting that it had taught him something that they didn't know about the things they saw every day. None of them knew what it meant to be in a place where there were delicacies to eat and new clothes to wear and look at, what it meant to be warm and out of the wind for a change, what it could mean merely to have water enough to pour on the ground and grass enough to cut down and throw away.

For the first time, seeing how the youngsters looked at him, he understood what that amounted to. There wasn't a one of them who wouldn't have traded places with him. There wasn't one that he would have traded places with, for all the haberdashery and fancy groceries in town. He turned down to the corrals, and old Apling held the gate open for him and remarked that he hadn't taken much time to it.

"You're sure you had enough of that ridin' through town?" he said. "It ain't the same when you do it a second time, remember."

"It'll last me," Beech said. "I wouldn't have missed it, and I wouldn't want it to be the same again. I'd sooner have things the way they run with us out in the high country. I'd sooner not have anything be the same a second time."

William Eastlake
1919-

Currently writer in residence at the University of Arizona, William Eastlake has taught in many colleges in the west, including USC and the University of New Mexico, though he never attended college himself. His stories and novels have been published in numerous countries, and a novel about the Viet Nam war, *The Bamboo Bed,* was published in 1969. "Something Big Is Happening To Me" is a story from his novel *Portrait Of An Artist With Twenty-Six Horses* and shows a deep love and concern for the Indian and the west. He treats the theme of death with humor and awe, and with respect for the dignity of the human spirit. "Our great west," he says, "the American promise, has been waiting for two hundred years to be discovered, and that has been my dedication and my delight, my Seven Cities of Cibola." Suggested readings: *The Bronc People* and *Castle Keep.*

SOMETHING BIG IS HAPPENING TO ME

Tomas Tomas, behind his round, cracked face and shallow-set, quick lizard eyes, was one hundred years old, or he was chasing one hundred, or one hundred was chasing him, no one knew, least of all Tomas Tomas. But early one morning nine months ago Tomas Tomas had gone down to the water hole in the arroyo and had come back dying.

It was cold for a September in New Mexico. The old Indian medicine man, Tomas Tomas, would never see another, warm or cold, and now he knew he would never see the end of this diamond-hard and dove-blue New Mexican day—he sat dreaming in front of his log and mud conical hogan; he sat dreaming that the white man never happened; he sat dreaming death never came.

His hogan was on a small bald rise beneath a fantastically purple butte. His home had not always been here; he had lived all around the Nation called Navajo Country. He got his name, Tomas Tomas—he had others—while a small boy and before he went to the United States government concentration camp at Bosque Redondo, when they rounded up all the Navajos during the last century to protect the settlers that were stealing Navajo land. That's the way most of the Navajos saw it, but Tomas Tomas thought and said very quietly otherwise. "We stole it," he said, "from the Anasazi People who built those cliff houses up there and the big houses in Chaco Canyon. Killed most of them. At least the Whites, at least they let us live to see the bug and iron bird arrive." Automobiles and airplanes he meant. "The tin bugs were not male nor female. We got under the big bugs and had a look. We know now they are made by people, like you make an axe or like you make a picture, or make noise, not like you make children. Although there is a clan among the Navajos who live mostly around Shiprock, the Red Stick Clan, who believe that children are sent by the child spirit and making love accomplishes nothing, or very little. That it's just funny, or fun. Exercise," Tomas Tomas added, not wanting to leave out some purpose to love-making entirely or altogether.

The other Navajo Indians had been expecting Tomas Tomas to die off and on for a hundred years. He was always being mortally wounded by a person or a horse and this day when he came back dying was not the first time that it had come to pass that Tomas Tomas was dead. The initiation rites into manhood of the Navajos in the Checkerboard Area kill an Indian boy so that he may be reborn again, reborn again even with a different name. The boy is killed in pantomime with a stone axe by the medicine man. You die and are reborn again by the medicine man, then all of the dream time is played out and the boy is shown all the magic that no woman knows, and in this manner and rite the boy dies and is reborn again as a man. But only after he has slept all naked in the night with a young girl, and that's important. If this is not done the boy is not reborn again and can never die. He is condemned to live forever in some form. Tomas Tomas did this very repeatedly and successfully and on his first night became a man among men, and now he could die.

When a Navajo dies he can have all his wives again in heaven. There is prosperity, joy and wit and wisdom in Navajo heaven. Navajo heaven is not a solemn gray high refuse heap for humble failures.

So when Tomas Tomas came back to his hogan dying he was not sweating cold in fear of judgment. He had been judged and found with much wisdom, many wives, three hogans, all in giant circles, and enough turquoise and silver to founder a horse, enough pride to have killed four plundering Whites, enough magic in his medicine bag to confound the universe and a long, never quite out of fashion turkey bonnet festooned with bright parrot feathers so long it dragged the ground.

One of his wives must catch a horse, Tomas Tomas thought with his arms grabbing his chest to contain the awful pain of death—also to keep the death from spreading before he got to the mountain. A Checker Clan

Navajo must die on the mountain, that's what mountains are made for. Mountains are for dying.

Tomas Tomas knelt down painfully in front of the Pendleton, yellow-striped blanket door of the hogan and made a cigarette; it was time to be calm and appraising. Death comes very seldom to a man and it must be taken with dignity and carefulness. It must be arranged, if it can be arranged, so that there is no messiness, no blood, no dreaming, no raving out loud so that everything is undone that was properly done in your life.

That's why the ascent of the mountain is so valuable at the end. Occupied instead of preoccupied. Gaining ever new heights in spreading splendor, not the visit of fading visitors between coming-together walls.

What was that? A horse. It was nice of the white man to send his horse. A black horse, but still a horse. Maybe he didn't send it. Maybe the horse just got away. Well, it's a fine horse for the occasion. That is, I always thought he'd make a good mountain horse. Luto—I think that's the name they call him. But some call him that black son of a bitch. That's a nice name too. Pretty name. "Come here, Pretty Name," Tomas Tomas called in White language to the white man's black horse. "Come here, you pretty black Luto son of a bitch," Tomas Tomas called softly.

Now he finished making the cigarette and licked the paper carefully, eyeing the horse and seeing into and beyond the old familiar place. The Navajo Nation had been an old familiar place for a long time. Tomas Tomas did not want to go to any unknown place, but things were beginning to repeat themselves here. The medicine man had travelled a great deal in his practice, into foreign countries as far as Arizona. His wives did not like travel, or they did not like horses, it was difficult to tell which. Someone should find out if the Whites' women would travel if they had to travel on a horse. What am I doing dreaming about such rubbish when I've got to be on the mountain to see another world before the sun goes down? I never saw such an accommodating horse, come all this way here to help me keep the appointment. I never saw the hogans and the piñons and the fires all around them and the great yellow rocks above them so fixed before. It is as though it will never change, like a drawing on the rock or a picture on a pot. It seems stopped forever now in this last time. Only she moves.

"Where do you go, Tomas Tomas?" one of his wives said.

"To the mountain now."

"Why, Tomas Tomas?"

"For the last time."

"It's growing cold up there."

"That's all right."

"Soon it will be winter."

"Yes, I know."

"Whose horse?"

"It belongs to a White."

"It's black."

"Yes, but it belongs to a White with red hair and blue eyes."

"And a green nose."

"The Whites are funny enough without making anything up."

"Look, Tomas Tomas," this one of his wives continued. She was Spotted Calf, with a soft face and curling a huge orange blanket around her youth. "Look, why go to the mountain?"

"Because it's best."

"Why not here in comfort?"

"Because comfort is not best. The mountain is best."

"I will bring you some soup before you start."

"No, I just want to look from here at everything. Here is for the last time, which is like the first time. The last time and the first time are really the only time we ever see anything."

"Shall I get the others?"

"No, I remember them."

"Shall I get your magic, Tomas Tomas?"

"No, I leave my magic to the world. Wouldn't it be something to arrive there with my medicine before the Big Magician? But I don't know. I have no good medicine."

"What, Tomas Tomas?"

"I will not take my magic. It's not much medicine."

"Are you sure, Tomas Tomas?"

"Yes!" That hurt him. It made a sharp axe sink deep within his chest to speak so firmly and it hurt Tomas Tomas around the heart to speak so sharply to Spotted Calf. "No, I will not take my magic," Tomas Tomas said quietly. "You get me packed up now, Eleventh Wife," Tomas Tomas said quietly in his pain. "And my empty medicine bundle."

"Yes, Tomas Tomas," and she disappeared into the hogan.

If I only had one piece of respectable medicine, the medicine man Tomas Tomas thought. Certainly He cannot object if I show off a little too. And there are a few things I want to find out. Why was I sentenced to earth? What will the white man's position be up there? Will the Whites have all the good land there too? But more important, why is all God's medicine a failure now? At one time I suppose He had very good magic and then He began to lose interest. He found the Indians no longer interesting. Something else I can bring up quietly with Him on the mountain: Why is the white man frightened of his God? What did his God do to him that makes the white man scared? "Do you know, Luto?" he asked towards the horse. "What is the white man afraid of? Is he afraid his God is not there? Where is my watch?" Tomas Tomas asked himself. The watch could not tell time. Tomas Tomas tied the watch around his wrist for fetish. The sun could tell time. "I must go to the mountain on time."

Tomas Tomas looked out over the long slow fire on the Navajo Nation that had been his home for so long and that now he was going to leave. The Checkerboard Area was shaped like a great horn, a horn of nothing. The wide open mouth of the horn lay along the flat Torreón and Cabazon country that was pricked with sharp white volcanic cores. The horn of volcanoes. The heavy middle sweep of the horn was checkered with flat high green-capped, copper-hued mesas that gave you the feeling that the world was on two levels, which it is in the Checkerboard. The horn of many levels. Here at the narrow tip of the horn the land was drinking from the narrow, quick, crazy mountain streams that cough past and were called La Jara, Los Pinos and San Jose, and finally all became a great—dry in most seasons—wash called the Puerco which crossed under Route 66 at Gallup and entered the Rio Grande among spider cactus at Hondo. The horn is a dry river. Not really, Tomas Tomas thought. The horn is none of these things. The horn is home. Home is where you breed and leave other persons to take your place.

Nature is no longer interested in a person past the breeding age. That's true, Tomas Tomas thought. The rest of the body begins to quit and you die. But it's also true that a man can breed a long time, longer than a wolf or a coyote or a goat. Because he drinks alcoholic drinks? Smokes cigarettes? Lies? That's it. He does it longer and lives long because he lies, Tomas Tomas thought. Although I may be an exception. Tomas Tomas allowed his weakening but still hawk-severe eyes to roam the faint-in-the-hard-distance Cabazon country. "Every man is an exception," he said.

"What, Tomas Tomas?"

"Have I been a good husband?"

"Best," she said in clear Navajo.

"Where are the other wives?"

"They went to wash in the Los Pinos. Shall I get them?"

"No," Tomas Tomas said. "I like arriving to people but not going from people. The wrong things are said when there is nothing that can be said. Don't bother to drag out the saddle. A saddle blanket will be enough. I didn't need a saddle to come into this world and I don't need one to leave." Indian, Tomas Tomas thought to himself, you're getting silly. But I still don't need a saddle, he thought. That Luto horse has a wide comfortable back. That horse was by no horse bred. A strange horse by no mare fed.

"Just a saddle blanket," he repeated and his youngest wife again disappeared into the hogan. "Listen, horse," he said to Luto, "why did you come? All right, I know why you came, but you're only taking one—me—and it took you a long time—a hundred years. You're only taking one, and for every one you take we breed three or four, sometimes five or six. A person like me, who knows how many? I guess about a hundred. You don't believe it? Possibly more. It's not important. The important thing is we Indians don't waste anything. We have enough wives. Do you know how many Navajos there are now? Eighty thousand. When I was a young boy there were only six thousand. Soon now millions. That's how we're going to defeat the Whites. One day there will be no room for the Whites. If you can't fight them off our land, —— them off. Would you like to see our secret weapons? That's a joke." Tomas Tomas used the Navajo word which sounded like laughter—adeesh. "Haven't you a sense of humor, horse?"

While the medicine man was leaning over in pain on one knee waiting for his youngest wife, Tomas Tomas tried to think something more that might be funny to work against this pain. It was a great pain. It was a new kind of pain deep in the chest as though something had entered him, something that had never been inside him before and only came once. No, he couldn't think of any joke to make against it but he could make this: Death will never get us all because the tribe has got something that the White hasn't got, a belief in the earth and in the world inside everyone, and like a bear or a coyote or an elk, the Indian is still part of the earth. And this, Tomas Tomas thought: Any Indian, me and every Indian I know in my clan, goes through a big time of his life believing it never happened. That's the only way an Indian can live. An Indian must spend a big time of his life in front of his hogan in the north part of New Mexico believing that the Whites never happened, that the white man never came.

Who are those two young white idiots coming towards me below the butte on those silly speckled horses? They are the magicians. Why can't they let an old Indian medicine man die in peace? No, I shouldn't say things like that. I should say, Who are those two silly speckled Whites coming towards me below the butte on idiot horses. Why can't they let an old Indian die with a little excitement of his own?

Tomas Tomas watched the door of the hogan for his youngest wife to appear with the saddle blanket. The black horse would not wait all day.

"Something big is happening to me," Tomas Tomas said as the riders pulled up.

"*Olá,* Tomas Tomas! We were looking for Luto."

"Some horse," Tomas Tomas said.

"We were trailing Luto and we trailed him to here."

"Don't bother. I'm going to use him now."

"For the mountains?"

"Yes."

"Already?"

"Already. Don't you think it's time?"

"But you've been here forever, Tomas Tomas," Ring said.

"Yes, I have."

"But not forever and ever?"

The young white man who asked this was accompanied by an Indian of about the same age. The medicine man knew the young white man's name was Ring Bowman and his father owned a ranch near the White Horse Trading Post. His Indian partner's name was The Son Of The Man With Twenty-six Horses.

"I was thinking," Tomas Tomas said, "we could not beat the white man but we can wait slowly and patiently like a woman and in time tame the Whites. In time."

"But now it's your time, Tomas Tomas."

Tomas Tomas looked out over all the staggering bright land that was forever lost. All the opportunities that would never come again. Where did the Indian make his mistake? In being born. Partly that. Partly that and partly not dying, staying around too long, trying to hang on to life when there was no life. The White is a knife. I have known some good Whites, but I have also known some good knives, some good looms, a good hatchet, and an excellent rope. But it's not the same as people. We were conquered by the knives. We defeated the Anasazi People and then we were defeated by knives. That's all right because there's nothing we can do about it but it would have been nice if I could leave the world to people. If people still peopled the world. "Do you agree?"

"Sure, Tomas Tomas."

"I was thinking how nice it would be in leaving it if people still peopled the world."

"Yes, Tomas Tomas."

"You think I'm an old medicine man with too many wives and cow shit talk."

"You leave the world in good hands, Tomas Tomas. Your world will be in good hands."

"Give me your hand." The medicine man took the white boy's hand and looked at it carefully. "Chalk hand. What do you expect to get done with this?"

"Nothing."

"That's right. You will get nothing done. It's not a hand that can make any magic."

"Did you hear that, Twenty-six Horses?"

"Yes, I heard it," Twenty-six Horses said. "Does that mean you are going to kill me?"

"Yes, it does."

"Right here?" Tomas Tomas asked.

"Yes," Ring said. "There will still be a lot of magic after you're gone, Tomas Tomas. I'm going to kill Twenty-six Horses right before your eyes."

"Yes, he is," Twenty-six Horses said.

"That's not magic," Tomas Tomas said. "Anyway you're not Twenty-six Horses, you're The Son Of The Man With Twenty-six Horses."

"Just the same," Ring said.

"Now, if you could kill twenty-six Whites that would be a trick."

"You're bitter, aren't you, Tomas Tomas?"

"No, I'm an Indian," Tomas Tomas said. The medicine man was still hunched forward in pain and he could not figure why the two young men did not understand that he had some very important business to take care of. "You should understand," Tomas Tomas said, hoping that he had picked up where he left off. "You should understand that I don't have much time. I must arrive on the mountain before it is too late."

"It will take just one shot to kill Twenty-six Horses."

"Believe him, it's true," Twenty-six Horses said.

"I believe him," Tomas Tomas said, raising his voice. "I believe that he can kill you, Twenty-six Horses, in one shot. But what is great magic about that?"

"The great magic, Tomas Tomas, is that I bring Twenty-six Horses back to life."

Tomas Tomas tried resting on one hand to ease the pain. "I know the missionary says the same thing. There was a man who died and came back again by magic, but no one saw it. I never met anyone who saw it. The missionary didn't see this magic. Did you?"

"No, but we can do it," Ring said.

"The both of you die?"

"No, just him," Ring said, hooking his thumb at Twenty-six Horses.

Tomas Tomas looked over at the hogan. "Ihda!" Tomas Tomas called toward the hogan door .

"The saddle blanket must be in the other hogan," Tomas Tomas' youngest wife called back. "I will go there and look."

"Hurry," the medicine man repeated in a guttural whisper. Then to the magicians, "Now?"

"Now," Ring said. "Twenty-six Horses will stand there on the rimrock."

"No," Tomas Tomas whispered.

"At about ten paces I will kill him."

"No, don't."

"Then bring him back to life."

"Sure?"

"Positive."

"Could you bring me back to life? Don't answer. I am going this time. I'm all prepared to go and I'm going. But if you have some good magic I would like to take that magic with me. Can I take it with me in my medicine bundle?"

"Yes," Ring said. "Now stand over there on the rimrock, Twenty-six Horses."

"Something I can take with me," the medicine man repeated. "I would like to take some good magic with me when I go and I go to the mountain now."

Tomas Tomas saw the young man called Ring, who was tall for his age and hard blue-eyed, withdraw from the saddle holster on the patient speckled Appaloosa a Marlin carbine.

"Just an ordinary thirty-thirty," Ring said to the dying medicine man, Tomas Tomas.

"Yes."

"Now I put the cartridge in the chamber. You notice it has a red tip."

"Why does the bullet have a red tip? Does it have something to do with the magic?"

Ring did not answer but slammed the shell home with a swift solid swing of the lever action.

The medicine man watched the young, arrogantly young, white man named Ring Bowman—who came from a near ranch with water and green grass that sleeked the cattle and the young man's cheeks, and demarked the boundaries of the Navajo Nation—raised the gun slowly and carefully until the bronze tipped front sight was perfectly down in the V of the rear sight and the front sight was exactly on the heart of the Indian called Twenty-six Horses.

"Now I will kill an Indian," Ring said.

"Wait!"

"Why?"

"Well, I have decided I don't need to take any magic with me."

"Oh, you'll need magic up there, Tomas Tomas, won't he, Twenty-six Horses?"

"Yes, you will, Tomas Tomas."

"All right. If Tomas Tomas is willing, go ahead and kill Twenty-six Horses with one shot." The medicine man was annoyed.

"One shot," Ring said and began to squeeze the trigger slowly. The roar was terrific, the noise came back again and again from the mesas and the dark canyons and Twenty-six Horses toppled down dead like the very dead and bled red from the stomach all over the ground.

"Get up!" Ring shouted.

The dead got up.

"Now give me the red bullet I fired."

Twenty-six Horses raised his bronzed hand to his mouth and spat out the red bullet.

"Now here is your magic to take to the mountain," Ring said, taking the red bullet and placing it in the quavering hand of Tomas Tomas.

"Do I dare? Sure I do," Tomas Tomas answered himself. "I will try it on Him as soon as I get to the mountain."

"Who is him?"

"The one who allowed the Whites to defeat us."

"You mean an ancestor?" the dead-alive and standing Twenty-six Horses asked.

"Yes," Tomas Tomas said, standing with great effort. "An ancestor. That's a good name, ancestor. Where's the horse?"

When Twenty-six Horses and Ring brought Luto over to the hogan Tomas Tomas was ready. His youngest wife placed the white saddle blanket on the very wide-backed black horse and Tomas Tomas mounted painfully by himself. Now she passed Tomas Tomas up a small dark bundle and Tomas Tomas placed the red bullet inside.

"If it does not work," the medicine man said down to the young men, "you will hear from me."

"Where you are going it will work," Ring said.

The black horse started slowly toward the easy foothills that began the big climb of the mountain. "Goodbye," Tomas Tomas waved to his youngest wife. "It has been good. Marry rich. Die old. Bring magic. I will see you. I will see you all. I climb dying. I climb dying. Something big is happening to me," Tomas Tomas called.

"We should have told him how it works," Twenty-six Horses said, watching the medicine man disappear.

"That there were two blank red bullets, one in my gun and one in your mouth, and catchup in your pants. No. No, it's not necessary because they will believe him."

"His ancestors?"

"Yes, Twenty-six Horses. Haven't we always believed he had eleven wives instead of five?"

"Yes."

"Well, if he wanted to believe eleven, then his ancestors will want to believe anything."

"I suppose," Twenty-six Horses said. "Let's get some more catchup."

"And bullets," Ring said.

In a few hours all the Navajo Indians from the Checkerboard Clan had gathered around Coyotes Love Me, who held a spy glass loaned to him by the trader.

"Where is the medicine man, Tomas Tomas, Coyotes Love Me?"

"He is on the Vallecito."

"Is he steady?"

"No, he seems sick in the saddle, as though he will fall."

"How is he now, Coyotes Love Me?"

Coyotes Love Me steadied the long scope. "Better. The black horse is trying to help. He stops and tries to steady Tomas Tomas, but I do not think Tomas Tomas will make it. . . ."

"Let me see." Afraid Of His Own Horses took the scope. "It's worse than Coyotes Love Me said. No, Tomas Tomas will never make it. The black horse seems very tired. The black horse cannot make it up and over the Gregorio Crest. Well, that's too bad. I guess the medicine man will fall off and die on the way up. It's a terrible thing, he won't make the mountain to die, but we don't have any magic for this."

"No, we don't," Coyotes Love Me agreed.

"I've got some," Ring said. "Will you hand me the rifle again, Twenty-six Horses?"

"Nothing will work now. There is nothing anyone can do now at this distance," Coyotes Love Me said.

Ring raised the gun very high, much too high most of the Indians thought, but a half second after the shot the great black horse, even at this distance with the naked eye, could be seen going over the top in furious desperate leaps as though fleeing a battle. The medicine man, Tomas Tomas, was on top. Home.

Afraid Of His Own Horses put down the scope and looked at Ring. "That was good magic."

"That was a good, while no one was looking, far-off long-distance kick in the ass," Coyotes Love Me said. "White medicine."

They found the body of Tomas Tomas two months later near a spring on the exact top of the mountain above a live oak knoll near the Las Vacas ranger cabin. There were tracks from where Tomas Tomas had dismounted, gone down to the spring, come back to the top dying and finally died.

There was never found any trace of his medicine bundle containing the red bullet. Twenty-six Horses and Ring went up to look all around the Las Vacas one day, spent the night and came down bright the next morning, but they never found the red bullet either.

"Do you suppose—?"

"No," Ring said. "You've got to realize, Twenty-six Horses, that dead is dead."

But Twenty-six Horses, besides being a Navajo who believed in magic in the afterworld, had been shot dead many times in this one, so all the way down the mountain and even after they had passed the hogan of Tomas Tomas in Navajo Country, Twenty-six Horses kept saying, "Do you suppose?"

And Ring kept saying, "No, I don't. I guess I don't."

Which is a good place to leave it, where we left it, Ring thought, a place where the world has always and will always leave it. Ring rode ahead on Luto carrying the gun and Twenty-six Horses followed on a small paint. The horses slipped down obliquely into the wide flat far-lost beauty of the Indian Country and disappeared in the hard purple and wild mesas that fell in steps through a fierce color continuity that was not dying, a fabulous and bright Navajo Nation that was not dead, the hushed song in the land, disappearing and faint but still an alive and still smoldering Indian incantation against white doom—singing that the white man never happened, chanting death never came.

FACING DEATH: THE SOUTH

William Faulkner
1897-1962

Without question, Faulkner was one of the most imposing literary figures America ever produced. Though he spent most of his life in and around his native Oxford, Mississippi, his name is known world-wide for his books. In them he created and populated an entire county, Yoknapatawapha. "Red Leaves" was published in Faulkner's first collection of stories, *These Thirteen,* and is about the Chickasaw Indians in the county's early days. It is a powerful story, again proceeding inevitably, and much of its power is derived from the characters' vivid, contrasting attitudes towards death. The tone is especially convincing, reflecting Faulkner's love and concern for the land. A Nobel Prize winner, Faulkner takes the reader, through his other books and stories, up to modern times, tracing the progress of several families. Suggested readings: *The Bear, The Sound And The Fury,* and *The Hamlet.*

RED LEAVES

I

The two Indians crossed the plantation toward the slave quarters. Neat with whitewash, of baked soft brick, the two rows of houses in which lived the slaves belonging to the clan faced one another across the mild shade of the lane marked and scored with naked feet and with a few homemade toys mute in the dust. There was no sign of life.

"I know what we will find," the first Indian said.

"What we will not find," the second said. Although it was noon, the lane was vacant, the doors of the cabins empty and quiet; no cooking smoke rose from any of the chinked and plastered chimneys.

"Yes. It happened like this when the father of him who is now the Man died."

"You mean, of him who was the Man."

"Yao."

The first Indian's name was Three Basket. He was perhaps sixty. They were both squat men, a little solid, burgherlike; paunchy, with big heads, big, broad, dust-colored faces of a certain blurred serenity like carved heads on a ruined wall in Siam or Sumatra, looming out of a mist. The sun had done it, the violent sun, the violent shade. Their hair looked like sedge grass on burnt-over land. Clamped through one ear Three Basket wore an enameled snuffbox.

"I have said all the time that this is not the good way. In the old days there were no quarters, no Negroes. A man's time was his own then. He had time. Now he must spend most of it finding work for them who prefer sweating to do."

"They are like horses and dogs."

"They are like nothing in this sensible world. Nothing contents them save sweat. They are worse than the white people."

"It is not as though the Man himself had to find work for them to do."

"You said it. I do not like slavery. It is not the good way. In the old days, there was the good way. But not now."

"You do not remember the old way either."

"I have listened to them who do. And I have tried this way. Man was not made to sweat."

"That's so. See what it has done to their flesh."

"Yes. Black. It has a bitter taste, too."

"You have eaten of it?"

"Once. I was young then, and more hardy in the appetite than now. Now it is different with me."

"Yes. They are too valuable to eat now."

"There is a bitter taste to the flesh which I do not like."

"They are too valuable to eat, anyway, when the white men will give horses for them."

They entered the lane. The mute, meager toys—the fetish-shaped objects made of wood and rags and feathers—lay in the dust about the patinaed doorsteps, among bones and broken gourd dishes. But there was no sound from any cabin, no face in any door; had not been since yesterday, when Issetibbeha died. But they already knew what they would find.

It was in the central cabin, a house a little larger than the others, where at certain phases of the moon the Negroes would gather to begin their ceremonies before removing after nightfall to the creek bottom, where they kept the drums. In this room they kept the minor accessories, the cryptic ornaments, the ceremonial records which consisted of sticks daubed with red clay in symbols. It had a hearth in the center of the floor, beneath a hole in the roof, with a few cold wood ashes and a suspended iron pot. The window shutters were closed; when the two Indians entered, after the abashless sunlight they could distinguish nothing with the eyes save a movement, shadow, out of which eyeballs rolled, so that the place appeared to be full of Negroes. The two Indians stood in the door.

"Yao," Basket said. "I said this is not the good way."

"I don't think I want to be here," the second said.

"That is black man's fear which you smell. It does not smell as ours does."

"I don't think I want to be here."

"Your fear has an odor too."

"Maybe it is Issetibba which we smell."

"Yao. He knows. He knows what we will find here. He knew when he died what we should find here today." Out of the rank twilight of the room the eyes, the smell, of Negroes rolled about them. "I am Three Basket, whom you know," Basket said into the room. "We are come from the Man. He whom we seek is gone?" The Negroes said nothing. The smell of them, of their bodies, seemed to ebb and flux in the still hot air. They seemed to be musing as one upon something remote, inscrutable. They were like a single octopus. They were like the roots of a huge tree uncovered, the earth broken momentarily upon the writhen, thick, fetid tangle of its lightless and outraged life. "Come," Basket said. "You know our errand. Is he whom we seek gone?"

"They are thinking something," the second said. "I do not want to be here."

"They are knowing something," Basket said.

"They are hiding him, you think?"

"No. He is gone. He has been gone since last night. It happened like this before, when the grandfather of him who is now the Man died. It took us three days to catch him. For three days Doom lay above the ground, saying, 'I see my horse and my dog. But I do not see my slave. What have you done with him that you will not permit me to lie quiet?' "

"They do not like to die."

"Yao. They cling. It makes trouble for us, always. A people without honor and without decorum. Always a trouble."

"I do not like it here."

"Nor do I. But then, they are savages; they cannot be expected to regard usage. That is why I say that this way is a bad way."

"Yao. They cling. They would even rather work in the sun than to enter the earth with a chief. But he is gone."

The Negroes had said nothing, made no sound. The white eyeballs rolled, wild, subdued; the smell was rank, violent. "Yes, they fear," the second said. "What shall we do now?"

"Let us go and talk with the Man."

"Will Moketubbe listen?"

"What can he do? He will not like to. But he is the Man now."

"Yao. He is the Man. He can wear the shoes with the red heels all the time now." They turned and went out. There was no door in the door frame. There were no doors in any of the cabins.

"He did that anyway," Basket said.

"Behind Issetibbeha's back. But now they are his shoes, since he is the Man."

"Yao. Issetibbeha did not like it. I have heard. I know that he said to Moketubbe: 'When you are the Man, the shoes will be yours. But until then, they are my shoes.' But now Moketubbe is the Man; he can wear them."

"Yao," the second said. "He is the Man now. He used to wear the shoes behind Issetibbeha's back, and it was not known if Issetibbeha knew this or not. And then Issetibbeha became dead, who was not old, and the shoes are Moketubbe's, since he is the Man now. What do you think of that?"

"I don't think about it," Basket said. "Do you?"

"No," the second said.

"Good," Basket said. "You are wise."

II

The house sat on a knoll, surrounded by oak trees. The front of it was one story in height, composed of the deck house of a steamboat which had gone ashore and which Doom, Issetibbeha's father, had dismantled with his slaves and hauled on cypress rollers twelve miles home overland. It took them five months. His house consisted at the time of one brick wall. He set the steamboat broadside on to the wall, where now the chipped and flaked gilding of the rococo cornices arched in faint splendor above the gilt lettering of the stateroom names above the jalousied doors.

Doom had been born merely a subchief, a Mingo, one of three children on the mother's side of the family. He made a journey—he was a young man then and New Orleans was a European city—from north Mississippi to New Orleans by keel boat, where he met the Chevalier Soeur Blonde de Vitry, a man whose social position, on its face, was as equivocal as Doom's own. In New Orleans, among the gamblers and cutthroats of the river front, Doom, under the tutelage of his patron, passed as the chief, the Man, the hereditary owner of that land which belonged to the male side of the family; it was the Chevalier de Vitry who spoke of him as *l'Homme or de l'Homme,* and hence Doom.

They were seen everywhere together—the Indian, the squat man with a bold, inscrutable, underbred face, and the Parisian, the expatriate, the friend, it was said, of Carondelet and the intimate of General Wilkinson. Then they disappeared, the two of them, vanishing from their old equivocal haunts and leaving behind them the legend of the sums which Doom was believed to have won, and some tale about a young woman, daughter of a fairly well-to-do West Indian family, the son and brother of whom sought Doom with a pistol about his old haunts for some time after his disappearance.

Six months later the young woman herself disappeared, boarding the Saint Louis packet, which put in one night at a wood landing on the north Mississippi side, where the woman, accompanied by a Negro maid, got off. Four Indians met her with a horse and wagon, and they traveled for three days, slowly, since she was already big with child, to the plantation, where she found that Doom was now chief. He never told her how he accomplished it, save that his uncle and his cousin had died suddenly. Before that time the house had consisted of a brick wall built by shiftless slaves, against which was propped a thatched lean-to divided into rooms and littered with bones and refuse, set in the center of ten thousand acres of matchless parklike forest where deer grazed like domestic cattle. Doom and the woman were married there a short time before Issetibbeha was born, by a combination itinerant minister and slave trader who arrived on a mule, to the saddle of which was lashed a cotton umbrella and a three-gallon demijohn of whiskey. After that, Doom began to acquire more slaves and to cultivate some of his land, as the white people did. But he never had enough for them to do. In utter idleness the majority of them led lives transplanted whole out of African jungles, save on the occasions when, entertaining guests, Doom coursed them with dogs.

When Doom died, Issetibbeha, his son, was nineteen. He became proprietor of the land and of the quintupled herd of blacks for which he had no use at all. Though the title of Man rested with him, there was a hierarchy of cousins and uncles who ruled the clan and who finally gathered in squatting conclave over the Negro question, squatting profoundly beneath the golden names above the doors of the steamboat.

"We cannot eat them," one said.

"Why not?"

"There are too many of them."

"That's true," a third said. "Once we started, we should have to eat them all. And that much flesh diet is not good for man."

"Perhaps they will be like deer flesh. That cannot hurt you."

"We might kill a few of them and not eat them," Issetibbeha said.

They looked at him for a while. "What for?" one said.

"That is true," a second said. "We cannot do that. They are too valuable; remember all the bother they have caused us, finding things for them to do. We must do as the white men do."

"How is that?" Issetibbeha said.

"Raise more Negroes by clearing more land to make corn to feed them, then sell them. We will clear the land and plant it with food and raise Negroes and sell them to the white men for money."

"But what will we do with this money?" a third said.

They thought for a while.

"We will see," the first said. They squatted, profound, grave.

"It means work," the third said.

"Let the Negroes do it," the first said.

"Yao. Let them. To sweat is bad. It is damp. It opens the pores."

"And then the night air enters."

"Yao. Let the Negroes do it. They appear to like sweating."

So they cleared the land with the Negroes and planted it in grain. Up to that time the slaves had lived in a huge pen with a lean-to roof over one corner, like a pen for pigs. But now they began to build quarters, cabins, putting the young Negroes in the cabins in pairs to mate; five years later Issetibbeha sold forty head to a Memphis trader, and he took the money and went abroad upon it, his maternal uncle from New Orleans conducting the trip. At that time the Chevalier Soeur Blonde de Vitry was an old man in Paris, in a toupee and a corset and a careful, toothless old face fixed in a grimace quizzical and profoundly tragic. He borrowed three hundred dollars from Issetibbeha and in return he introduced him into certain circles; a year later Issetibbeha returned home with a gilt bed, a pair of girandoles by whose light it was said that Pompadour arranged her hair while Louis smirked at his mirrored face across her powdered shoulder, and a pair of slippers with red heels. They were too small for him, since he had not worn shoes at all until he reached New Orleans on his way abroad.

He brought the slippers home in tissue paper and kept them in the remaining pocket of a pair of saddlebags filled with cedar shavings, save when he took them out on occasion for his son, Moketubbe, to play with. At three years of age Moketubbe had a broad, flat, Mongolian face that appeared to exist in a complete and unfathomable lethargy, until confronted by the slippers.

Moketubbe's mother was a comely girl whom Issetibbeha had seen one day working in her shift in a melon patch. He stopped and watched her for a while—the broad, solid thighs, the sound back, the serene face. He was on his way to the creek to fish that day, but he didn't go any farther; perhaps while he stood there watching the unaware girl he may have remembered his own mother, the city woman, the fugitive with her fans and laces and her Negro blood, and all the tawdry shabbiness of that sorry affair. Within the year Moketubbe was born; even at three he could not get his feet into the slippers. Watching him in the still, hot afternoons as he struggled with the slippers with a certain monstrous repudiation of fact, Issetibbeha laughed quietly to himself. He laughed at Moketubbe's antics with the shoes for several years, because Moketubbe did not give up trying to put them on until he was sixteen. Then he quit. Or Issetibbeha thought he had. But he had merely quit trying in Issetibbeha's presence. Issetibbeha's newest wife told him that Moketubbe had stolen and hidden the shoes. Issetibbeha quit laughing then, and he sent the woman away, so that he was alone. "Yao," he said. "I too like being alive, it seems." He sent for Moketubbe. "I give them to you," he said.

Moketubbe was twenty-five then, unmarried. Issetibbeha was not tall, but he was taller by six inches than his son and almost a hundred pounds lighter. Moketubbe was already diseased with flesh, with a pale, broad, inert face and dropsical hands and feet. "They are yours now," Issetibbeha said, watching him. Moketubbe had looked at him once when he entered, a glance brief, discreet, veiled.

"Thanks," he said.

Issetibbeha looked at him. He could never tell if Moketubbe saw anything, looked at anything. "Why will it not be the same if I give the slippers to you?"

"Thanks," Moketubbe said. Issetibbeha was using snuff at the time; a white man had shown him how to put the powder into his lip and scour it against his teeth with a twig of gum or of alphea.

"Well," he said, "a man cannot live forever." He looked at his son, then his gaze went blank in turn, unseeing, and he mused for an instant. You could not tell what he was thinking, save that he said half aloud: "Yao. But Doom's uncle had no shoes with red heels." He looked at his son again, fat, inert. "Beneath all that, a man might think of doing anything and it not be known until too late." He sat in a splint chair hammocked with deer thongs. "He cannot even get them on; he and I are both frustrated by the same gross meat which he wears. He cannot even get them on. But is that my fault?"

He lived for five years longer, then he died. He was sick one night, and though the doctor came in a skunk-skin vest and burned sticks, Issetibbeha died before noon.

That was yesterday; the grave was dug, and for twelve hours now the People had been coming in wagons and carriages and on horseback and afoot, to eat the baked dog and the succotash and the yams cooked in ashes and to attend the funeral.

III

"It will be three days," Basket said, as he and the other Indian returned to the house. "It will be three days and the food will not be enough; I have seen it before."

The second Indian's name was Louis Berry. "He will smell too, in this weather."

"Yao. They are nothing but a trouble and a care."

"Maybe it will not take three days."

"They run far. Yao. We will smell this Man before he enters the earth. You watch and see if I am not right."

They approached the house.

"He can wear the shoes now," Berry said. "He can wear them now in man's sight."

"He cannot wear them for a while yet," Basket said. Berry looked at him. "He will lead the hunt."

"Moketubbe?" Berry said. "Do you think he will? A man to whom even talking is travail?"

"What else can he do? It is his own father who will soon begin to smell."

"That is true," Berry said. "There is even yet a price he must pay for the shoes. Yao. He has truly bought them. What do you think?"

"What do you think?"

"What do you think?"

"I think nothing."

"Nor do I. Issetibbeha will not need the shoes now. Let Moketubbe have them; Issetibbeha will not care."

"Yao. Man must die."

"Yao. Let him; there is still the Man."

The bark roof of the porch was supported by peeled cypress poles, high above the texas of the steamboat, shading an unfloored banquette where on the trodden earth mules and horses were tethered in bad weather. On the forward end of the steamboat's deck sat an old man and two women. One of the women was dressing a fowl, the other was shelling corn. The old man was talking. He was barefoot, in a long linen frock coat and a beaver hat.

"This world is going to the dogs," he said. "It is being ruined by white men. We got along fine for years and years, before the white men foisted their Negroes upon us. In the old days the old men sat in the shade and ate stewed deer's flesh and corn and smoked tobacco and talked of honor and grave affairs; now what do we do? Even the old wear themselves into the grave taking care of them that like sweating." When Basket and Berry crossed the deck he ceased and looked up at them. His eyes were querulous, bleared; his face was myriad with tiny wrinkles. "He is fled also," he said.

"Yes," Berry said, "he is gone."

"I knew it. I told them so. It will take three weeks, like when Doom died. You watch and see."

"It was three days, not three weeks," Berry said.

"Were you there?"

"No," Berry said. "But I have heard."

"Well, I was there," the old man said. "For three whole weeks, through the swamps and the briers—" They went on and left him talking.

What had been the saloon of the steamboat was now a shell, rotting slowly; the polished mahogany, the carving glinting momentarily and fading through the mold in figures cabalistic and profound; the gutted windows were like cataracted eyes. It contained a few sacks of seed or grain, and the fore part of the running gear of a barouche, to the axle of which two C-springs rusted in graceful curves, supporting nothing. In one corner a fox cub ran steadily and soundlessly up and down a willow cage; three scrawny gamecocks moved in the dust, and the place was pocked and marked with their dried droppings.

They passed through the brick wall and entered a big room of chinked logs. It contained the hinder part of the barouche, and the dismantled body lying on its side, the window slatted over with willow withes, through which protruded the heads, the still, beady, outraged eyes and frayed combs of still more game chickens. It was floored with packed clay; in one corner leaned a crude plow and two hand-hewn boat paddles. From the ceiling, suspended by four deer thongs, hung the gilt bed which Issetibbeha had fetched from Paris. It had neither mattress nor springs, the frame criss-crossed now by a neat hammocking of thongs.

Issetibbeha had tried to have his newest wife, the young one, sleep in the bed. He was congenitally short of breath himself, and he passed the nights half reclining in his splint chair. He would see her to bed and, later, wakeful, sleeping as he did but three or four hours a night, he would sit in the darkness and simulate slumber and listen to her sneak infinitesimally from the gilt and ribboned bed, to lie on a quilt pallet on the floor until just before daylight. Then she would enter the bed quietly again and in turn simulate slumber, while in the darkness beside her Issetibbeha quietly laughed and laughed.

The girandoles were lashed by thongs to two sticks propped in a corner where a ten-gallon whiskey keg lay also. There was a clay hearth; facing it, in the splint chair, Moketubbe sat. He was maybe an inch better than five feet tall, and he weighed two hundred and fifty pounds. He wore a broadcloth coat and no shirt, his round, smooth copper balloon of belly swelling above the bottom piece of a suit of linen underwear. On his feet were the slippers with the red heels. Behind his chair stood a stripling with a punkah-like fan made of fringed paper. Moketubbe sat motionless, with his broad, yellow face with its closed eyes and flat nostrils, his flipperlike arms extended. On his face was an expression profound, tragic, and inert. He did not open his eyes when Basket and Berry came in.

"He has worn them since daylight?" Basket said.

"Since daylight," the stripling said. The fan did not cease. "You can see."

"Yao," Basket said. "We can see." Moketubbe did not move. He looked like an effigy, like a Malay god in frock coat, drawers, naked chest, the trivial scarlet-heeled shoes.

"I wouldn't disturb him, if I were you," the stripling said.

"Not if I were you," Basket said. He and Berry squatted. The stripling moved the fan steadily. "O Man," Basket said, "listen." Moketubbe did not move. "He is gone," Basket said.

"I told you so," the stripling said. "I knew he would flee. I told you."

"Yao," Basket said. "You are not the first to tell us afterward what we should have known before. Why is it that some of you wise men took no steps yesterday to prevent this?"

"He does not wish to die," Berry said.

"Why should he not wish it?" Basket said.

"Because he must die some day is no reason," the stripling said. "That would not convince me either, old man."

"Hold your tongue," Berry said.

"For twenty years," Basket said, "while others of his race sweat in the fields, he served the Man in the shade. Why should he not wish to die, since he did not wish to sweat?"

"And it will be quick," Berry said. "It will not take long."

"Catch him and tell him that," the stripling said.

"Hush," Berry said. They squatted, watching Moketubbe's face. He might have been dead himself. It was as though he were cased so in flesh that even breathing took place too deep within him to show.

"Listen, O Man," Basket said. "Issetibbeha is dead. He waits. His dog and his horse we have. But his slave has fled. The one who held the pot for him, who ate of his food, from his dish, is fled. Issetibbeha waits."

"Yao," Berry said.

"This is not the first time," Basket said. "This happened when Doom, thy grandfather, lay waiting at the door of the earth. He lay waiting three days, saying, 'Where is my Negro?' And Issetibbeha, thy father, answered, 'I will find him. Rest; I will bring him to you so that you may begin the journey.'"

"Yao," Berry said.

Moketubbe had not moved, had not opened his eyes.

"For three days Issetibbeha hunted in the bottom," Basket said. "He did not even return home for food, until the Negro was with him; then he said to Doom, his father, 'Here is thy dog, thy horse, thy Negro; rest.' Issetibbeha, who is dead since yesterday, said it. And now Issetibbeha's Negro is fled. His horse and his dog wait with him, but his Negro is fled."

"Yao," Berry said.

Moketubbe had not moved. His eyes were closed; upon his supine monstrous shape there was a colossal inertia, something profoundly immobile, beyond and impervious to flesh. They watched his face, squatting.

"When thy father was newly the Man, this happened," Basket said. "And it was Issetibbeha who brought back the slave to where his father waited to enter the earth." Moketubbe's face had not moved, his eyes had not moved. After a while Basket said, "Remove the shoes."

The stripling removed the shoes. Moketubbe began to pant, his bare chest moving deep, as though he were rising from beyond his unfathomed flesh back into life, like up from the water, the sea. But his eyes had not opened yet.

Berry said, "He will lead the hunt."

"Yao," Basket said. "He is the Man. He will lead the hunt."

IV

All that day the Negro, Issetibbeha's body servant, hidden in the barn, watched Issetibbeha's dying. He was forty, a Guinea man. He had a flat nose, a close, small head; the inside corners of his eyes showed red a little, and his prominent gums were a pale bluish red above his square, broad teeth. He had been taken at fourteen by a trader off Kamerun, before his teeth had been filed. He had been Issetibbha's body servant for twenty-three years.

On the day before, the day on which Issetibbeha lay sick, he returned to the quarters at dusk. In that unhurried hour the smoke of the cooking fires blew slowly across the street from door to door, carrying into the opposite one the smell of the identical meat and bread. The women tended them; the men were gathered at the head of the lane, watching him as he came down the slope from the house, putting his naked feet down carefully in a strange dusk. To the waiting men his eyeballs were a little luminous.

"Issetibbeha is not dead yet," the headman said.

"Not dead," the body servant said. "Who not dead?"

In the dusk they had faces like his, the different ages, the thoughts sealed inscrutable behind faces like the death masks of apes. The smell of the fires, the cooking, blew sharp and slow across the strange dusk, as from another world, above the lane and the pickaninnies naked in the dust.

"If he lives past sundown, he will live until daybreak," one said.

"Who says?"

"Talk says."

"Yao. Talk says. We know but one thing." They looked at the body servant as he stood among them, his eyeballs a little luminous. He was breathing slow and deep. His chest was bare; he was sweating a little. "He knows. He knows it."

"Let us let the drums talk."

"Yao. Let the drums tell it."

The drums began after dark. They kept them hidden in the creek bottom. They were made of hollowed cypress knees, and the Negroes kept them hidden; why, none knew. They were buried in the mud on the bank of a slough; a lad of fourteen guarded them. He was undersized, and a mute; he squatted in the mud there all day, clouded over with mosquitoes, naked save for the mud with which he coated himself against the mosquitoes, and about his neck a fiber bag containing a pig's rib to which black shreds of flesh still adhered, and two scaly barks on a wire. He slobbered onto his clutched knees, drooling; now and then Indians came noiselessly out of the bushes behind him and stood there and contemplated him for a while and went away, and he never knew it.

From the loft of the stable where he lay hidden until dark and after, the Negro could hear the drums. They were three miles away, but he could hear them as though they were in the barn itself below him, thudding and thudding. It was as though he could see the fire too, and the black limbs turning into and out of the flames in copper gleams. Only there would be no fire. There would be no more light there than where he lay in the dusty loft, with the whispering arpeggios of rat feet along the warm and immemorial ax-squared rafters. The only fire there would be the smudge against mosquitoes where the women with nursing children crouched, their heavy, sluggish breasts nippled full and smooth into the mouths of men children; contemplative, oblivious of the drumming, since a fire would signify life.

There was a fire in the steamboat, where Issetibbeha lay dying among his wives, beneath the lashed girandoles and the suspended bed. He could see the smoke, and just before sunset he saw the doctor come out, in a waistcoat made of skunk skins, and set fire to two clay-daubed sticks at the bows of the boat deck. "So he is not dead yet," the Negro said into the whispering gloom of the loft, answering himself; he could hear the two voices, himself and himself:

"Who not dead?"

"You are dead."

"Yao, I am dead," he said quietly. He wished to be where the drums were. He imagined himself springing out of the bushes, leaping among the drums on his bare, lean, greasy, invisible limbs. But he could not do that, because man leaped past life, into where death was; he dashed into death and did not die because when death took a man, it took him just this side of the end of living. It was when death overran him from behind, still in life. The thin whisper of rat feet died in fainting gusts along the rafters. Once he had eaten rat. He was a boy then, but just come to America. They had lived ninety days in a three-foot-high 'tween deck in tropic latitudes, hearing from topside the drunken New England captain intoning aloud from a book which he did not recognize for ten years afterward to be the Bible. Squatting in the stable so, he had watched the rat, civilized, by association with man reft of its inherent cunning of limb and eye; he had caught it without difficulty, with scarce a movement of his hand, and he ate it slowly, wondering how any of the rats had escaped so long. At that time he was still wearing the single white garment which the trader, a deacon in the Unitarian church, had given him, and he spoke then only his native tongue.

He was naked now, save for a pair of dungaree pants bought by Indians from white men, and an amulet slung on a thong about his hips. The amulet consisted of one half of a mother-of-pearl lorgnon which Issetibbeha had brought back from Paris, and the skull of a cottonmouth moccasin. He had killed the snake himself and eaten it, save the poison head. He lay in the loft, watching the house, the steamboat, listening to the drums, thinking of himself among the drums.

He lay there all night. The next morning he saw the doctor come out, in his skunk vest, and get on his mule and ride away, and he became quite still and watched the final dust from beneath the mule's delicate feet die away, and then he found that he was still breathing and it seemed strange to him that he still breathed air, still needed air. Then he lay and watched quietly, waiting to move, his eyeballs a little luminous, but with a quiet light, and his breathing light and regular, and saw Louis Berry come out and look at the sky. It was good light then, and already five Indians squatted in their Sunday clothes along the steamboat deck; by noon there were twenty-five there. That afternoon they dug the trench in which the meat would be baked, and the yams; by that time there were almost a hundred guests—decorous, quiet, patient in their stiff European finery—and he watched Berry lead Issetibbeha's mare from the stable and tie her to a tree, and then he watched Berry emerge from the house with the old hound which lay beside Issetibbeha's chair. He tied the hound to the tree too, and it sat there, looking gravely about at the faces. Then it began to howl. It was still howling at sundown, when the Negro climbed down the back wall of the barn and entered the spring branch, where it was already dusk. He began to run then. He could hear the hound howling behind him, and near the spring, already running, he passed another Negro. The two men, the one motionless and the other running, looked for an instant at each other as though across an actual boundary between two different worlds. He ran on into full darkness, mouth closed, fists doubled, his broad nostrils bellowing steadily.

He ran on in the darkness. He knew the country well, because he had hunted it often with Issetibbeha, following on his mule the course of the fox or the cat beside Issetibbeha's mare; he knew it as well as did the men who would pursue him. He saw them for the first time shortly before sunset of the second day. He had run thirty miles then, up the creek bottom, before doubling back; lying in a pawpaw thicket he saw the pursuit for the first time. There were two of them, in shirts and straw hats, carrying their neatly rolled trousers under their arms, and they had no weapons. They were middle-aged, paunchy, and they could not have moved very fast anyway; it would be twelve hours before they could return to where he lay watching them. "So I will have until midnight to rest," he said. He was near enough to the plantation to smell the cooking fires, and he thought how he ought to be hungry, since he had not eaten in thirty hours. "But it is more important to rest," he told himself. He continued to tell himself that, lying in the pawpaw thicket, because the effort of resting, the need and the haste to rest, made his heart thud the same as the running had done. It was as though he had forgot how to rest, as though the six hours were not long enough to do it in, to remember again how to do it.

As soon as dark came he moved again. He had thought to keep going steadily and quietly through the night, since there was nowhere for him to go, but as soon as he moved he began to run at top speed, breasting his panting chest, his broad-flaring nostrils through the choked and whipping darkness. He ran for an hour, lost by then, without direction, when suddenly he stopped, and after a time his thudding heart unraveled from the sound of the drums. By the sound they were not two miles away; he followed the sound until he could smell the smudge fire and taste the acrid smoke. When he stood among them the drums did not cease; only the headman came to him where he stood in the drifting smudge, panting, his nostrils flaring and pulsing, the hushed glare of his ceaseless eyeballs in his mud-daubed face as though they were worked from lungs.

"We have expected thee," the headman said. "Go, now."

"Go?"

"Eat, and go. The dead may not consort with the living; thou knowest that."

"Yao. I know that." They did not look at one another. The drums had not ceased.

"Wilt thou eat?" the headman said.

"I am not hungry. I caught a rabbit this afternoon, and ate while I lay hidden."

"Take some cooked meat with thee, then."

He accepted the cooked meat, wrapped in leaves, and entered the creek bottom again; after a while the sound of the drums ceased. He walked steadily until daybread. "I have twelve hours," he said. "Maybe more, since the trail was followed by night." He squatted and ate the meat and wiped his hands on his thighs. Then he rose and removed the dungaree pants and squatted again beside a slough and coated himself with mud—face, arms, body and legs—and squatted again, clasping his knees, his head bowed. When it was light enough to see, he moved back into the swamp and squatted again and went to sleep so. He did not dream at all. It was well that he moved, for, waking suddenly in board daylight and the high sun, he saw the two Indians. They still carried their neatly rolled trousers; they stood opposite the place where he lay hidden, paunchy, thick, soft-looking, a little ludicrous in their straw hats and shirt tails.

"This is wearying work," one said.

"I'd rather be at home in the shade myself," the other said. "But there is the Man waiting at the door to the earth."

"Yao." They looked quietly about; stooping, one of them removed from his shirt tail a clot of cockleburs. "Damn that Negro," he said.

"Yao. When have they ever been anything but a trial and a care to us?"

In the early afternoon, from the top of a tree, the Negro looked down into the plantation. He could see Issetibbeha's body in a hammock between the two trees where the horse and the dog were tethered, and the concourse about the steamboat was filled with wagons and horses and mules, with carts and saddle-horses, while in bright clumps the women and the smaller children and the old men squatted about the long trench where the smoke from the barbecuing meat blew slow and thick. The men and the big boys would all be down there in the creek bottom behind him, on the trail, their Sunday clothes rolled carefully up and wedged into tree crotches. There was a clump of men near the door to the house, to the saloon of the steamboat, though, and he watched them, and after a while he saw them bring Moketubbe out in a litter made of buckskin and persimmon poles; high hidden in his leafed nook the Negro, the quarry, looked quietly down upon his irrevocable doom with an expression as profound as Moketubbe's own. "Yao," he said quietly. "He will go then. That man whose body has been dead for fifteen years, he will go also."

In the middle of the afternoon he came face to face with an Indian. They were both on a footlog across a slough—the Negro gaunt, lean, hard, tireless and desperate; the Indian thick, soft-looking, the apparent embodiment of the ultimate and the supreme reluctance and inertia. The

Indian made no move, no sound; he stood on the log and watched the Negro plunge into the slough and swim ashore and crash away into the undergrowth.

Just before sunset he lay behind a down log. Up the log in slow procession moved a line of ants. He caught them and ate them slowly, with a kind of detachment, like that of a dinner guest eating salted nuts from a dish. They too had a salt taste, engendering a salivary reaction out of all proportion. He ate them slowly, watching the unbroken line move up the log and into oblivious doom with a steady and terrific undeviation. He had eaten nothing else all day; in his caked mud mask his eyes rolled in reddened rims. At sunset, creeping along the creek bank toward where he had spotted a frog, a cottonmouth moccasin slashed him suddenly across the forearm with a thick, sluggish blow. It struck clumsily, leaving two long slashes across his arm like two razor slashes, and half sprawled with its own momentum and rage, it appeared for the moment utterly helpless with its own awkwardness and choleric anger. "Olé, Grandfather," the Negro said. He touched its head and watched it slash him again across his arm, and again, with thick, raking, awkward blows. "It's that I do not wish to die," he said. Then he said it again—"It's that I do not wish to die"—in a quiet tone, of slow and low amaze, as though it were something that, until the words had said themselves, he found that he had not known, or had not known the depth and extent of his desire.

V

Moketubbe took the slippers with him. He could not wear them very long while in motion, not even in the litter where he was slung reclining, so they rested upon a square of fawnskin upon his lap—the cracked, frail slippers a little shapeless now, with their scaled patentleather surface and buckleless tongues and scarlet heels, lying upon the supine, obese shape just barely alive, carried through swamp and brier by swinging relays of men who bore steadily all day long the crime and its object, on the business of the slain. To Moketubbe it must have been as though, himself immortal, he were being carried rapidly through hell by doomed spirits which, alive, had contemplated his disaster, and, dead, were oblivious partners to his damnation.

After resting for a while, the litter propped in the center of the squatting circle and Moketubbe motionless in it, with closed eyes and his face at once peaceful for the instant and filled with inescapable foreknowledge, he could wear the slippers for a while. The stripling put them on him, forcing his big, tender, dropsical feet into them; whereupon into his face came again that expression, tragic, passive, and profoundly attentive, which dyspeptics wear. Then they went on. He made no move, no sound, inert in the rhythmic litter out of some reserve of inertia, or maybe if some kingly virtue such as courage or fortitude. After a time they set the litter down and looked at him, at the yellow face like that of an idol, beaded over with sweat. Then Three Basket or Louis Berry would say: "Take them off. Honor has been served." They would remove the shoes. Moketubbe's face would not alter, but only then would his breathing become perceptible, going in and out of his pale lips with a faint ah-ah-ah sound, and they would squat again while the couriers and the runners came up.

"Not yet?"

"Not yet. He is going east. By sunset he will reach Mouth of Tippah. Then he will turn back. We may take him tomorrow."

"Let us hope so. It will not be too soon."

"Yao. It has been three days now."

"When Doom died, it took only three days."

"But that was an old man. This one is young."

"Yao. A good race. If he is taken tomorrow, I will win a horse."

"May you win it."

"Yao. This work is not pleasant."

That was the day on which the food gave out at the plantation. The guests returned home and came back the next day with more food, enough for a week longer. On that day Issetibbeha began to smell; they could smell him for a long way up and down the bottom when it got hot toward noon and the wind blew. But they didn't capture the Negro on that day, nor on the next. It was about dusk on the sixth day when the couriers came up to the litter; they had found blood. "He has injured himself."

"Not bad, I hope," Basket said. "We cannot send with Issetibbeha one who will be of no service to him."

"Nor whom Issetibbeha himself will have to nurse and care for," Berry said.

"We do not know," the courier said. "He has hidden himself. He has crept back into the swamp. We have left pickets."

They trotted with the litter now. The place where the Negro had crept into the swamp was an hour away. In the hurry and excitement they had forgotten that Moketubbe still wore the slippers; when they reached the place Moketubbe had fainted. They removed the slippers and brought him to.

With dark, they formed a circle about the swamp. They squatted, clouded over with gnats and mosquitoes; the evening star burned low and close down the west, and the constellations began to wheel overhead. "We will give him time," they said. "Tomorrow is just another name for today."

"Yao. Let him have time." Then they ceased, and gazed as one into the darkness where the swamp lay. After a while the noise ceased, and soon the courier came out of the darkness.

"He tried to break out."

"But you turned him back?"

"He turned back. We feared for a moment, the three of us. We could smell him creeping in the darkness, and we could smell something else, which we did not know. That was why we feared, until he told us. He said to slay him there, since it would be dark and he would not have to see the face when it came. But it was not that which we smelled; he told us what it was. A snake had struck him. That was two days ago. The arm swelled, and it smelled bad. But it was not that which we smelled then, because the swelling had gone down and his arm was no larger than that of a child. He showed us. We felt the arm, all of us did; it was no larger than that of a child. He said to give him a hatchet so he could chop the arm off. But tomorrow is today also."

"Yao. Tomorrow is today."

"We feared for a while. Then he went back into the swamp."

"That is good."

"Yao. We feared. Shall I tell the Man?"

"I will see," Basket said. He went away. The courier squatted, telling again about the Negro. Basket returned. "The Man says that it is good. Return to your post."

The courier crept away. They squatted about the litter; now and then they slept. Sometime after midnight the Negro waked them. He began to shout and talk to himself, his voice coming sharp and sudden out of the darkness, then he fell silent. Dawn came; a white crane flapped slowly across the jonquil sky. Basket was awake. "Let us go now," he said. "It is today."

Two Indians entered the swamp, their movements noisy. Before they reached the Negro they stopped, because he began to sing. They could see him, naked and mud-caked, sitting on a log, singing. They squatted silently a short distance away, until he finished. He was chanting something in his own language, his face lifted to the rising sun. His voice was clear, full, with a quality wild and sad. "Let him have time," the Indians said, squatting, patient, waiting. He ceased and they approached. He looked back and up at them through the cracked mud mask. His eyes were bloodshot, his lips cracked upon his square short teeth. The mask of mud appeared to be loose on his face, as if he might have lost flesh since he put it there; he held his left arm close to his breast. From the elbow down it was caked and shapeless with black mud. They could smell him, a rank smell. He watched them quietly until one touched him on the arm. "Come," the Indian said. "You ran well. Do not be ashamed."

VI

As they neared the plantation in the tainted bright morning, the Negro's eyes began to roll a little, like those of a horse. The smoke from the cooking pit blew low along the earth and upon the squatting and waiting guests about the yard and upon the steamboat deck, in their bright, stiff, harsh finery; the women, the children, the old men. They had sent couriers along the bottom, and another on ahead, and Issetibbeha's body had already been removed to where the grave waited, along with the horse and the dog, though they could still smell him in death about the house where he had lived in life. The guests were beginning to move toward the grave when the bearers of Moketubbe's litter mounted the slope.

The Negro was the tallest there, his high, close, mud-caked head looming above them all. He was breathing hard, as though the desperate effort of the six suspended and desperate days had capitulated upon him at once; although they walked slowly, his naked scarred chest rose and fell above the close-clutched left arm. He looked this way and that continuously, as if he were not seeing, as though sight never quite caught up with the looking. His mouth was open a little upon his big white teeth; he began to pant. The already moving guests halted, pausing, looking back, some with pieces of meat in their hands, as the Negro looked about at their faces with his wild, restrained, unceasing eyes.

"Will you eat first?" Basket said. He had to say it twice.

"Yes," the Negro said. "That's it. I want to eat."

The throng had begun to press back toward the center; the word passed to the outermost: "He will eat first."

They reached the steamboat. "Sit down," Basket said. The Negro sat on the edge of the deck. He was still panting, his chest rising and falling, his head ceaseless with its white eyeballs, turning from side to side. It was as if the inability to see came from within, from hopelessness, not from absence of vision. They brought food and watched quietly as he tried to eat it. He put the food into his mouth and chewed it, but chewing, the half-masticated matter began to emerge from the corners of his mouth and to drool down his chin, onto his chest, and after a while he stopped chewing and sat there, naked, covered with dried mud, the plate on his knees, and his mouth filled with a mass of chewed food, open, his eyes wide and unceasing, panting and panting. They watched him, patient, implacable, waiting.

"Come," Basket said at last.

"It's water I want," the Negro said. "I want water."

The well was a little way down the slope toward the quarters. The slope lay dappled with the shadows of noon, of that peaceful hour when, Issetibbeha napping in his chair and waiting for the noon meal and the long afternoon to sleep in, the Negro, the body servant, would be free. He would sit in the kitchen door then, talking with the women that prepared the food. Beyond the kitchen the lane between the quarters would be quiet, peaceful, with the women talking to one another across the lane and the smoke of the dinner fires blowing upon the pickaninnies like ebony toys in the dust.

"Come," Basket said.

The Negro walked among them, taller than any. The guests were moving on toward where Issetibbeha and the horse and the dog waited. The Negro walked with his high ceaseless head, his panting chest. "Come," Basket said. "You wanted water."

"Yes," the Negro said. "Yes." He looked back at the house, then down to the quarters, where today no fire burned, no face showed in any door, no pickaninny in the dust, panting. "It struck me here, raking me across this arm; once, twice, three times. I said, 'Olé, Grandfather.' "

"Come now," Basket said. The Negro was still going through the motion of walking, his knee action high, his head high, as though he were on a treadmill. His eyeballs had a wild, restrained glare, like those of a horse. "You wanted water," Basket said. "Here it is."

There was a gourd in the well. They dipped it full and gave it to the Negro, and they watched him try to drink. His eyes had not ceased rolling as he tilted the gourd slowly against his caked face. They could watch his throat working and the bright water cascading from either side of the gourd, down his chin and breast. Then the water stopped. "Come," Basket said.

"Wait," the Negro said. He dipped the gourd again and tilted it against his face, beneath his ceaseless eyes. Again they watched his throat working and the unswallowed water sheathing broken and myriad down his chin, channeling his caked chest. They waited, patient, grave, decorous, implacable; clansman and guest and kin. Then the water ceased, though still the empty gourd tilted higher and higher, and still his black throat aped the vain motion of his frustrated swallowing. A piece of water-loosened mud carried away from his chest and broke at his muddy feet, and in the empty gourd they could hear his breath: ah-ah-ah.

"Come," Basket said, taking the gourd from the Negro and hanging it back in the well.

Flannery O'Connor
1925-1964

One of the most respected female writers of modern America, Flannery O'Connor was born in Georgia and wrote almost exclusively about the south. Her concerns with that land were essentially religious and mysterious, but the characters she painted were often humorous, in a countrified, macabre way. She was aware of her own approaching death to the extent that her last collection of stories, *Everything That Rises Must Converge,* seems to strongly reflect that awareness. Those stories are bleak and despairing, though many of them are excellent regardless. "A Good Man Is Hard To Find" is one of her best and well displays the force of her work, as we see in the character of the grandmother and her fear of death. Suggested readings: *Three By Flannery O'Connor* ("Wise Blood," "A Good Man Is Hard To Find," and "The Violent Bear It Away.")

A GOOD MAN IS HARD TO FIND

The grandmother didn't want to go to Florida. She wanted to visit some of her connections in east Tennessee and she was seizing at every chance to change Bailey's mind. Bailey was the son she lived with, her only boy. He was sitting on the edge of his chair at the table, bent over the orange sports section of the *Journal.* "Now look here, Bailey," she said, "see here, read this," and she stood with one hand on her thin hip and the other rattling the newspaper at his bald head. "Here this fellow that calls himself The Misfit is aloose from the Federal Pen and headed toward Florida and you read here what it says he did to these people. Just you read it. I wouldn't take my children in any direction with a criminal like that aloose in it. I couldn't answer to my conscience if I did."

Bailey didn't look up from his reading so she wheeled around then and faced the children's mother, a young woman in slacks, whose face was as broad and innocent as a cabbage and was tied around with a green head-kerchief that had two points on the top like a rabbit's ears. She was sitting on the sofa, feeding the baby his apricots out of a jar.

"The children have been to Florida before," the old lady said. "You all ought to take them somewhere else for a change so they would see different parts of the world and be broad. They never have been to east Tennessee."

The children's mother didn't seem to hear her but the eight-year-old boy, John Wesley, a stocky child with glasses, said, "If you don't want to go to Florida, why dontcha stay at home?" He and the little girl, June Star, were reading the funny papers on the floor.

"She wouldn't stay at home to be queen for a day," June Star said without raising her yellow head.

"Yes and what would you do if this fellow, the Misfit, caught you?" the grandmother asked.

"I'd smack his face," John Welsley said.

"She wouldn't stay at home for a million bucks," June Star said. "Afraid she'd miss something. She has to go everywhere we go."

"All right, Miss," the grandmother said. "Just remember that the next time you want me to curl your hair."

June Star said her hair was naturally curly.

The next morning the grandmother was the first one in the car, ready to go. She had her big black valise that looked like the head of a hippopotamus in one corner, and underneath it she was hiding a basket with Pitty Sing, the cat, in it. She didn't intend for the cat to be left alone in the house for three days because he would miss her too much and she was afraid he might brush against one of the gas burners and accidentally asphyxiate himself. Her son, Bailey, didn't like to arrive at a motel with a cat.

She sat in the middle of the back seat with John Wesley and June Star on either side of her. Bailey and the children's mother and the baby sat in front and they left Atlanta at eighty forty-five with the mileage on the car at 55890. The grandmother wrote this down because she thought it would be interesting to say how many miles they had been when they got back. It took them twenty minutes to reach the outskirts of the city.

The old lady settled herself comfortably, removing her white cotton gloves and putting them up with her purse on the shelf in front of the back window. The children's mother still had on slacks and still had her head tied up in a green kerchief, but the grandmother had on a navy blue straw sailor hat with a bunch of white violets on the brim and a navy blue dress with a small white dot in the print. Her collars and cuffs were white organdy trimmed with lace and at her neckline she had pinned a purple spray of cloth violets containing a sachet. In case of an accident, anyone seeing her dead on the highway would know at once that she was a lady.

She said she thought it was going to be a good day for driving, neither too hot nor too cold, and she cautioned Bailey that the speed limit was fifty-five miles an hour and that the patrolmen hid themselves behind billboards and small clumps of trees and sped out after you before you had a chance to slow down. She pointed out interesting details of the scenery: Stone Mountain; the blue granite that in some places came up to both sides of the highway; the brilliant red clay banks slightly streaked with purple; and the various crops that made rows of green lace-work on the ground. The trees were full of silver-white sunlight and the meanest of them sparkled. The children were reading comic magazines and their mother had gone back to sleep.

"Let's go through Georgia fast so we won't have to look at it much," John Welsey said.

"If I were a little boy," said the grandmother, "I wouldn't talk about my native state that way. Tennessee has the mountains and Georgia has the hills."

"Tennessee is just a hillbilly dumping ground," John Wesley said, "and Georgia is a lousy state too."

"You said it," June Star said.

"In my time," said the grandmother, folding her thin veined fingers, "children were more respectful of their native states and their parents and everything else. People did right then. Oh look at the cute little pickaninny!" she said and pointed to a Negro child standing in the door of a shack. "Wouldn't that make a picture, now?" she asked and they all turned and looked at the little Negro out of the back window. He waved.

"He didn't have any britches on," June Star said.

"He probably didn't have any," the grandmother explained. "Little niggers in the country don't have things like we do. If I could paint, I'd paint that picture," she said.

The children exchanged comic books.

The grandmother offered to hold the baby and the children's mother passed him over the front seat to her. She set him on her knee and bounced him and told him about the things they were passing. She rolled her eyes and screwed up her mouth and stuck her leathery thin face into his smooth bland one. Occasionally he gave her a faraway smile. They passed a large cotton field with five or six graves fenced in the middle of it, like a small island. "Look at the graveyard!" the grandmother said, pointing it out. "That was the old family burying ground. That belonged to the plantation."

"Where's the plantation?" John Welsey asked.

"Gone With the Wind," said the grandmother. "Ha. Ha."

When the children finished all the comic books they had brought, they opened the lunch and ate it. The grandmother ate a peanut butter sandwich and an olive and would not let the children throw the box and the paper napkins out the window. When there was nothing else to do they played a game by choosing a cloud and making the other two guess what shape it suggested. John Wesley took one the shape of a cow and June Star guessed a cow and John Wesley said, no, an automobile, and June Star said he didn't play fair, and they began to slap each other over the grandmother.

The grandmother said she would tell them a story if they would keep quiet. When she told a story, she rolled her eyes and waved her head and was very dramatic. She said once when she was a maiden lady she had been courted by a Mr. Edgar Atkins Teagarden from Jasper, Georgia. She said he was a very good-looking man and a gentleman and that he brought her a watermelon every Saturday afternoon with his initials cut in it, E. A. T. Well, one Saturday, she said, Mr. Teagarden brought the watermelon and there was nobody at home and he left it on the front porch and returned in his buggy to Jasper, but she never got the watermelon, she said, because a nigger boy ate it when he saw the initials, E. A. T.! This story tickled John Wesley's funny bone and he giggled and giggled but June Star didn't think it was any good. She said she wouldn't marry a man that just brought her a watermelon on Saturday. The grandmother said she would have done well to marry Mr. Teagarden because he was a gentleman and had bought Coca-Cola stock when it first came out and that he had died only a few years ago, a very wealthy man.

They stopped at The Tower for barbecued sandwiches. The Tower was a part stucco and part wood filling station and dance hall set in a clearing outside of Timothy. A fat man named Red Sammy Butts ran it and there were signs stuck here and there on the building and for miles up and down the highway saying, TRY RED SAMMY'S FAMOUS BARBECUE. NONE LIKE FAMOUS RED SAMMYS! RED SAM! THE FAT BOY WITH THE HAPPY LAUGH. A VETERAN! RED SAMMY'S YOUR MAN!

Red Sammy was lying on the bare ground outside The Tower with his head under a truck while a gray monkey about a foot high, chained to a small chinaberry tree, chattered nearby. The monkey sprang back into the tree and got on the highest limb as soon as he saw the children jump out of the car and run toward him.

Inside, The Tower was a long dark room with a counter at one end and tables at the other and dancing space in the middle. They all sat down at a board table next to the nickelodeon and Red Sam's wife, a tall burnt-brown woman with hair and eyes lighter than her skin, came and took their order. The children's mother put a dime in the machine and played "The Tennessee Waltz," and the grandmother said that tune always made her want to dance. She asked Bailey if he would like to dance but he only glared at her. He didn't have a naturally sunny disposition like she did and trips made him nervous. The grandmother's brown eyes were very bright. She swayed her head from side to side and pretended she was dancing in her chair. June Star said play something she could tap to so the children's mother put in another dime and played a fast number and June Star stepped out onto the dance floor and did her tap routine.

"Ain't she cute?" Red Sam's wife said, leaning over the counter. "Would you like to come be my little girl?"

"No I certainly wouldn't," June Star said. "I wouldn't live in a broken-down place like this for a million bucks!" and she ran back to the table.

"Ain't she cute?" the woman repeated, stretching her mouth politely.

"Aren't you ashamed?" hissed the grandmother.

Red Sam came in and told his wife to quit lounging on the counter and hurry up with these people's order. His khaki trousers reached just to his hip bones and his stomach hung over them like a sack of meal swaying under his shirt. He came over and sat down at a table nearby and let out a combination sigh and yodel. "You can't win," he said. "You can't win," and he wiped his sweating red face off with a gray handkerchief. "These days you don't know who to trust," he said. "Ain't that the truth?"

"People are certainly not nice like they used to be," said the grandmother.

"Two fellers came in here last week," Red Sammy said, "driving a Chrysler. It was a old beat-up car but it was a good one and these boys looked all right to me. Said they worked at the mill and you know I let them fellers charge the gas they bought? Now why did I do that?"

"Because you're a good man!" the grandmother said at once.

"Yes'm, I suppose so," Red Sam said as if he were struck with this answer.

His wife brought the orders, carrying the five plates all at once without a tray, two in each hand and one balanced on her arm. "It isn't a soul in this green world of God's that you can trust," she said. "And I don't count nobody out of that, not nobody," she repeated, looking at Red Sammy.

"Did you read about that criminal, The Misfit, that's escaped?" asked the grandmother.

"I wouldn't be a bit surprised if he didn't attact this place right here," said the woman. "If he hears about it being here, I wouldn't be none surprised to see him. If he hears it's two cents in the cash register, I wouldn't be a tall surprised if he . . ."

"That'll do," Red Sam said. "Go bring these people their Co'-Colas," and the woman went off to get the rest of the order.

"A good man is hard to find," Red Sammy said. 'Everything is getting terrible. I remember the day you could go off and leave your screen door unlatched. Not no more."

He and the grandmother discussed better times. The old lady said that in her opinion Europe was entirely to blame for the way things were now. She said the way Europe acted you would think we were made of money and Red Sam said it was no use talking about it, she was exactly right. The children ran outside into the white sunlight and looked at the monkey in the lacy chinaberry tree. He was busy catching fleas on himself and biting each one carefully between his teeth as if it were a delicacy.

They drove off again into the hot afternoon. The grandmother took cat naps and woke up every few minutes with her own snoring. Outside of Toombsboro she woke up and recalled an old plantation that she had visited in this neighborhood once when she was a young lady. She said the house had six white columns across the front and that there was an avenue of oaks leading up to it and two little wooden trellis arbors on either side in front where you sat down with your suitor after a stroll in the garden. She recalled exactly which road to turn off to get to it. She knew that Bailey would not be willing to lose any time looking at an old house, but the more she talked about it, the more she wanted to see it once again and find out if the little twin arbors were still standing. "There was a secret panel in this house," she said craftily, not telling the truth but wishing that she were, "and the story went that all the family silver was hidden in it when Sherman came through but it was never found . . ."

"Hey!" John Wesley said. "Let's go see it! We'll find it! We'll poke all the woodwork and find it! Who lives there? Where do you turn off at? Hey Pop, can't we turn off there?"

"We never have seen a house with a secret panel!" June Star shrieked. "Let's go to the house with the secret panel! Hey Pop, can't we go see the house with the secret panel!"

"It's not far from here, I know," the grandmother said. "It wouldn't take over twenty minutes."

Bailey was looking straight ahead. His jaw was as rigid as a horseshoe. "No," he said.

The children began to yell and scream that they wanted to see the house with the secret panel. John Wesley kicked the back of the front seat and June Star hung over her mother's shoulder and whined desperately into her ear that they never had any fun even on their vacation, that they could never do what THEY wanted to do. The baby began to scream and John Welsey kicked the back of the seat so hard that his father could feel the blows in his kidney.

"All right!" he shouted and drew the car to a stop at the side of the road. "Will you all shut up? Will you all just shut up for one second? If you don't shut up, we won't go anywhere."

"It would be very educational for them," the grandmother murmured.

"All right," Bailey said, "but get this: this is the only time we're going to stop for anything like this. This is the one and only time."

"The dirt road that you have to turn down is about a mile back," the grandmother directed. "I marked it when we passed."

"A dirt road," Bailey groaned.

After they had turned around and were headed toward the dirt road, the grandmother recalled other points about the house, the beautiful glass over the front doorway and the candle-lamp in the hall. John Wesley said that the secret panel was probably in the fireplace.

"You can't go inside this house," Bailey said. "You don't know who lives there."

"While you all talk to the people in front, I'll run around behind and get in a window," John Wesley suggested.

"We'll all stay in the car," his mother said.

They turned onto the dirt road and the car raced roughly along in a swirl of pink dust. The grandmother recalled the times when there were no paved roads and thirty miles was a day's journey. The dirt road was hilly and there were sudden washes in it and sharp curves on dangerous embankments. All at once they would be on a hill, looking down over the blue tops of trees for miles around, then the next minute, they would be in a red depression with the dust-coated trees looking down on them.

"This place had better turn up in a minute," Bailey said, "or I'm going to turn around."

The road looked as if no one had traveled on it in months.

"It's not much farther," the grandmother said and just as she said it, a horrible thought came to her. The thought was so embarrassing that she turned red in the face and her eyes dilated and her feet jumped up, upsetting her valise in the corner. The instant the valise moved, the newspaper top she had over the basket under it rose with a snarl and Pitty Sing, the cat, sprang onto Bailey's shoulder.

The children were thrown to the floor and their mother, clutching the baby, was thrown out the door onto the ground; the old lady was thrown into the front seat. The car turned over once and landed right-side-up in a gulch off the side of the road. Bailey remained in the driver's seat with the cat—gray-striped with a broad white face and an orange nose—clinging to his neck like a caterpillar.

As soon as the children saw they could move their arms and legs, they scrambled out of the car, shouting, "We've had an ACCIDENT!" The grandmother was curled up under the dashboard, hoping she was injured so that Bailey's wrath would not come down on her all at once. The horrible thought she had had before the accident was that the house she had remembered so vividly was not in Georgia but in Tennessee.

Bailey removed the cat from his neck with both hands and flung it out the window against the side of a pine tree. Then he got out of the car and started looking for the children's mother. She was sitting against the side of the red gutted ditch, holding the screaming baby, but she only had a cut down her face and a broken shoulder. "We've had an ACCIDENT!" the children screamed in a frenzy of delight.

"But nobody's killed," June Star said with disappointment as the grandmother limped out of the car, her hat still pinned to her head but the broken front brim standing up at a jaunty angle and the violet spray hanging off the side. They all sat down in the ditch, except the children, to recover from the shock. They were all shaking.

"Maybe a car will come along," said the children's mother hoarsely.

"I believe I have injured an organ," said the grandmother, pressing her side, but no one answered her. Bailey's teeth were clattering. He had on a yellow sport shirt with bright blue parrots designed in it and his face was as yellow as the shirt. The grandmother decided that she would not mention that the house was in Tennessee.

The road was about ten feet above and they could see only the tops of the trees on the other side of it. Behind the ditch they were sitting in there were more woods, tall and dark and deep. In a few minutes they saw a car some distance away on top of a hill, coming slowly as if the occupants were watching them. The grandmother stood up and waved both arms dramatically to attract their attention. The car continued to come on slowly, disappeared around a bend and appeared again, moving even slower, on top of the hill they had gone over. It was a big black battered hearse-like automobile. There were three men in it.

It came to a stop just over them and for some minutes, the driver looked down with a steady expressionless gaze to where they were sitting, and didn't speak. Then he turned his head and muttered something to the other two and they got out. One was a fat boy in black trousers and a red sweat shirt with a silver stallion embossed on the front of it. He moved around on the right side of them and stood staring, his mouth partly open in a kind of loose grin. The other had on khaki pants and a blue striped coat and a gray hat pulled down very low, hiding most of his face. He came around slowly on the left side. Neither spoke.

The driver got out of the car and stood by the side of it, looking down at them. He was an older man than the other two. His hair was just beginning to gray and he wore silver-rimmed spectacles that gave him a scholarly look. He had a long creased face and didn't have on any shirt or undershirt. He had on blue jeans that were too tight for him and was holding a black hat and a gun. The two boys also had guns.

"We've had an ACCIDENT!" the children screamed.

The grandmother had the peculiar feeling that the bespectacled man was someone she knew. His face was as familiar to her as if she had known him all her life but she could not recall who he was. He moved away from the car and began to come down the embankment, placing his feet carefully so that he wouldn't slip. He had on tan and white shoes and no socks, and his ankles were red and thin. "Good afternoon," he said. "I see you all had you a little spill."

"We turned over twice!" said the grandmother.

"Oncet," he corrected. "We seen it happen. Try their car and see will it run, Hiram," he said quietly to the boy with the gray hat.

"What you got that gun for?" John Welsey asked. "Whatcha gonna do with that gun?"

"Lady," the man said to the children's mother, "would you mind calling them children to sit down by you? Children make me nervous. I want all you all to sit down right together there where you're at."

"What are you telling US what to do for?" June Star asked.

Behind them the line of woods gaped like a dark open mouth. "Come here," said their mother.

"Look here now," Bailey began suddenly, "we're in a predicament! We're in . . ."

The grandmother shrieked. She scrambled to her feet and stood staring. "You're The Misfit!" she said. "I recognized you at once!"

"Yes'm," the man said, smiling slightly as if he were pleased in spite of himself to be known, "but it would have been better for all of you, lady, if you hadn't of reckernized me."

Bailey turned his head sharply and said something to his mother that shocked even the children. The old lady began to cry and The Misfit reddened.

"Lady," he said, "don't you get upset. Sometimes a man says things he don't mean. I don't reckon he meant to talk to you thataway."

"You wouldn't shoot a lady, would you?" the grandmother said and removed a clean handkerchief from her cuff and began to slap at her eyes with it.

The Misfit pointed the toe of his shoe into the ground and made a little hole and then covered it up again. "I would hate to have to," he said.

"Listen," the grandmother almost screamed, "I know you're a good man. You don't look a bit like you have common blood. I know you must come from nice people!"

"Yes mam," he said, "finest people in the world." When he smiled he showed a row of strong white teeth. "God never made a finer woman than my mother and my daddy's heart was pure gold," he said. The boy with the red sweat shirt had come around behind them and was standing with his gun at his hip. The Misfit squatted down on the ground. "Watch them children, Bobby Lee," he said. "You know they make me nervous." He looked at the six of them huddled together in front of him and he seemed to be embarrassed as if he couldn't think of anything to say. "Ain't a cloud in the sky," he remarked, looking up at it. "Don't see no sun but don't see no cloud neither."

"Yes, it's a beautiful day," said the grandmother. "Listen," she said, "you shouldn't call yourself The Misfit because I know you're a good man at heart. I can just look at you and tell."

"Hush!" Bailey yelled. "Hush! Everybody shut up and let me handle this!" He was squatting in the position of a runner about to sprint forward but he didn't move.

"I pre-chate that, lady," The Misfit said and drew a little circle in the ground with the butt of his gun.

"It'll take a half a hour to fix this here car," Hiram called, looking over the raised hood of it.

"Well, first you and Bobby Lee get him and that little boy to step over yonder with you," The Misfit said, pointing to Bailey and John Wesley. "The boys want to ast you something," he said to Bailey. "Would you mind stepping back in them woods there with them?"

"Listen," Bailey began, "we're in a terrible predicament! Nobody realizes what this is," and his voice cracked. His eyes were as blue and intense as the parrots in his shirt and he remained perfectly still.

The grandmother reached up to adjust her hat brim as if she were going to the woods with him but it came off in her hand. She stood staring at it and after a second she let it fall on the ground. Hiram pulled Bailey up by the arm as if he were assisting an old man. John Wesley caught hold of his father's hand and Bobby Lee followed. They went off toward the woods and just as they reached the dark edge, Bailey turned and supporting himself against a gray naked pine trunk, he shouted, "I'll be back in a minute, Mamma, wait on me!"

"Come back this instant!" his mother shrilled but they all disappeared into the woods.

"Bailey Boy!" the grandmother called in a tragic voice but she found she was looking at The Misfit squatting on the ground in front of her. "I just know you're a good man," she said desperately. "You're not a bit common!"

"Nome. I ain't a good man." The Misfit said after a second as if he had considered her statement carefully, "but I ain't the worst in the world neither. My daddy said I was a different breed of dog from my brothers and sisters. 'You know,' Daddy said, 'it's some that can live their whole life out without asking about it and it's others has to know why it is, and this boy is one of the latters. He's going to be into everything!'" He put on his black hat and looked up suddenly and then away deep into the woods as if he were embarrassed again. "I'm sorry I don't have on a shirt before you ladies," he said, hunching his shoulders slightly. "We buried our clothes that we had on when we escaped and we're just making do until we can get better. We borrowed these from some folks we met," he explained.

"That's perfectly all right," the grandmother said. "Maybe Bailey has an extra shirt in his suitcase."

"I'll look and see terrectly," The Misfit said.

"Where are they taking him?" the children's mother screamed.

"Daddy was a card himself," The Misfit said. "You couldn't put anything over on him. He never got in trouble with the Authorities though. Just had the knack of handling them."

"You could be honest too if you'd only try," said the grandmother. "Think how wonderful it would be to settle down and live a comfortable life and not have to think about somebody chasing you all the time."

The Misfit kept scratching in the ground with the butt of his gun as if he were thinking about it. "Yes'm, somebody is always after you," he murmured.

The grandmother noticed how thin his shoulder blades were just behind his hat because she was standing up looking down on him. "Do you ever pray?" she asked.

He shook his head. All she saw was the black hat wiggle between his shoulder blades. "Nome," he said.

There was a pistol shot from the woods, followed closely by another. Then silence. The old lady's head jerked around. She could hear the wind move through the tree tops like a long satisfied insuck of breath. "Bailey Boy!" she called.

"I was a gospel singer for a while," The Misfit said. "I been most everything. Been in the arm service, both land and sea, at home and abroad, been twict married, been an undertaker, been with the railroads, plowed Mother Earth, been in a tornado, seen a man burnt alive oncet," and he looked up at the children's mother and the little girl who were sitting close together, their faces white and their eyes glassy; "I even seen a woman flogged," he said.

"Pray, pray," the grandmother began, "pray, pray . . ."

"I never was a bad boy that I remember of," The Misfit said in an almost dreamy voice, "but somewheres along the line I done something wrong and got sent to the penitentiary. I was buried alive," and he looked up and held her attention to him by a steady-stare.

"That's when you should have started to pray," she said. "What did you do to get sent to the penitentiary that first time?"

"Turn to the right, it was a wall," The Misfit said, looking up again at the cloudless sky. "Turn to the left, it was a wall. Look up it was a ceiling, look down it was a floor. I forget what I done, lady. I set there and set there, trying to remember what it was I done and I ain't recalled it to this day. Oncet in a while, I would think it was coming to me, but it never come."

"Maybe they put you in by mistake," the old lady said vaguely.

"Nome," he said. "It wasn't no mistake. They had the papers on me."

"You must have stolen something," she said.

The Misfit sneered slightly. "Nobody had nothing I wanted," he said. "It was a head-doctor at the penitentiary said what I had done was kill my daddy but I known that for a lie. My daddy died in nineteen ought nineteen of the epidemic flu and I never had a thing to do with it. He was buried in the Mount Hopewell Baptist churchyard and you can go there and see for yourself."

"If you would pray," the old lady said, "Jesus would help you."

"That's right," The Misfit said.

"Well then, why don't you pray?" she asked trembling with delight suddenly.

"I don't want no hep," he said. "I'm doing all right by myself."

Bobby Lee and Hiram came ambling back from the woods. Bobby Lee was dragging a yellow shirt with bright blue parrots in it.

"Thow me that shirt, Bobby Lee," The Misfit said. The shirt came flying at him and landed on his shoulder and he put it on. The grandmother couldn't name what the shirt reminded her of. "No, lady," The Misfit said while he was buttoning it up. "I found out the crime don't matter. You can do one thing or you can do another, kill a man or take a tire off his car, because sooner or later you're going to forget what it was you done and just be punished for it."

The children's mother had begun to make heaving noises as if she couldn't get her breath. "Lady," he asked, "would you and that little girl like to step off yonder with Bobby Lee and Hiram and join your husband?"

"Yes, thank you," the mother said faintly. Her left arm dangled helplessly and she was holding the baby, who had gone to sleep, in the other. "Hep that lady up, Hiram," The Misfit said as she struggled to climb out of the ditch, "and Bobby Lee, you hold onto that little girl's hand."

"I don't want to hold hands with him," June Star said. "He reminds me of a pig."

The fat boy blushed and laughed and caught her by the arm and pulled her off into the woods after Hiram and her mother.

Alone with The Misfit, the grandmother found that she had lost her voice. There was not a cloud in the sky nor any sun. There was nothing around her but woods. She wanted to tell him that he must pray. She opened and closed her mouth several times before anything came out. Finally she found herself saying, "Jesus, Jesus," meaning, Jesus will help you, but the way she was saying it, it sounded as if she might be cursing.

"Yes'm," The Misfit said as if he agreed. "Jesus thown everything off balance. It was the same case with Him as with me except He hadn't committed any crime and they could prove I had committed one because they had the papers on me. Of course," he said, "they never shown me my papers. That's why I sign myself now. I said long ago, you get you a signature and sign everything you do and keep a copy of it. Then you'll know what you done and you can hold up the crime to the punishment and see do they match and in the end you'll have something to prove you ain't been treated right. I call myself The Misfit," he said, "because I can't make what all I done wrong fit what all I gone through in punishment."

There was a piercing scream from the woods, followed closely by a pistol report. "Does it seem right to you, lady, that one is punished a heap and another ain't punished at all?"

"Jesus!" the old lady cried. "You've got good blood! I know you wouldn't shoot a lady! I know you come from nice people! Pray! Jesus, you ought not to shoot a lady. I'll give you all the money I've got!"

"Lady," The Misfit said, looking beyond her far into the woods, "there never was a body that give the undertaker a tip."

There were two more pistol reports and the grandmother raised her head like a parched old turkey hen crying for water and called, "Bailey Boy, Bailey Boy!" as if her heart would break.

"Jesus was the only One that ever raised the dead," The Misfit continued, "and He shouldn't have done it. He thown everything off balance. If He did what He said, then it's nothing for you to do but thow away everything and follow Him, and if He didn't, then it's nothing for you to do but enjoy the few minutes you got left the best way you can—by killing somebody or burning down his house or doing some other meanness to him. No pleasure but meanness," he said and his voice had become almost a snarl.

"Maybe He didn't raise the dead," the old lady mumbled, not knowing what she was saying and feeling so dizzy that she sank down in the ditch with her legs twisted under her.

"I wasn't there so I can't say He didn't," The Misfit said. "I wisht I had of been there," he said, hitting the ground with his fist. "It ain't right I wasn't there because if I had of been there I would of known. Listen lady," he said in a high voice. "If I had of been there I would of known and I wouldn't be like I am now." His voice seemed about to crack and the grandmother's head cleared for an instant. She saw the man's face twisted close to her own as if he were going to cry and she murmured, "Why you're one of my babies. You're one of my own children!" She reached out and touched him on the shoulder. The Misfit sprang back as if a snake had bitten him and shot her three times through the chest. Then he put his gun down on the ground and took off his glasses and began to clean them.

Hiram and Bobby Lee returned from the woods and stood over the ditch, looking down at the grandmother who half sat and half lay in a puddle of blood with her legs crossed under her like a child's and her face smiling up at the cloudless sky.

Without his glasses, The Misfit's eyes were red-rimmed and pale and defenseless-looking. "Take her off and thow her where you thown the others, he said, picking up the cat that was rubbing itself against his leg.

"She was a talker, wasn't she?" Bobby Lee said, sliding down the ditch with a yodel.

"She would of been a good woman," The Misfit said, "if it had been somebody there to shoot her every minute of her life."

"Some fun!" Bobby Lee said.

"Shut up, Bobby Lee," The Misfit said. "It's no real pleasure in life."

SOLDIERS

Philip Roth
1933-

Roth's first novel, *Goodbye, Columbus and Five Short Stories,* won the National Book Award in 1960. He was born in Newark, New Jersey, received his Master's degree from the University of Chicago, and taught there as well as at the Iowa Writer's Workshop, Princeton, and other universities. "Defender Of The Faith" is an army story and in that respect may not be typical of Roth's work; but it does deal with the conflicts of the "new Jews"—between themselves and with modern, predominantly Christian America. The reader will note the irony here as the protagonist is forced to become the "defender of the faith." Suggested readings: *Goodbye, Columbus and Five Short Stories* and *Portnoy's Complaint.*

DEFENDER OF THE FAITH

In May of 1945, only a few weeks after the fighting had ended in Europe, I was rotated back to the States, where I spent the remainder of the war with a training company at Camp Crowder, Missouri. Along with the rest of the Ninth Army, I had been racing across Germany so swiftly during the late winter and spring that when I boarded the plane, I couldn't believe its destination lay to the west. My mind might inform me otherwise, but there was an inertia of the spirit that told me we were flying to a new front, where we would disembark and continue our push eastward—eastward until we'd circled the globe, marching through villages along whose twisting, cobbled streets crowds of the enemy would watch us take possession of what, up till then, they'd considered their own. I had changed enough in two years not to mind the trembling of the old people, the crying of the very young, the uncertainty and fear in the eyes of the once arrogant. I had been fortunate enough to develop an infantryman's heart, which, like his feet, at first aches and swells but finally grows horny enough for him to travel the weirdest paths without feeling a thing.

Captain Paul Barrett was my C. O. in Camp Crowder. The day I reported for duty, he came out of his office to shake my hand. He was short, gruff, and fiery, and—indoors or out—he wore his polished helmet liner pulled down to his little eyes. In Europe, he had received a battlefield commission and a serious chest wound, and he'd been returned to the States only a few months before. He spoke easily to me, and at the evening formation he introduced me to the troops. "Gentlemen," he said, "Sergeant Thurston, as you know, is no longer with this company. Your new first sergeant is Sergeant Nathan Marx, here. He is a veteran of the European theater, and consequently will expect to find a company of soldiers here, and not a company of *boys*."

I sat up late in the orderly room that evening, trying halfheartedly to solve the riddle of duty rosters, personnel forms, and morning reports. The Charge of Quarters slept with his mouth open on a mattress on the floor. A trainee stood reading the next day's duty roster, which was posted on the bulletin board just inside the screen door. It was a warm evening, and I could hear radios playing dance music over in the barracks. The trainee, who had been staring at me whenever he thought I wouldn't notice, finally took a step in my direction.

"Hey, Sarge—we having a G.I. party tomorrow night?" he asked. A G.I. party is a barracks cleaning.

"You usually have them on Friday nights?" I asked him.

"Yes," he said, and then he added, mysteriously, "that's the whole thing."

"Then you'll have a G.I. party."

He turned away, and I heard him mumbling. His shoulders were moving, and I wondered if he was crying.

"What's your name, soldier?" I asked.

He turned, not crying at all. Instead, his green-speckled eyes, long and narrow, flashed like fish in the sun. He walked over to me and sat on the edge of my desk. He reached out a hand. "Sheldon," he said.

"Stand on your feet, Sheldon."

Getting off the desk, he said, "Sheldon Grossbart." He smiled at the familiarity into which he'd led me.

"You against cleaning the barracks Friday night, Grossbart?" I said. "Maybe we shouldn't have G.I. parties. Maybe we should get a maid." My tone startled me. I felt I sounded like every top sergeant I had ever known.

"No, Sergeant." He grew serious, but with a seriousness that seemed to be only the stifling of a smile. "It's just—G.I. parties on Friday night, of all nights."

He slipped up onto the corner of the desk again—not quite sitting, but not quite standing, either. He looked at me with those speckled eyes flashing, and then made a gesture with his hand. It was very slight—no more than a movement back and forth of the wrist—and yet it managed to exclude from our affairs everything else in the orderly room, to make the two of us the center of the world. It seemed, in fact, to exclude everything even about the two of us except our hearts.

"Sergeant Thurston was one thing," he whispered, glancing at the sleeping C.Q., "but we thought that with you here things might be a little different."

"We?"

"The Jewish personnel."

"Why?" I asked, harshly. "What's on your mind?" Whether I was still angry at the "Sheldon" business, or now at something else, I hadn't time to tell, but clearly I was angry.

"We thought you—Marx, you know, like Karl Marx. The Marx Brothers. Those guys are all—M-a-r-x. Isn't that how *you* spell it, Sergeant?"

"M-a-r-x."

"Fishbein said—" He stopped. "What I mean to say, Sergeant—" His face and neck were red, and his mouth moved but no words came out. In a moment, he raised himelf to attention, gazing down at me. It was as though he had suddenly decided he could expect no more sympathy from me than from Thurston, the reason being that I was of Thurston's faith, and not his. The young man had managed to confuse himself as to what my faith really was, but I felt no desire to straighten him out. Very simply, I didn't like him.

When I did nothing but return his gaze, he spoke, in an altered tone. "You see, Sergeant," he explained to me, "Friday nights, Jews are supposed to go to services."

"Did Sergeant Thurston tell you you couldn't go to them when there was a G.I. party?"

"No."

"Did he say you had to stay and scrub the floors?"

"No, Sergeant."

"Did the Captain say you had to stay and scrub the floors?"

"That isn't it, Sergeant. It's the other guys in the barracks." He leaned toward me. "They think we're goofing off. But we're not. That's when Jews go to services, Friday night. We have to."

"Then go."

"But the other guys make accusations. They have no right."

"That's not the Army's problem, Grossbart. It's a personal problem you'll have to work out yourself."

"But it's un*fair*."

I got up to leave. "There's nothing I can do about it," I said.

Grossbart stiffened and stood in front of me. "But this is a matter of *religion*, sir."

"Sergeant," I said.

"I mean 'Sergeant,' " he said, almost snarling.

"Look, go see the chaplain. You want to see Captain Barrett, I'll arrange an appointment."

"No, no. I don't want to make trouble, Sergeant. That's the first thing they throw up to you. I just want my rights!"

"Damn it, Grossbart, stop whining. You have your rights. You can stay and scrub floors or you can go to shul—"

The smile swam in again. Spittle gleamed at the corners of his mouth. "You mean church, Sergeant."

"I mean shul, Grossbart!"

I walked past him and went outside. Near me, I heard the scrunching of a guard's boots on gravel. Beyond the lighted windows of the barracks, young men in T shirts and fatigue pants were sitting on their bunks, polishing their rifles. Suddenly there was a light rustling behind me. I turned and saw Grossbart's dark frame fleeing back to the barracks, racing to tell his Jewish friends that they were right—that, like Karl and Harpo, I was one of them.

The next morning, while chatting with Captain Barrett, I recounted the incident of the previous evening. Somehow, in the telling, it must have seemed to the Captain that I was not so much explaining Grossbart's position as defending it. "Marx, I'd fight side by side with a nigger if the fella proved to me he was a man. I pride myself," he said, looking out the window, "that I've got an open mind. Consequently, Sergeant, nobody gets special treatment here, for the good *or* the bad. All a man's got to do is prove himself. A man fires well on the range, I give him a weekend pass. He scores high in P.T., he gets a weekend pass. He *earns* it." He turned from the window and pointed a finger at me. "You're a Jewish fella, am I right, Marx?"

"Yes, sir."

"And I admire you. I admire you because of the ribbons on your chest. I judge a man by what he shows me on the field of battle, Sergeant. It's what he's got *here*," he said, and then, though I expected he would point to his heart, he jerked a thumb toward the buttons straining to hold his blouse across his belly. "Guts," he said.

"O.K., sir. I only wanted to pass on to you how the men felt."

"Mr. Marx, you're going to be old before your time if you worry about how the men feel. Leave that stuff to the chaplain—that's his business, not yours. Let's us train these fellas to shoot straight. If the Jewish personnel feels the other men are accusing them of goldbricking—well, I just don't know. Seems awful funny that suddenly the Lord is calling so loud in Private Grossman's ear he's just got to run to church."

"Synagogue," I said.

"Synagogue is right, Sergeant. I'll write that down for handy reference. Thank you for stopping by."

That evening, a few minutes before the company gathered outside the orderly room for the chow formation, I called the C.Q., Corporal Robert LaHill, in to see me. LaHill was a dark, burly fellow whose hair curled out of his clothes wherever it could. He had a glaze in his eyes that made one think of caves and dinosaurs. "LaHill," I said, "when you take the formation, remind the men that they're free to attend church services *whenever* they are held, provided they report to the orderly room before they leave the area."

LaHill scratched his wrist, but gave no indication that he'd heard or understood.

"LaHill," I said, "*church*. You remember? Church, priest, Mass, confession."

He curled one lip into a kind of smile; I took it for a signal that for a second he had flickered back up into the human race.

"Jewish personnel who want to attend services this evening are to fall out in front of the orderly room at 1900," I said. Then, as an afterthought, I added, "By order of Captain Barrett."

A little while later, as the day's last light—softer than any I had seen that year—began to drop over Camp Crowder, I heard LaHill's thick, inflectionless voice outside my window: "Give me your ears, troopers. Toppie says for me to tell you that at 1900 hours all Jewish personnel is to fall out in front, here, if they want to attend the Jewish Mass."

At seven o'clock, I looked out the orderly-room window and saw three soldiers in starched khakis standing on the dusty quadrangle. They looked at their watches and fidgeted while they whispered back and forth. It was getting dimmer, and, alone on the otherwise deserted field, they looked tiny. When I opened the door, I heard the noises of the G.I. party coming from the surrounding barracks—bunks being pushed to the walls, faucets pounding water into buckets, brooms whisking at the wooden floors, cleaning the dirt away for Saturday's inspection. Big puffs of cloth moved round and round on the windowpanes. I walked outside, and the moment my foot hit the ground I thought I heard Grossbart call to the others, " 'Ten-*hut!*" Or maybe, when they all three jumped to attention, I imagined I heard the command.

Grossbart stepped forward. "Thank you, sir," he said.

" 'Sergeant,' Grossbart," I reminded him. "You call officers 'sir.' I'm not an officer. You've been in the Army three weeks—you know that."

He turned his palms out at his sides to indicate that, in truth, he and I lived beyond convention. "Thank you, anyway," he said.

"Yes," a tall boy behind him said. "Thanks a lot."

And the third boy whispered, "Thank you," but his mouth barely fluttered, so that he did not alter by more than a lip's movement his posture of attention.

"For what?" I asked.

Grossbart snorted happily. "For the announcement. The Corporal's announcement. It helped. It made it—"

"Fancier." The tall boy finished Grossbart's sentence.

Grossbart smiled. "He means formal, sir. Public," he said to me. "Now it won't seem as though we're just taking off—goldbricking because the work has begun."

"It was by order of Captain Barrett," I said.

"Aaah, but you pull a little weight," Grossbart said. "So we thank you." Then he turned to his companions. "Sergeant Marx, I want you to meet Larry Fishbein."

The tall boy stepped forward and extended his hand. I shook it. "You from New York?" he asked.

"Yes."

"Me, too." He had a cadaverous face that collapsed inward from his cheekbone to his jaw, and when he smiled—as he did at the news of our communal attachment—revealed a mouthful of bad teeth. He was blinking his eyes a good deal, as though he were fighting back tears. "What borough?" he asked.

I turned to Grossbart. "It's five after seven. What time are services?"

"Shul," he said, smiling, "is in ten minutes. I want you to meet Mickey Halpern. This is Nathan Marx, our sergeant."

The third boy hopped forward. "Private Michael Halpern." He saluted.

"Salute officers, Halpern," I said. The boy dropped his hand, and, on its way down, in his nervousness, checked to see if his shirt pockets were buttoned.

"Shall I march them over, sir?" Grossbart asked. "Or are you coming along?"

From behind Grossbart, Fishbein piped up. "Afterward, they're having refreshments. A ladies' auxiliary from St. Louis, the rabbi told us last week."

"The chaplain," Halpern whispered.

"You're welcome to come along," Grossbart said.

To avoid his plea, I looked away, and saw, in the windows of the barracks, a cloud of faces staring out at the four of us. "Hurry along, Grossbart," I said.

"O.K., then," he said. He turned to the others. "Double time, *march!*"

They started off, but ten feet away Grossbart spun around and, running backward, called to me, "Good *shabbus,* sir!" And then the three of them were swallowed into the alien Missouri dusk.

Even after they had disappeared over the parade ground, whose green was now a deep blue, I could hear Grossbart singing the double-time cadence, and as it grew dimmer and dimmer, it suddenly touched a deep memory—as did the slant of the light—and I was remembering the shrill sounds of a Bronx playground where, years ago, beside the Grand Concourse, I had played on long spring evenings such as this. It was a pleasant memory for a young man so far from peace and home, and it brought so many recollections with it that I began to grow exceedingly tender about myself. In fact, I indulged myself in a reverie so strong that I felt as though a hand were reaching down inside me. It had to reach so very far to touch me! It had to reach past those days in the forests of Belgium, and past the dying I'd refused to weep over; past the nights in German farmhouses whose books we'd burned to warm us; past endless stretches when I had shut off all softness I might feel for my fellows, and had managed even to deny myself the posture of a conqueror—the swagger that I, as a Jew, might well have worn as my boots whacked against the rubble of Wesel, Münster, and Braunschweig.

But now one night noise, one rumor of home and time past, and memory plunged down through all I had anesthetized, and came to what I suddenly remembered was myself. So it was not altogether curious that, in search of more of me, I found myself following Grossbart's tracks to Chapel No. 3, where the Jewish services were being held.

I took a seat in the last row, which was empty. Two rows in front of me sat Grossbart, Fishbein, and Halpern, holding little white Dixie cups. Each row of seats was raised higher than the one in front of it, and I could see clearly what was going on. Fishbein was pouring the contents of his cup into Grossbart's, and Grossbart looked mirthful as the liquid made a purple arc between Fishbein's hand and his. In the glaring yellow light, I saw the chaplain standing on the platform at the front; he was chanting the first line of the responsive reading. Grossbart's prayer book remained closed on his lap; he was swishing the cup around. Only Halpern responded to the chant by praying. The fingers of his right hand were spread wide across the cover of his open book. His cap was pulled down low onto his brow, which made it round, like a yarmulke. From time to time, Grossbart wet his lips at the cup's edge; Fishbein, his long yellow face a dying light bulb, looked from here to there, craning forward to catch sight of the faces down the row, then of those in front of him, then behind. He saw me, and his eyelids beat a tattoo. His elbow slid into Grossbart's side, his neck inclined toward his friend, he whispered something, and then, when the congregation next responded to the chant, Grossbart's voice was among the others. Fishbein looked into his book now, too; his lips, however, didn't move.

Finally, it was time to drink the wine. The chaplain smiled down at them as Grossbart swigged his in one long gulp, Halpern sipped, meditating, and Fishbein faked devotion with an empty cup. "As I look down amongst the congregation"—the chaplain grinned at the word—"this night, I see many new faces, and I want to welcome you to Friday-night services here at Camp Crowder. I am Major Leo Ben Ezra, your chaplain." Though an American, the chaplain spoke deliberately—syllable by syllable, almost—as though to communicate, above all, with the lip readers in his audience. "I have only a few words to say before we adjourn to the refreshment room, where the kind ladies of the Temple Sinai, St. Louis, Missouri, have a nice setting for you."

Applause and whistling broke out. After another momentary grin, the chaplain raised his hands, palms out, his eyes flicking upward a moment, as if to remind the troops where they were and Who Else might be in attendance. In the sudden silence that followed, I thought I heard Grossbart cackle, "Let the goyim clean the floors!" Were those the words? I wasn't sure, but Fishbein, grinning, nudged Halpern. Halpern looked dumbly at him, then went back to his prayer book, which had been occupying him all through the rabbi's talk. One hand tugged at the black kinky hair that stuck out under his cap. His lips moved.

The rabbi continued. "It is about the food that I want to speak to you for a moment. I know, I know, I know," he intoned, wearily, "how in the mouths of most of you the *trafe* food tastes like ashes. I know how you gag, some of you, and how your parents suffer to think of their children eating foods unclean and offensive to the palate. What can I tell you? I can only say, close your eyes and swallow as best you can. Eat what you must to live, and throw away the rest. I wish I could help more. For those of you who find this impossible, may I ask that you try and try, but then come to see me in private. If your revulsion is so great, we will have to seek aid from those higher up."

A round of chatter rose and subsided. Then everyone sang "Ain Kelohainu"; after all those years, I discovered I still knew the words. Then, suddenly, the service over, Grossbart was upon me. "Higher up? He means the General?"

"Hey, Shelly," Fishbein said, "he means God." He smacked his face and looked at Halpern. "How high can you go!"

"Sh-h-h!" Grossbart said. "What do you think, Sergeant?"

"I don't know," I said. "You better ask the chaplain."

"I'm going to. I'm making an appointment to see him in private. So is Mickey."

Halpern shook his head. "No, no, Sheldon—"

"You have rights, Mickey," Grossbart said. "They can't push us around."

"It's O.K.," said Halpern. "It bothers my mother, not me."

Grossbart looked at me. "Yesterday he threw up. From the hash. It was all ham and God knows what else."

"I have a cold—that was why," Halpern said. He pushed his yarmulke back into a cap.

"What about you, Fishbein?" I asked. "You kosher, too?"

He flushed. "A little. But I'll let it ride. I have a very strong stomach, and I don't eat a lot anyway." I continued to look at him, and he held up his wrist to reinforce what he'd just said; his watch strap was tightened to the last hole, and he pointed that out to me.

"But services are important to you?" I asked him.

He looked at Grossbart. "Sure, sir."

" 'Sergeant.' "

"Not so much at home," said Grossbart, stepping between us, "but away from home it gives one a sense of his Jewishness."

"We have to stick together," Fishbein said.

I started to walk toward the door; Halpern stepped back to make way for me.

"That's what happened in Germany," Grossbart was saying, loud enough for me to hear. "They didn't stick together. They let themselves get pushed around."

I turned. "Look, Grossbart. This is the Army, not summer camp."

He smiled. "So?"

Halpern tried to sneak off, but Grossbart held his arm.

"Grossbart, how old are you?" I asked.

"Nineteen."

"And you?" I said to Fishbein.

"The same. The same month, even."

"And what about him?" I pointed to Halpern, who had by now made it safely to the door.

"Eighteen," Grossbart whispered. "But like he can't tie his shoes or brush his teeth himself. I feel sorry for him."

"I feel sorry for all of us, Grossbart," I said, "but just act like a man. Just don't overdo it."

"Overdo what, sir?"

"The 'sir' business, for one thing. Don't overdo that," I said.

I left him standing there. I passed by Halpern, but he did not look at me. Then I was outside, but, behind, I heard Grossbart call, "Hey, Mickey, my *leben*, come on back. Refreshments!"

"*Leben!*" My grandmother's word for me!

One morning a week later, while I was working at my desk, Captain Barrett shouted for me to come into his office. When I entered, he had his helmet liner squashed down so far on his head that I couldn't even see his eyes. He was on the phone, and when he spoke to me, he cupped one hand over the mouthpiece. "Who the hell is Grossbart?"

"Third platoon, Captain," I said. "A trainee."

"What's all this stink about food? His mother called a goddam congressman about the food." He uncovered the mouthpiece and slid his helmet up until I could see his bottom eyelashes. "Yes, sir," he said into the phone. "Yes, sir. I'm still here, sir. I'm asking Marx, here, right now—"

He covered the mouthpiece again and turned his head back toward me. "Lightfoot Harry's on the phone," he said, between his teeth. "This congressman calls General Lyman, who calls Colonel Sousa, who calls the Major, who calls me. They're just dying to stick this thing on me. Whatsa matter?" He shook the phone at me. "I don't feed the troops? What the hell is this?"

"Sir, Grossbart is strange—" Barrett greeted that with a mockingly indulgent smile. I altered my approach. "Captain, he's a very orthodox Jew, and so he's only allowed to eat certain foods."

"He throws up, the congressman said. Every time he eats something, his mother says, he throws up!"

"He's accustomed to observing the dietary laws, Captain."

"So why's his old lady have to call the White House?"

"Jewish parents, sir—they're apt to be more protective than you expect. I mean, Jews have a very close family life. A boy goes away from home, sometimes the mother is liable to get very upset. Probably the boy mentioned something in a letter, and his mother misinterpreted."

"I'd like to punch him one right in the mouth," the Captain said. "There's a goddam war on, and he wants a silver platter!"

"I don't think the boy's to blame, sir. I'm sure we can straighten it out by just asking him. Jewish parents worry—"

"*All* parents worry, for Christ's sake. But they don't get on their high horse and start pulling strings—"

I interrupted, my voice higher, tighter than before. "The home life, Captain, is very important—but you're right, it may sometimes get out of hand. It's a very wonderful thing, Captain, but because it's so close, this kind of thing . . ."

He didn't listen any longer to my attempt to present both myself and Lightfoot Harry with an explanation for the letter. He turned back to the phone. "Sir?" he said. "Sir—Marx, here, tells me Jews have a tendency to be pushy. He says he thinks we can settle it right here in the company. . . . Yes, sir. . . . I *will* call back, sir, soon as I can." He hung up. "Where are the men, Sergeant?"

"On the range."

With a whack on the top of his helmet, he crushed it down over his eyes again, and charged out of his chair. "We're going for a ride," he said.

The Captain drove, and I sat beside him. It was a hot spring day, and under my newly starched fatigues I felt as though my armpits were melting down onto my sides and chest. The roads were dry, and by the time we reached the firing range, my teeth felt gritty with dust, though my mouth had been shut the whole trip. The Captain slammed the brakes on and told me to get the hell out and find Grossbart.

I found him on his belly, firing wildly at the five-hundred-feet target. Waiting their turns behind him were Halpern and Fishbein. Fishbein, wearing a pair of steel-rimmed G.I. glasses I hadn't seen on him before, had the appearance of an old peddler who would gladly have sold you his rifle and the cartridges that were slung all over him. I stood back by the ammo boxes, waiting for Grossbart to finish spraying the distant targets. Fishbein straggled back to stand near me.

"Hello, Sergeant Marx," he said.

"How are you?" I mumbled.

"Fine, thank you. Sheldon's really a good shot."

"I didn't notice."

"I'm not so good, but I think I'm getting the hang of it now. Sergeant, I don't mean to, you know, ask what I shouldn't—" The boy stopped. He was trying to speak intimately, but the noise of the shooting forced him to shout at me.

"What is it?" I asked. Down the range, I saw Captain Barrett standing up in the jeep, scanning the line for me and Grossbart.

"My parents keep asking and asking where we're going," Fishbein said. "Everybody says the Pacific. I don't care, but my parents— If I could relieve their minds, I think I could concentrate more on my shooting."

"I don't know where, Fishbein. Try to concentrate anyway."

"Sheldon says you might be able to find out."

"I don't know a thing, Fishbein. You just take it easy, and don't let Sheldon—"

"*I'm* taking it easy, Sergeant. It's at home—"

Grossbart had finished on the line, and was dusting his fatigues with one hand. I called to him. "Grossbart, the Captain wants to see you."

He came toward us. His eyes blazed and twinkled. "Hi!"

"Don't point that goddam rifle!" I said.

"I wouldn't shoot you, Sarge." He gave me a smile as wide as a pumpkin, and turned the barrel aside.

"Damn you, Grossbart, this is no joke! Follow me."

I walked ahead of him, and had the awful suspicion that, behind me, Grossbart was *marching*, his rifle on his shoulder, as though he were a one-man detachment. At the jeep, he gave the Captain a rifle salute. "Private Sheldon Grossbart, sir."

"At ease, Grossman." The Captain sat down, slid over into the empty seat, and, crooking a finger, invited Grossbart closer.

"Bart, sir. Sheldon Gross*bart*. It's a common error." Grossbart nodded at me; *I* understood, he indicated. I looked away just as the mess truck pulled up to the range, disgorging a half-dozen K.P.s with rolled-up sleeves. The mess sergeant screamed at them while they set up the chow-line equipment.

"Grossbart, your mama wrote some congressman that we don't feed you right. Do you know that?" the Captain said.

"It was my father, sir. He wrote to Representative Franconi that my religion forbids me to eat certain foods."

"What religion is that, Grossbart?"

"Jewish."

" 'Jewish, *sir*,' " I said to Grossbart.

"Excuse me, sir. Jewish, sir."

"What have you been living on?" the Captain asked. "You've been in the Army a month already. You don't look to me like you're falling to pieces."

"I eat because I have to, sir. But Sergeant Marx will testify to the fact that I don't eat one mouthful more than I need to in order to survive."

"Is that so, Marx?" Barrett asked.

"I've never seen Grossbart eat, sir," I said.

"But you heard the rabbi," Grossbart said. "He told us what to do, and I listened."

The Captain looked at me. "Well, Marx?"

"I still don't know what he eats and doesn't eat, sir."

Grossbart raised his arms to plead with me, and it looked for a moment as though he were going to hand me his weapon to hold. "But, Sergeant—"

"Look, Grossbart, just answer the Captain's questions," I said sharply.

Barrett smiled at me, and I resented it. "All right, Grossbart," he said. "What is it you want? The little piece of paper? You want out?"

"No, sir. Only to be allowed to live as a Jew. And for the others, too."

"What others?"

"Fishbein, sir, and Halpern."

"They don't like the way we serve, either?"

"Halpern throws up, sir. I've seen it."

"I thought *you* throw up."

"Just once, sir. I didn't know the sausage was sausage."

"We'll give menus, Grossbart. We'll show training films about the food, so you can identify when we're trying to poison you."

Grossbart did not answer. The men had been organized into two long chow lines. At the tail end of one, I spotted Fishbein—or, rather, his glasses spotted me. They winked sunlight back at me. Halpern stood next to him, patting the inside of his collar with a khaki handkerchief. They moved with the line as it began to edge up toward the food. The mess sergeant was still screaming at the K.P.s. For a moment, I was actually terrified by the thought that somehow the mess sergeant was going to become involved in Grossbart's problem.

"Marx," the Captain said, "you're a Jewish fella—am I right?"

I played straight man. "Yes, sir."

"How long you been in the Army? Tell this boy."

"Three years and two months."

"A year in combat, Grossbart. Twelve goddam months in combat all through Europe. I admire this man." The Captain snapped a wrist against my chest. "Do you hear him peeping about the food? Do you? I want an answer, Grossbart. Yes or no."

"No, sir."

"And why not? He's a Jewish fella."

"Some things are more important to some Jews than other things to other Jews."

Barrett blew up. "Look, Grossbart. Marx, here, is a good man—a goddam hero. When you were in high school, Sergeant Marx was killing Germans. Who does more for the Jews—you, by throwing up over a lousy piece of sausage, a piece of first-cut meat, or Marx, by killing those Nazi bastards? If I was a Jew, Grossbart, I'd kiss this man's feet. He's a goddam hero, and *he* eats what we give him. Why do you have to cause trouble is what I want to know! What is it you're buckin' for—a discharge?"

"No, sir."

"I'm talking to a wall! Sergeant, get him out of my way." Barrett swung himself back into the driver's seat. "I'm going to see the chaplain." The engine roared, the jeep spun around in a whirl of dust, and the Captain was headed back to camp.

For a moment, Grossbart and I stood side by side, watching the jeep. Then he looked at me and said, "I don't want to start trouble. That's the first thing they toss up to us."

When he spoke, I saw that his teeth were white and straight, and the sight of them suddenly made me understand that Grossbart actually did have parents—that once upon a time someone had taken little Sheldon to the dentist. He was their son. Despite all the talk about his parents, it was hard to believe in Grossbart as a child, an heir—as related by blood to anyone, mother, father, or, above all, to me. This realization led me to another.

"What does your father do, Grossbart?" I asked as we started to walk back toward the chow line.

"He's a tailor."

"An American?"

"Now, yes. A son in the Army," he said, jokingly.

"And your mother?" I asked.

He winked. "A *ballabusta.* She practically sleeps with a dustcloth in her hand."

"She's also an immigrant?"

"All she talks is Yiddish, still."

"And your father, too?"

"A little English. 'Clean,' 'Press,' 'Take the pants in.' That's the extent of it. But they're good to me."

"Then, Grossbart—" I reached out and stopped him. He turned toward me, and when our eyes met, his seemed to jump back, to shiver in their sockets. "Grossbart—you were the one who wrote that letter, weren't you?"

It took only a second or two for his eyes to flash happy again. "Yes." He walked on, and I kept pace. "It's what my father *would* have written if he had known how. It was his name, though. *He* signed it. He even mailed it. I sent it home. For the New York postmark."

I was astonished, and he saw it. With complete seriousness, he thrust his right arm in front of me. "Blood is blood, Sergeant," he said, pinching the blue vein in his wrist.

"What the hell *are* you trying to do, Grossbart?" I asked. "I've seen you eat. Do you know that? I told the Captain I don't know what you eat, but I've seen you eat like a hound at chow."

"We work hard, Sergeant. We're in training. For a furnace to work, you've got to feed it coal."

"Why did you say in the letter that you threw up all the time?"

"I was really talking about Mickey there. I was talking *for* him. He would never write, Sergeant, though I pleaded with him. He'll waste away to nothing if I don't help. Sergeant, I used my name—my father's name—but it's Mickey, and Fishbein, too, I'm watching out for."

"You're a regular Messiah, aren't you?"

We were at the chow line now.

"That's a good one, Sergeant," he said, smiling. "But who knows? Who can tell? Maybe you're the Messiah—a little bit. What Mickey says is the Messiah is a collective idea. He went to Yeshiva, Mickey, for a while. He says *together* we're the Messiah. Me a little bit, you a little bit. You should hear that kid talk, Sergeant, when he gets going."

"Me a little bit, you a little bit," I said. "You'd like to believe that, wouldn't you, Grossbart? That would make everything so clean for you."

"It doesn't seem too bad a thing to believe, Sergeant. It only means we should all *give* a little, is all."

I walked off to eat my rations with the other noncoms.

Two days later, a letter addressed to Captain Barrett passed over my desk. It had come through the chain of command—from the office of Congressman Franconi where it had been received, to General Lyman, to Colonel Sousa, to Major Lamont, now to Captain Barrett. I read it over twice. It was dated May 14, the day Barrett had spoken with Grossbart on the rifle range.

> *Dear Congressman:*
>
> *First let me thank you for your interest in behalf of my son, Private Sheldon Grossbart. Fortunately, I was able to speak with Sheldon on the phone the other night, and I think I've been able to solve our problem. He is, as I mentioned in my last letter, a very religious boy, and it was only with the greatest difficulty that I could persuade him that the religious thing to do—what God Himself would want Sheldon to do—would be to suffer the pangs of religious remorse for the good of his country and all mankind. It took some doing, Congressman, but finally he saw the light. In fact, what he said (and I wrote down the words on a scratch pad so as never to forget), what he said was "I guess you're right, Dad. So many millions of my fellow-Jews gave up their lives to the enemy, the least I can do is live for a while minus a bit of my heritage so as to help end this struggle and regain for all the children of God dignity and humanity." That, Congressman, would make any father proud.*
>
> *By the way, Sheldon wanted me to know—and to pass on to you—the name of a soldier who helped him reach this decision: SERGEANT NATHAN MARX. Sergeant Marx is a combat veteran who is Sheldon's first sergeant. This man has helped Sheldon over some of the first hurdles he's had to face in the Army, and is in part responsible for Sheldon's changing his mind about the dietary laws. I know Sheldon would appreciate any recognition Marx could receive.*
>
> *Thank you and good luck. I look forward to seeing your name on the next election ballot.*
>
> *Respectfully,*
> *Samuel E. Grossbart*

Attached to the Grossbart communiqué was another, addressed to General Marshall Lyman, the post commander, and signed by Representative Charles E. Franconi, of the House of Representatives. The communiqué informed General Lyman that Sergeant Nathan Marx was a credit to the U.S. Army and the Jewish people.

What was Grossbart's motive in recanting? Did he feel he'd gone too far? Was the letter a strategic retreat—a crafty attempt to strengthen what he considered our alliance? Or had he actually changed his mind, via an imaginary dialogue between Grossbart *père* and Grossbart *fils*? I was puzzled, but only for a few days—that is, only until I realized that, whatever his reasons, he had actually decided to disappear from my life; he was going to allow himself to become just another trainee. I saw him at inspection, but he never winked; at chow formations, but he never flashed me a sign. On Sundays, with the other trainees, he would sit around watching the noncoms' softball team, for which I pitched, but not once did he speak an unnecessary word to me. Fishbein and Halpern retreated, too—at Grossbart's command, I was sure. Apparently he had seen that wisdom lay in turning back before he plunged over into the ugliness of privilege undeserved. Our separation allowed me to forgive him our past encounters, and, finally, to admire him for his good sense.

Meanwhile, free of Grossbart, I grew used to my job and my administrative tasks. I stepped on a scale one day, and discovered I had truly become a noncombatant; I had gained seven pounds. I found patience to get past the first three pages of a book. I thought about the future more and more, and wrote letters to girls I'd known before the war. I even got a few answers. I sent away to Columbia for a Law School catalogue. I continued to follow the war in the Pacific, but it was not my war. I thought I could see the end, and sometimes, at night, I dreamed that I was walking on the streets of Manhattan—Broadway, Third Avenue, 116th Street, where I had lived the three years I attended Columbia. I curled myself around these dreams and I began to be happy.

And then, one Saturday, when everybody was away and I was alone in the orderly room reading a month-old copy of the *Sporting News*, Grossbart reappeared.

"You a baseball fan, Sergeant?"

I looked up. "How are you?"

"Fine," Grossbart said. "They're making a soldier out of me."

"How are Fishbein and Halpern?"

"Coming along," he said. "We've got no training this afternoon. They're at the movies."

"How come you're not with them?"

"I wanted to come over and say hello."

He smiled—a shy, regular-guy smile, as though he and I well knew that our friendship drew its sustenance from unexpected visits, remembered birthdays, and borrowed lawnmowers. At first it offended me, and then the feeling was swallowed by the general uneasiness I felt at the thought that everyone on the post was locked away in a dark movie theater and I was here alone with Grossbart. I folded up my paper.

"Sergeant," he said, "I'd like to ask a favor. It is a favor, and I'm making no bones about it."

He stopped, allowing me to refuse him a hearing—which, of course, forced me into a courtesy I did not intend. "Go ahead."

"Well, actually it's two favors."

I said nothing.

"The first one's about these rumors. Everybody says we're going to the Pacific."

"As I told your friend Fishbein, I don't know," I said. "You'll just have to wait to find out. Like everybody else."

"You think there's a chance of any of us going East?"

"Germany?" I said. "Maybe."

"I meant New York."

"I don't think so, Grossbart. Offhand."

"Thanks for the information, Sergeant," he said.

"It's not information, Grossbart. Just what I surmise."

"It certainly would be good to be near home. My parents—you know." He took a step toward the door and then turned back. "Oh, the other thing. May I ask the other?"

"What is it?"

"The other thing is—I've got relatives in St. Louis, and they say they'll give me a whole Passover dinner if I can get down there. God, Sergeant, that'd mean an awful lot to me."

I stood up. "No passes during basic, Grossbart."

"But we're off from now till Monday morning, Sergeant. I could leave the post and no one would even know."

"I'd know. You'd know."

"But that's all. Just the two of us. Last night, I called my aunt, and you should have heard her. 'Come—come,' she said. 'I got gefilte fish, *chrain*—the works!' Just a day, Sergeant. I'd take the blame if anything happened."

"The Captain isn't here to sign a pass."

"You could sign."

"Look, Grossbart—"

"Sergeant, for two months, practically, I've been eating *trafe* till I want to die."

"I thought you'd made up your mind to live with it. To be minus a little bit of heritage."

He pointed a finger at me. "You!" he said. "That wasn't for you to read."

"I read it. So what?"

"That letter was addressed to a congressman."

"Grossbart, don't feed me any baloney. You *wanted* me to read it."

"Why are you persecuting me, Sergeant?"

"Are you kidding!"

"I've run into this before," he said, "but never from my own!"

"Get out of here, Grossbart! Get the hell out of my sight!"

He did not move. "Ashamed, that's what you are," he said. "So you take it out on the rest of us. They say Hitler himself was half a Jew. Hearing you, I wouldn't doubt it."

"What are you trying to do with me, Grossbart?" I asked him. "What are you after? You want me to give you special privileges, to change the food, to find out about your orders, to give you weekend passes."

"You even talk like a goy!" Grossbart shook his fist. "Is this just a weekend pass I'm asking for? Is a Seder sacred, or not?"

Seder! It suddenly occurred to me that Passover had been celebrated weeks before. I said so.

"That's right," he replied. "Who says no? A month ago—and I was in the field eating hash! And now all I ask is a simple favor. A Jewish boy I thought would understand. My aunt's willing to go out of her way—to make a Seder a month later. . . ." He turned to go, mumbling.

"Come back here!" I called. He stopped and looked at me. "Grossbart, why can't you be like the rest? Why do you have to stick out like a sore thumb?"

"Because I'm a Jew, Sergeant. I *am* different. Better, maybe not. But different."

"This is a war, Grossbart. For the time being *be* the same."

"I refuse."

"What?"

"I refuse. I can't stop being me, that's all there is to it." Tears came to his eyes. "It's a hard thing to be a Jew. But now I understand what Mickey says—it's a harder thing to stay one." He raised a hand sadly toward me. "Look at *you*."

"Stop crying!"

"Stop this, stop that, stop the other thing! *You* stop, Sergeant. Stop closing your heart to your own!" And, wiping his face with his sleeve, he ran out the door. "The least we can do for one another—the least."

An hour later, looking out of the window, I saw Grossbart headed across the field. He wore a pair of starched khakis and carried a little leather ditty bag. I went out into the heat of the day. It was quiet; not a soul was in sight except, over by the mess hall, four K.P.s sitting around a pan, sloped forward from their waists, gabbing and peeling potatoes in the sun.

"Grossbart!" I called.

He looked toward me and continued walking.

"Grossbart, get over here!"

He turned and came across the field. Finally, he stood before me.

"Where are you going?" I asked.

"St. Louis. I don't care."

"You'll get caught without a pass."

"So I'll get caught without a pass."

"You'll go to the stockade."

"I'm in the stockade." He made an about-face and headed off.

I let him go only a step or two. "Come back here," I said, and he followed me into the office, where I typed out a pass and signed the Captain's name, and my own initials after it.

He took the pass and then, a moment later, reached out and grabbed my hand. "Sergeant, you don't know how much this means to me."

"O.K.," I said. "Don't get in any trouble."

"I wish I could show you how much this means to me."

"Don't do me any favors. Don't write any more congressmen for citations."

He smiled. "You're right. I won't. But let me do something."

"Bring me a piece of that gefilte fish. Just get out of here."

"I will," he said. "With a slice of carrot and a little horseradish. I won't forget."

"All right. Just show your pass at the gate. And don't tell *anybody*."

"I won't. It's a month late, but a good Yom Tov to you."

"Good Yom Tov, Grossbart," I said.

"You're a good Jew, Sergeant. You like to think you have a hard heart, but underneath you're a fine, decent man. I mean that."

Those last three words touched me more than any words from Grossbart's mouth had the right to. "All right, Grossbart," I said. "Now call me 'sir,' and get the hell out of here."

He ran out the door and was gone. I felt very pleased with myself; it was a great relief to stop fighting Grossbart, and it had cost me nothing. Barrett would never find out, and if he did, I could manage to invent some excuse. For a while, I sat at my desk, comfortable in my decision. Then the screen door flew back and Grossbart burst in again. "Sergeant!" he said. Behind him I saw Fishbein and Halpern, both in starched khakis, both carrying ditty bags like Grossbart's.

"Sergeant, I caught Mickey and Larry coming out of the movies. I almost missed them."

"Grossbart—did I say tell no one?" I said.

"But my aunt said I could bring friends. That I should, in fact."

"*I'm* the Sergeant, Grossbart—not your aunt!"

Grossbart looked at me in disbelief. He pulled Halpern up by his sleeve. "Mickey, tell the Sergeant what this would mean to you."

Halpern looked at me and, shrugging, said, "A lot."

Fishbein stepped forward without prompting. "This would mean a great deal to me and my parents, Sergeant Marx."

"No!" I shouted.

Grossbart was shaking his head. "Sergeant, I could see you denying me, but how you can deny Mickey, a Yeshiva boy—that's beyond me."

"I'm not denying Mickey anything," I said. "You just pushed a little too hard, Grossbart. *You* denied him."

"I'll give him my pass, then," Grossbart said. "I'll give him my aunt's address and a little note. At least let him go."

In a second, he had crammed the pass into Halpern's pants pocket. Halpern looked at me, and so did Fishbein. Grossbart was at the door, pushing it open. "Mickey, bring me a piece of gefilte fish, at least," he said, and then he was outside again.

The three of us looked at one another, and then I said, "Halpern, hand that pass over."

He took it from his pocket and gave it to me. Fishbein had now moved to the doorway, where he lingered. He stood there for a moment with his mouth slightly open, and then he pointed to himself. "And me?" he asked.

His utter ridiculousness exhausted me. I slumped down in my seat and felt pulses knocking at the back of my eyes. "Fishbein," I said, "you understand I'm not trying to deny you anything, don't you? If it was my Army, I'd serve gefilte fish in the mess hall. I'd sell *kugel* in the PX, honest to God."

Halpern smiled.

"You understand, don't you, Halpern?"

"Yes, Sergeant."

"And you, Fishbein? I don't want enemies. I'm just like you—I want to serve my time and go home. I miss the same things you miss."

"Then, Sergeant," Fishbein said, "why don't you come, too?"

"Where?"

"To St. Louis. To Shelly's aunt. We'll have a regular Seder. Play hide-the-matzoh." He gave me a broad, black-toothed smile.

I saw Grossbart again, on the other side of the screen.

"Pst!" He waved a piece of paper. "Mickey, here's the address. Tell her I couldn't get away."

Halpern did not move. He looked at me, and I saw the shrug moving up his arms into his shoulders again. I took the cover off my typewriter and made out passes for him and Fishbein. "Go," I said. "The three of you."

I thought Halpern was going to kiss my hand.

That afternoon, in a bar in Joplin, I drank beer and listened with half an ear to the Cardinal game. I tried to look squarely at what I'd become involved in, and began to wonder if perhaps the struggle with Grossbart wasn't as much my fault as his. What was I that I had to *muster* generous feelings? Who was I to have been feeling so grudging, so tight-hearted? After all, I wasn't being asked to move the world. Had I a right, then, or a reason, to clamp down on Grossbart, when that meant clamping down on Halpern, too? And Fishbein—that ugly, agreeable soul? Out of the many recollections of my childhood that had tumbled over me these past few days I heard my grandmother's voice: "What are you making a *tsimmes?*" It was what she would ask my mother when, say, I had cut myself while doing something I shouldn't have done, and her daughter was busy bawling me out. I needed a hug and a kiss, and my mother would moralize. But my grandmother knew—mercy overrides justice. I should have known it, too. Who was Nathan Marx to be such a penny pincher with kindness? Surely, I thought, the Messiah himself—if He should ever come—won't niggle over nickels and dimes. God willing, he'll hug and kiss.

The next day, while I was playing softball over on the parade ground, I decided to ask Bob Wright, who was noncom in charge of Classification and Assignment, where he thought our trainees would be sent when their cycle ended, in two weeks. I asked casually, between innings, and he said, "They're pushing them all into the Pacific. Shulman cut the orders on your boys the other day."

The news shocked me, as though I were the father of Halpern, Fishbein, and Grossbart.

That night, I was just sliding into sleep when someone tapped on my door. "Who is it?" I asked.

"Sheldon."

He opened the door and came in. For a moment, I felt his presence without being able to see him. "How was it?" I asked.

He popped into sight in the near-darkness before me. "Great, Sergeant." Then he was sitting on the edge of the bed. I sat up.

"How about you?" he asked. "Have a nice weekend?"

"Yes."

"The others went to sleep." He took a deep, paternal breath. We sat silent for a while, and a homey feeling invaded my ugly little cubicle; the door was locked, the cat was out, the children were safely in bed.

"Sergeant, can I tell you something? Personal?"

I did not answer, and he seemed to know why. "Not about me. About Mickey. Sergeant, I never felt for anybody like I feel for him. Last night I heard Mickey in the bed next to me. He was crying so, it could have broken your heart. Real sobs."

"I'm sorry to hear that."

"I had to talk to him to stop him. He held my hand, Sergeant—he wouldn't let it go. He was almost hysterical. He kept saying if he only knew where we were going. Even if he knew it *was* the Pacific, that would be better than nothing. Just to know."

Long ago, someone had taught Grossbart the sad rule that only lies can get the truth. Not that I couldn't believe in the fact of Halpern's crying; his eyes *always* seemed red-rimmed. But, fact or not, it became a lie when Grossbart uttered it. He was entirely strategic. But then—it came with the force of indictment—so was I! There are strategies of aggression, but there are strategies of retreat as well. And so, recognizing that I myself had not been without craft and guile, I told him what I knew. "It is the Pacific."

He let out a small gasp, which was not a lie. "I'll tell him. I wish it was otherwise."

"So do I."

He jumped on my words. "You mean you think you could do something? A change, maybe?"

"No, I couldn't do a thing."

"Don't you know anybody over at C. and A.?"

"Grossbart, there's nothing I can do," I said. "If your orders are for the Pacific, then it's the Pacific."

"But Mickey—"

"Mickey, you, me—everybody, Grossbart. There's nothing to be done. Maybe the war'll end before you go. Pray for a miracle."

"But—"

"Good night, Grossbart." I settled back, and was relieved to feel the springs unbend as Grossbart rose to leave. I could see him clearly now; his jaw had dropped, and he looked like a dazed prizefighter. I noticed for the first time a little paper bag in his hand.

"Grossbart." I smiled. "My gift?"

"Oh, yes, Sergeant. Here—from all of us." He handed me the bag. "It's egg roll."

"Egg roll?" I accepted the bag and felt a damp grease spot on the bottom. I opened it, sure that Grossbart was joking.

"We thought you'd probably like it. You know—Chinese egg roll. We thought you'd probably have a taste for—"

"Your aunt served egg roll?"

"She wasn't home."

"Grossbart, she invited you. You told me she invited you and your friends."

"I know," he said. "I just reread the letter. *Next* week."

I got out of bed and walked to the window. "Grossbart," I said. But I was not calling to him.

"What?"

"What are you, Grossbart? Honest to God, what are you?"

I think it was the first time I'd asked him a question for which he didn't have an immediate answer.

"How can you do this to people?" I went on.

"Sergeant, the day away did us all a world of good. Fishbein, you should see him, he *loves* Chinese food."

"But the Seder," I said.

"We took second best, Sergeant."

Rage came charging at me. I didn't sidestep. "Grossbart, you're a liar!" I said. "You're a schemer and a crook. You've got no respect for anything. Nothing at all. Not for me, for the truth—not even for poor Halpern! You use us all—"

"Sergeant, Sergeant, I feel for Mickey. Honest to God, I do. I *love* Mickey. I try—"

"You try! You feel!" I lurched toward him and grabbed his shirt front. I shook him furiously. "Grossbart, get out! Get out and stay the hell away from me. Because if I see you, I'll make your life miserable. *You understand that?*"

"Yes."

I let him free, and when he walked from the room, I wanted to spit on the floor where he had stood. I couldn't stop the fury. It engulfed me, owned me, till it seemed I could only rid myself of it with tears or an act of violence. I snatched from the bed the bag Grossbart had given me and, with all my strength, threw it out the window. And the next morning, as the men policed the area around the barracks, I heard a great cry go up from one of the trainees, who had been anticipating only his morning handful of cigarette butts and candy wrappers. "Egg roll!" he shouted. "Holy Christ, Chinese goddam egg roll!"

A week later, when I read the orders that had come down from C. and A., I couldn't believe my eyes. Every single trainee was to be shipped to Camp Stoneman, California, and from there to the Pacific—every trainee but one. Private Sheldon Grossbart. He was to be sent to Fort Monmouth, New Jersey. I read the mimeographed sheet several times. Dee, Farrell, Fishbein, Fuselli, Flypowycz, Glinicki, Gromke, Guewa, Halpern, Hardy, Helebrandt, right down to Anton Zygadlo—all were to be headed West before the month was out. All except Grossbart. He had pulled a string, and I wasn't it.

I lifted the phone and called C. and A.

The voice on the other end said smartly, "Corporal Shulman, sir."

"Let me speak to Sergeant Wright."

"Who is this calling, sir?"

"Sergeant Marx."

And, to my surprise, the voice said, "*Oh!*" Then, "Just a minute, Sergeant."

Shulman's "*Oh!*" stayed with me while I waited for Wright to come to the phone. Why "*Oh!*"? Who was Shulman? And then, so simply, I knew I'd discovered the string that Grossbart had pulled. In fact, I could hear Grossbart the day he'd discovered Shulman in the PX, or in the bowling alley, or maybe even at services. "Glad to meet you. Where you from? Bronx? Me, too. Do you know So-and-So? And So-and-So? Me, too! You work at C. and A.? Really? Hey, how's chances of getting East? Could you do something? Change something? Swindle, cheat, lie? We gotta help each other, you know. If the Jews in Germany . . ."

Bob Wright answered the phone. "How are you, Nate? How's the pitching arm?"

"Good. Bob, I wonder if you could do me a favor." I heard clearly my own words, and they so reminded me of Grossbart that I dropped more easily than I could have imagined into what I had planned. "This may sound crazy, Bob, but I got a kid here on orders to Monmouth who wants them changed. He had a brother killed in Europe, and he's hot to go to the Pacific. Says he'd feel like a coward if he wound up Stateside. I don't know, Bob—can anything be done? Put somebody else in the Monmouth slot?"

"Who?" he asked cagily.

"Anybody. First guy in the alphabet. I don't care. The kid just asked if something could be done."

"What's his name?"

"Grossbart, Sheldon."

Wright didn't answer.

"Yeah," I said. "He's a Jewish kid, so he thought I could help him out. You know."

"I guess I can do something," he finally said. "The Major hasn't been around here for weeks. Temporary duty to the golf course. I'll try, Nate, that's all I can say."

"I'd appreciate it, Bob. See you Sunday." And I hung up, perspiring.

The following day, the corrected orders appeared: Fishbein, Fuselli, Fylypowycz, Glinicki, Gromke, Grossbart, Guewa, Halpern, Hardy . . . Lucky Private Harley Alton was to go to Fort Monmouth, New Jersey, where, for some reason or other, they wanted an enlisted man with infantry training.

After chow that night, I stopped back at the orderly room to straighten out the guard-duty roster. Grossbart was waiting for me. He spoke first.

"You son of a bitch!"

I sat down at my desk, and while he glared at me, I began to make the necessary alterations in the duty roster.

"What do you have against me?" he cried. "Against my family? Would it kill you for me to be near my father, God knows how many months he has left to him?"

"Why so?"

"His heart," Grossbart said. "He hasn't had enough troubles in a lifetime, you've got to add to them. I curse the day I ever met you, Marx! Shulman told me what happened over there. There's no limit to your anti-Semitism, is there? The damage you've done here isn't enough. You have to make a special phone call! You really want me dead!"

I made the last few notations in the duty roster and got up to leave. "Good night, Grossbart."

"You owe me an explanation!" He stood in my path.

"Sheldon, you're the one who owes explanations."

He scowled. "To *you?*"

"To me, I think so—yes. Mostly to Fishbein and Halpern."

"That's right, twist things around. I owe nobody nothing, I've done all I could do for them. Now I think I've got the right to watch out for myself."

"For each other we have to learn to watch out, Sheldon. You told me yourself."

"You call this watching out for me—what you did?"

"No. For all of us."

I pushed him aside and started for the door. I heard his furious breathing behind me, and it sounded like steam rushing from an engine of terrible strength.

"*You'll* be all right," I said from the door. And, I thought, so would Fishbein and Halpern be all right, even in the Pacific, if only Grossbart continued to see—in the obsequiousness of the one, the soft spirituality of the other—some profit for himself.

I stood outside the orderly room, and I heard Grossbart weeping behind me. Over in the barracks, in the lighted windows, I could see the boys in their T shirts sitting on their bunks talking about their orders, as they'd been doing for the past two days. With a kind of quiet nervousness, they polished shoes, shined belt buckles, squared away underwear, trying as best they could to accept their fate. Behind me, Grossbart swallowed hard, accepting his. And then, resisting with all my will an impulse to turn and seek pardon for my vindictiveness, I accepted my own.

Richard Yates
1926-

Presently teaching at the Iowa Writer's Workshop, Yates was born February 3 in Yonkers, New York. Earlier in his life he was a public relations man and a UP writer, and in 1962 he wrote the screenplay for William Styron's *Lie Down In Darkness.* "Jody Rolled The Bones" provides an excellent comparison with the preceding story, "Defender Of The Faith," because both are concerned with similar circumstances, but the mood, tone and realization of each story is vastly different. In "Jody Rolled The Bones" the reader nostalgically encounters the paradoxical roughness and delicacy found in the company of men and is allowed to experience the transition from recruit to soldier, the growth of "esprit de corps." Suggested readings: *Revolutionary Road* and *Eleven Kinds Of Loneliness.*

JODY ROLLED THE BONES

Sergeant Reece was a slim, quiet Tennessean who always managed to look neat in fatigues, and he wasn't exactly what we'd expected an infantry platoon sergeant to be. We learned soon enough that he was typical—almost a prototype—of the men who had drifted into the Regular Army in the thirties and stayed to form the cadres of the great wartime training centers, but at the time he surprised us. We were pretty naïve, and I think we'd all expected more of a Victor McLaglen—burly, roaring and tough, but lovable, in the Hollywood tradition. Reece was tough, all right, but he never roared and we didn't love him.

He alienated us on the first day by butchering our names. We were all from New York, and most of our names did require a little effort, but Reece made a great show of being defeated by them. His thin features puckered over the roster, his little mustache twitching at each unfamiliar syllable. "Dee—Dee Alice—" he stammered. "Dee Alice—"

"Here," D'Allessandro said, and it went like that with almost every name. At one point, after he'd grappled with Schacht, Scoglio, and Sizscovicz, he came to Smith. "Hey, Smith," he said, looking up with a slow grin. "What the hell *yew* doin' heah 'mong all these gorillas?" Nobody thought it was funny. At last he finished and tucked the clipboard under his arm. "All right," he told us. "My name's Sahjint Reece and I'm your platoon sahjint. That means when I say do somethin', do it." He gave us a long, appraising glare. "P'toon!" he snapped, making his diaphragm jump. "Tetch—*hut!*" And his tyranny began. By the end of that day and for many days thereafter we had him firmly fixed in our minds as, to use D'Allessandro's phrase, a dumb Rebel bastard.

I had better point out here that we were probably not very lovable either. We were all eighteen, a confused, platoon-sized bunch of city kids determined to be unenthusiastic about Basic Training. Apathy in boys of that age may be unusual—it is certainly unattractive—but this was 1944, the war was no longer new, and bitterness was the fashionable mood. To throw yourself into army life with gusto only meant you were a kid who didn't know the score, and nobody wanted to be that. Secretly we may have yearned for battle, or at least for ribbons, but on the surface we were shameless little wise guys about everything. Trying to make us soldiers must have been a staggering job, and Reece bore the brunt of it.

But of course that side of the thing didn't occur to us, at first. All we knew was that he rode us hard and we hated his guts. We saw very little of our lieutenant, a plump collegiate youth who showed up periodically to insist that if we played ball with him, he would play ball with us, and even less of our company commander (I hardly remember what he looked like, except that he wore glasses). But Reece was always there, calm and contemptuous, never speaking except to give orders and never smiling except in cruelty. And we could tell by observing the other platoons that he was exceptionally strict; he had, for instance, his own method of rationing water.

It was summer, and the camp lay flat under the blistering Texas sun. A generous supply of salt tablets was all that kept us conscious until nightfall; our fatigues were always streaked white from the salt of our sweat and we were always thirsty, but the camp's supply of drinking water had to be transported from a spring many miles away, so there was a standing order to go easy on it. Most noncoms were thirsty enough themselves to construe the regulation loosely, but Reece took it to heart. "If yew men don't learn nothin' else about soldierin'," he would say, "you're gonna learn water discipline." The water hung in Lister bags, fat canvas udders placed at intervals along the roads, and although it was warm and acrid with chemicals, the high point of every morning and every afternoon was the moment when we were authorized a break to fill our canteens with it. Most platoons would attack a Lister bag in a jostling, wallowing rush, working its little steel teats until the bag hung limp and wrinkled, and a dark stain of waste lay in the dust beneath it. Not us. Reece felt that half a canteenful at a time was enough for any man, and he would stand by the Lister bag in grim supervision, letting us at it in an orderly column of twos. When a man held his canteen too long under the bag, Reece would stop everything, pull the man out of line, and say, "Pour that out. All of it."

"I'll be *God damned* if I will!" D'Allessandro shot back at him one day, and we all stood fascinated, watching them glare at each other in the dazzling heat. D'Allessandro was a husky boy with fierce black eyes who had in a few weeks become our spokesman; I guess he was the only one brave enough to stage a scene like this. "Whaddya think I am," he shouted, "a goddamn *camel*, like you?" We giggled.

Reece demanded silence from the rest of us, got it, and turned back to D'Allessandro, squinting and licking his dry lips. "All right," he said quietly, "drink it. All of it. The resta yew men keep away from that bag, keep your hands off your canteens. I want y'all to watch this. Go on, drink it."

D'Allessandro gave us a grin of nervous triumph and began to drink, pausing only to catch his breath with the water dribbling on his chest. "Drink it," Reece would snap each time he stopped. It made us desperately thirsty to watch him, but we were beginning to get the idea. When the canteen was empty Reece told him to fill it up again. He did, still smiling but looking a little worried. "Now drink that," Reece said. "Fast. Faster." And when he was finished, gasping, with the empty canteen in his hand, Reece said, "Now get your helmet and rifle. See that barracks over there?" A white building shimmered in the distance, a couple of hundred yards away. "You're gonna proceed on the double to that barracks, go around it and come back on the double. Meantime your buddies're gonna be waitin' here, ain't none of 'em gonna get nothin' to drink till yew get back. All right, now, move. *Move.* On the *double.*"

In loyalty to D'Allessandro none of us laughed, but he did look absurd trotting heavily out across the drill field, his helmet wobbling. Before he reached the barracks we saw him stop, crouch, and vomit up the water. Then he staggered on, a tiny figure in the faraway dust, disappeared around the building, and finally emerged at the other side to begin the long trip back. At last he arrived and fell exhausted on the ground. "Now," Reece said softly. "Had enough to drink?" Only then were the rest of us allowed to use the Lister bag, two at a time. When we were all through, Reece squatted nimbly and drew half a canteenful for himself without spilling a drop.

That was the kind of thing he did, every day, and if anyone had suggested he was only doing his job our response would have been a long and unanimous Bronx cheer.

I think our first brief easing of hostility toward him occurred quite early in the training cycle, one morning when one of the instructors, a strapping first lieutenant, was trying to teach us the bayonet. We felt pretty sure that in the big, modern kind of war for which we were bound we probably would not be called on to fight with bayonets (and that if we ever were it wouldn't make a hell of a lot of difference whether we'd mastered the finer points of parry and thrust), and so our lassitude that morning was even purer than usual. We let the instructor talk to us, then got up and fumbled through the various positions he had outlined.

The other platoons looked as bad as we did, and faced with such dreary incompetence on a company scale the instructor rubbed his mouth. "No," he said. "No, no, you men haven't got the idea at all. Fall back to your places and sit down. Sergeant Reece front and center, please."

Reece had been sitting with the other platoon sergeants in their customary bored little circle, aloof from the lecture, but he rose promptly and came forward.

"Sergeant, I'd like you to show these people what a bayonet is all about," the instructor said. And from the moment Reece hefted a bayoneted rifle in his hands we knew, grudgingly or not, that we were going to see something. It was the feeling you get at a ball game when a heavy hitter selects a bat. At the instructor's commands he whipped smartly into each of the positions, freezing into a slim statue while the officer crouched and weaved around him, talking, pointing out the distribution of his weight and the angles of his limbs, explaining that this was how it should be done. Then, to climax the performance, the instructor sent Reece alone through the bayonet course. He went through it fast, never off balance and never wasting a motion, smashing blocks of wood off their wooden shoulders with his rifle butt, driving his blade deep into a shuddering torso of bundled sticks and ripping it out to bear down on the next one. He looked good. It would be too much to say that he kindled our admiration, but there is an automatic pleasure in watching a thing done well. The other platoons were clearly impressed, and although nobody in our platoon said anything, I think we were a little proud of him.

But the next period that day was close-order drill, at which the platoon sergeants had full command, and within half an hour Reece had nagged us into open resentment again. "What the hell's he think," Schacht muttered in the ranks, "he's some kind of a big deal now, just because he's a hotshot with that stupid bayonet?" And the rest of us felt a vague shame that we had so nearly been taken in.

When we eventually did change our minds about him it did not seem due, specifically, to any act of his, but to an experience that changed our minds about the army in general, and about ourselves. This was the rifle range, the only part of our training we thoroughly enjoyed. After so many hours of drill and calisthenics, of droning lectures in the sun and training films run off in sweltering clapboard buildings, the prospect of actually going out and shooting held considerable promise, and when the time came it proved to be fun. There was a keen pleasure in sprawling prone on the embankment of the firing line with a rifle stock nestled at your cheek and the oily, gleaming clips of ammunition close at hand; in squinting out across a great expanse of earth at your target and waiting for the signal from a measured voice on the loud-speaker. "Ready on the right. Ready on the left. Ready on the firing line. . . . The flag is up. The flag is waving. The flag is down. Commence—*fire!*" There would be a blast of many rifles in your ears, a breathless moment as you squeezed the trigger and a sharp jolt as you fired. Then you'd relax and watch the target slide down in the distance, controlled by unseen hands in the pit beneath it. When it reappeared a moment later a colored disc would be thrust up with it, waved and withdrawn, signaling your score. The man kneeling behind you with the score card would mutter "Nice going" or "Tough," and you'd squirm in the sand and take aim again. Like nothing else we had found in the army, this was something to rouse a competitive instinct, and when it took the form of wanting our platoon to make a better showing than the others, it brought us as close to a genuine *esprit de corps* as anything could.

We spent a week or so on the range, leaving early every morning and staying all day, taking our noon meal from a field kitchen that was in itself a refreshing change from the mess hall. Another good feature—at first it seemed the best of all—was that the range gave us a respite from Sergeant Reece. He marched us out there and back, and he supervised the cleaning of our rifles in the barracks, but for the bulk of the day he turned us over to the range staff, an impersonal, kindly crowd, much less concerned with petty discipline than with marksmanship.

Still, Reece had ample opportunity to bully us in the hours when he was in charge, but after a few days on the range we found he was easing up. When we counted cadence on the road now, for instance, he no longer made us do it over and over, louder each time, until our dry throats burned from yelling "HUT, WHO, REEP, HOE!" He would quit after one or two counts like the other platoon sergeants, and at first we didn't know what to make of it. "What's the deal?" we asked each other, baffled, and I guess the deal was simply that we'd begun to do it right the first time, loud enough and in perfect unison. We were marching well, and this was Reece's way of letting us know it.

The trip to the range was several miles, and a good share of it was through the part of camp where marching at attention was required—we were never given route-step until after we'd cleared the last of the company streets and buildings. But with our new efficiency at marching we got so that we almost enjoyed it, and even responded with enthusiasm to Reece's marching chant. It had always been his habit, after making us count cadence, to go through one of those traditional sing-song chants calling for traditional shouts of reply, and we'd always resented it before. But now the chant seemed uniquely stirring, an authentic piece of folklore from older armies and older wars, with roots deep in the life we were just beginning to understand. He would begin by expanding his ordinary nasal "Left . . . left . . . left" into a mournful little tune: "Oh *yew had* a good *home* and *yew left—*" to which we would answer "RIGHT!" as our right feet fell: We would go through several variations on this theme:—

"Oh yew had a good job and yew left—"

"RIGHT!"

"Oh yew had a good gal and yew left—"

"RIGHT!"

And then he'd vary the tune a little: "Oh Jody rolled the bones when yew left—"

"RIGHT!" we'd yell in soldierly accord. Jody was your faithless friend, the soft civilian to whom the dice-throw of chance had given everything you held dear; and the next verses, a series of taunting couplets, made it clear that he would always have the last laugh. You might march and shoot and learn to perfection your creed of disciplined force, but Jody was a force beyond control, and the fact had been faced by generations of proud, lonely men like this one, this splendid soldier who swung along beside our ranks in the sun and bawled the words from a twisted mouth: "Ain't no use in goin' home—Jody's got your gal and gone. Sound off—"

"HUT, WHO!"

"Sound off—"

"REEP, HOE!"

"Ever' time yew stand Retreat, Jody gets a piece of meat. Sound off—"

"HUT, WHO!"

"Sound off—"

"REEP, HOE!" It was almost a disappointment when he gave us route-step on the outskirts of camp and we became individuals again, cocking back our helmets and slouching along out of step, with the fine unanimity of the chant left behind. When we returned from the range dusty and tired, our ears numb from the noise of fire, it was somehow bracing to swing into formal cadence again for the last leg of the journey, heads up, backs straight, and split the cooling air with our roars of response.

A good part of our evenings, after chow, would be spent cleaning our rifles with the painstaking care that Reece demanded. The barracks would fill with the sharp, good smells of bore cleaner and oil as we worked, and when the job had been done to Reece's satisfaction we would usually drift out to the front steps for a smoke while we waited our turns at the showers. One night a group of us lingered there more quietly than usual, finding, I think, that the customary small talk of injustice and complaint was inadequate, unsuited to the strange well-being we had all begun to feel these last few days. Finally Fogarty put the mood into words. He was a small, serious boy, the runt of the platoon and something of a butt of jokes, and I guess he had nothing much to lose by letting his guard down. "Ah, I dunno," he said, leaning back against the doorjamb with a sigh, "I dunno about you guys, but I like this —going out to the range, marching and all. Makes you feel like you're really soldiering, you know what I mean?"

It was a dangerously naïve thing to say—"soldiering" was Reece's favorite word—and we looked at him uncertainly for a second. But then D'Allessandro glanced dead-pan around the group, defying anyone to laugh, and we relaxed. The idea of soldiering had become respectable, and because the idea as well as the word was inseparable in our minds from Sergeant Reece, he became respectable too.

Soon the change had come over the whole platoon. We were working with Reece now, instead of against him, trying instead of pretending to try. We wanted to be soldiers. The intensity of our effort must sometimes have been ludicrous, and might have caused a lesser man to suspect we were kidding—I remember earnest little choruses of "Okay, Sergeant" whenever he dispatched an order—but Reece took it all straight-faced, with that air of unlimited self-assurance that is the first requisite of good leadership. And he was as fair as he was strict, which must surely be the second requisite. In appointing provisional squad leaders, for example, he coolly passed over several men who had all but licked his shoes for recognition, and picked those he knew could hold our respect—D'Allessandro was one, and the others were equally well chosen. The rest of his formula was classically simple: he led by being excellent, at everything from cleaning a rifle to rolling a pair of socks, and we followed by trying to emulate him.

But if excellence is easy to admire it is hard to like, and Reece refused to make himself likable. It was his only failing, but it was a big one, for respect without affection can't last long—not, at least, where the sentimentality of adolescent minds is involved. Reece rationed kindness the way he rationed water: we might cherish each drop out of all proportion to its worth, but we never got enough or anything like enough to slake our thirst. We were delighted when he suddenly began to get our names right at roll call, and when we noticed that he was taking the edge of insult off most of his reprimands, for we knew these signs to be acknowledgments of our growth as soldiers, but somehow we felt a right to expect more.

We were delighted too at the discovery that our plump lieutenant was afraid of him; we could barely hide our pleasure at the condescending look that came over Reece's face whenever the lieutenant appeared, or at the tone of the young officer's voice—uneasy, almost apologetic—when he said, "All right, Sergeant." It made us feel close to Reece in a proud soldierly alliance, and once or twice he granted us the keen compliment of a wink behind the lieutenant's back, but only once or twice. We might imitate his walk and his squinting stare, get the shirts of our suntans tailored skintight like his and even adopt some of his habits of speech, Southern accent and all, but we could never quite consider him a Good Joe. He just wasn't the type. Formal obedience, in working hours, was all he wanted, and we hardly knew him at all.

On the rare evenings when he stayed on the post he would sit either alone or in the unapproachable company of one or two other cadre men as taciturn as himself, drinking beer in the PX. Most nights and all weekends he disappeared into town. I'm sure none of us expected him to spend his free time with us—the thought would never have occurred to us, in fact—but the smallest glimpse into his personal life would have helped. If he had ever reminisced with us about his home, for instance, or related the conversations of his PX friends, or told us of a bar he liked in town, I think we would all have been touchingly grateful, but he never did. And what made it worse was that, unlike him, we had no real life outside the day's routine. The town was a small, dusty maze of clapboard and neon, crawling with soldiers, and to most of us it yielded only loneliness, however we may have swaggered down its avenues. There wasn't enough town to go around; whatever delights it held remained the secrets of those who had found them first, and if you were young, shy, and not precisely sure what you were looking for anyway, it was a dreary place. You could hang around the U.S.O. and perhaps get to dance with a girl long hardened against a callow advance; you could settle for the insipid pleasures of watermelon stands and penny arcades, or you could prowl aimlessly in groups through the dark back streets, where all you met as a rule were other groups of soldiers on the aimless prowl. "So whaddya wanna *do?*" we would ask each other impatiently, and the only answer was, "Ah, I dunno. Cruise around awhile, I guess." Usually we'd drink enough beer to be drunk, or sick, on the bus back to camp, grateful for the promise of an orderly new day.

It was probably not surprising, then, that our emotional life became ingrown. Like frustrated suburban wives we fed on each other's discontent; we became divided into mean little cliques and subdivided into jealously shifting pairs of buddies, and we pieced out our idleness with gossip. Most of the gossip was self-contained; for news from the extraplatoon world we relied largely on the company clerk, a friendly, sedentary man who liked to dispense rumors over a carefully balanced cup of coffee as he strolled from table to table in the mess hall. "I got this from Personnel," he would say in preface to some improbable hearsay about the distant brass (the colonel had syphilis; the stockade commander had weaseled out of a combat assignment; the training program had been cut short and we'd all be overseas in a month). But one Saturday noon he had something less remote; he had gotten it from his own company orderly room, and it sounded plausible. For weeks, he told us, the plump lieutenant had been trying to get Reece transferred; now it appeared to be in the works, and next week might well be Reece's last as a platoon sergeant. "His days are numbered," the clerk said darkly.

"Whaddya mean, transferred?" D'Allessandro asked. "Transferred where?"

"Keep your voice down," the clerk said, with an uneasy glance toward the noncoms' table, where Reece bent stolidly over his food. "I dunno. That part I dunno. Anyway, it's a lousy trick. You kids got the best damn platoon sergeant on the post, if you wanna know something. He's too *damn* good, in fact; that's his trouble. Too good for a half-assed second lieutenant to handle. In the army it never pays to be that good."

"You're right," D'Allessandro said solemnly. "It never pays."

"Yeah?" Schacht inquired, grinning. "Is that right, Squad Leader? Tell us about it, Squad Leader." And the talk at our table degenerated into wisecracks. The clerk drifted away.

Reece must have heard the story about the same time we did; at any rate that weekend marked a sudden change in his behavior. He left for town with the tense look of a man methodically planning to get drunk, and on Monday morning he almost missed Reveille. He nearly always had a hangover on Monday mornings, but it had never before interfered with his day's work; he had always been there to get us up and out with his angry tongue. This time, though, there was an odd silence in the barracks as we dressed. "Hey, he isn't *here,*" somebody called from the door of Reece's room near the stairs. "Reece isn't *here.*" The squad leaders were admirably quick to take the initiative. They coaxed and prodded until we had all tumbled outside and into formation in the dark, very nearly as fast as we'd have done it under Reece's supervision. But the night's C.Q., in making his rounds, had already discovered Reece's absence and run off to rouse the lieutenant.

The company officers rarely stood Reveille, particularly on Mondays, but now as we stood leaderless in the company street our lieutenant came jogging around the side of the barracks. By the lights of the building we could see that his shirt was half buttoned and his hair wild; he looked puffy with sleep and badly confused. Still running, he called, "All right, you men, uh—"

All the squad leaders drew their breath to call us to attention, but they got no further than a ragged "Tetch—" when Reece emerged out of the gloaming, stepped up in front of the lieutenant, and said, "P'toon! Tetch—*hut!*" There he was, a little winded from running, still wearing the wrinkled suntans of the night before, but plainly in charge. He called the roll by squads; then he kicked out one stiff leg in the ornate, Regular Army way of doing an about-face, neatly executed the turn and ended up facing the lieutenant in a perfect salute. "All presen'accounted for, sir," he said.

The lieutenant was too startled to do anything but salute back, sloppily, and mumble "All right, Sergeant." I guess he felt he couldn't even say "See that this doesn't happen again," since, after all, nothing very much had happened, except that he'd been gotten out of bed for Reveille. And I guess he spent the rest of the day wondering whether he should have reprimanded Reece for being out of uniform; he looked as if the question were already bothering him as he turned to go back to his quarters. Dismissed, our formation broke up in a thunderclap of laughter that he pretended not to hear.

But Sergeant Reece soon spoiled the joke. He didn't even thank the squad leaders for helping him out of a tight spot, and for the rest of the day he treated us to the kind of petty nagging we thought we had outgrown. On the drill field he braced little Fogarty and said, "When'd yew shave last?"

Like many of our faces, Fogarty's bore only a pale fuzz that hardly needed shaving at all. "About a week ago," he said.

" 'Bout a week ago, *Sahjint,*" Reece corrected.

"About a week ago, Sergeant," Fogarty said.

Reece curled back his thin lips. "Yew look lak a mangey ole mungrel bitch," he said. "Doan yew know you're s'posed to shave ever' day?"

"I wouldn't have nothing to *shave* every day."

"Wouldn't have nothin' to shave, *Sahjint.*"

Fogarty swallowed, blinking. "Nothing to shave, Sergeant," he said.

We all felt badly let down. "What the hell's he think we are," Schacht demanded that noon, "a bunch of rookies?" And D'Allessandro grumbled in mutinous agreement.

A bad hangover might have excused Reece that day, but it could hardly have accounted for the next day and the day after that. He was bullying us without reason and without relief, and he was destroying everything he had built up so carefully in the many weeks before; the whole delicate structure of our respect for him crumbled and fell.

"It's final," the company clerk said grimly at supper Wednesday night. "The orders are cut. Tomorrow's his last day."

"So?" Schacht inquired. "Where's he going?"

"Keep your voice down," the clerk said. "Gonna work with the instructors. Spend part of his time out on the bivouac area and part on the bayonet course."

Schacht laughed, nudging D'Allessandro. "Hod damn," he said, "he'll eat that up, won't he? Specially the bayonet part. Bastard'll get to show off every day. He'll like that."

"Whaddya, *kidding?*" the clerk asked, offended. "Like it my ass. That guy loved his job. You think I'm kidding? He *loved* his job, and it's a lousy break. You kids don't know when you're well off."

D'Allessandro took up the argument, narrowing his eyes. "Yeah?" he said. "You think so? You oughta seen him out there every day this week. Every day."

The clerk leaned forward so earnestly that some of his coffee spilled. "Listen," he said. "He's known about this all week—how the hellya *want* him to act? How the hell would *you* act if you knew somebody was screwing you out of the thing you liked best? Can'tcha see he's under a strain?"

But that, we all told him with our surly stares, was no excuse for being a dumb Rebel bastard.

"Some of you kids act too big for your pants," the clerk said, and went away in a sulk.

"Ah, don't believe everything you hear," Schacht said. "I'll believe he's transferred when I see it."

But it was true. That night Reece sat up late in his room, drinking morosely with one of his cronies. We could hear their low, blurred voices in the darkness, and the occasional clink of their whiskey bottle. The following day he was neither easy nor hard on us in the field, but brooding and aloof as if he had other things on his mind. And when he marched us back that evening he kept us standing in formation in front of the barracks for a few moments, at ease, before dismissing us. His restless glance seemed to survey all our faces in turn. Then he began to speak in a voice more gentle than any we had ever heard him use. "I won't be seein' yew men any more after today," he said. "I'm bein' transferred. One thing yew can always count on in th' army, and that is, if yew find somethin' good, some job yew like, they always transfer your ass somewheres else."

I think we were all touched—I know I was; it was the closest he had ever come to saying he liked us. But it was too late. Anything he said or did now would have been too late, and our predominant feeling was relief. Reece seemed to sense this, and seemed to cut short the things he had planned to say.

"I know there ain't no call for me to make a speech," he said, "and I ain't gonna make one. Onliest thing I want to say is—" He lowered his eyes and stared at his dusty service shoes. "I want to wish all yew men a lot of luck. Y'all keep your nose clean, hear? And stay outa trouble?" The next words could scarcely be heard. "And doan let nobody push y'around."

A short, painful silence followed, as painful as the parting of disenchanted lovers. Then he drew himself straight. "P'toon! Tetch—*hut!*" He looked us over once more with hard and glittering eyes. "*Dis*-missed."

And when we came back from chow that night we found he had already packed his barracks bags and cleared out. We didn't even get to shake his hand.

Our new platoon sergeant was there in the morning, a squat, jolly cab driver from Queens who insisted that we call him only by his first name, which was Ruby. He was every inch a Good Joe. He turned us loose at the Lister bags every chance he got, and confided with a giggle that, through a buddy of his in the PX, he often got his own canteen filled with Coca-Cola and crushed ice. He was a slack drill master, and on the road he never made us count cadence except when we passed an officer; never made us chant or sing anything except a ragged version of "Give My Regards to Broadway," which he led with fervor although he didn't know all the words.

It took us a little while to adjust to him, after Reece. Once when the lieutenant came to the barracks to give one of his little talks about playing ball, ending up with his usual "All right, Sergeant," Ruby hooked his thumbs in his cartridge belt, slouched comfortably, and said, "Fellas, I hope yez all listened and gave ya attention to what the lieutenant said. I think I can speak fa yez all as well as myself when I say, Lieutenant, we're *gonna* play ball wit' you, like you said, because this here is one platoon that knows a Good Joe when we see one."

As flustered by this as he had ever been by Reece's silent scorn, the lieutenant could only blush and stammer, "Well, uh—thank you, Sergeant. Uh—I guess that's all, then. Carry on." And as soon as the lieutenant was out of sight we all began to make loud retching noises, to hold our noses or go through the motions of shoveling, as if we stood knee-deep in manure. "Christ, Ruby," Schacht cried, "what the hella *you* buckin' for?"

Ruby hunched his shoulders and spread his hands, bubbling with good-natured laughter. "To stay alive," he said. "To stay alive, whaddya think?" And he defended the point vigorously over the mounting din of our ridicule. "Whatsa matta?" he demanded. "Whatsa matta? Don'tcha think he does it to the captain? Don'tcha think the captain does it up at Battalion? Listen, wise up, will yez? *Evvybody* does it! *Evvybody* does it! What the hellya think makes the army *go?*" Finally he dismissed the whole subject with cab-driverly nonchalance. "Arright, arright, just stick around. *Yull* find out. Wait'll you kids got *my* time in the army, *then* yez can talk." But by that time we were all laughing with him; he had won our hearts.

In the evenings, at the PX, we would cluster around him while he sat behind a battery of beer bottles, waving his expressive hands and talking the kind of relaxed, civilian language we could all understand. "Ah, I got this brother-in-law, a real smott bastid. Know how *he* got outa the army? Know how *he* got out?" There would follow an involved, unlikely tale of treachery to which the only expected response was a laugh. "Sure!" Ruby would insist, laughing. "Don'tcha believe me? Don'tcha believe me? And this other guy I know, boy, talk about bein' *smott*—I'm tellin' ya, this bastid's *really* smott. Know how *he* got out?"

Sometimes our allegiance wavered, but not for long. One evening a group of us sat around the front steps, dawdling over cigarettes before we pushed off to the PX, and discussing at length—as if to convince ourselves—the many things that made life with Ruby so enjoyable. "Well yeah," little Fogarty said, "but I dunno. With Ruby it don't seem much like soldiering any more."

This was the second time Fogarty had thrown us into a momentary confusion, and for the second time D'Allessandro cleared the air. "So?" he said with a shrug. "Who the hell wants to soldier?"

That said it perfectly. We could spit in the dust and amble off toward the PX now, round-shouldered, relieved, confident that Sergeant Reece would not haunt us again. Who the hell wanted to soldier? "Not *me,*" we could all say in our hearts, "not *this* chicken," and our very defiance would dignify the attitude. An attitude was all we needed anyway, all we had ever needed, and this one would always sit more comfortably than Reece's stern, demanding creed. It meant, I guess, that at the end of our training cycle the camp delivered up a bunch of shameless little wise guys to be scattered and absorbed into the vast disorder of the army, but at lease Reece never saw it happen, and he was the only one who might have cared.

WHAT *IS* REAL?

Bernard Malamud
1914-

Much of Malamud's concern has been with what is happening to the "new Jews"—those who have successfully moved from the lower to the middle classes in America. Schwartz, the Jewbird in the Cohen household, can be seen as a representative of the Jewish tradition, perhaps an elderly relative. The irony of the persecution Schwartz endures from Harry Cohen makes a statement about these new Jews. Note the matter-of-fact way in which Malamud presents the Jewbird. This allows the reader to become involved with other, more important things in the story, rather than with the surprise of a talking bird. Malamud was born in Brooklyn. He has taught in many universities and is the author of numerous short stories and novels. Suggested readings: *The Assistant* and *The Magic Barrel.*

THE JEWBIRD

The window was open so the skinny bird flew in. Flappity-flap with its frazzled black wings. That's how it goes. It's open, you're in. Closed, you're out and that's your fate. The bird wearily flapped through the open kitchen window by Harry Cohen's top-floor apartment on First Avenue near the lower East River. On a rod on the wall hung an escaped canary cage, its door wide open, but this black-type longbeaked bird—its ruffled head and small dull eyes, crossed a little, making it look like a dissipated crow—landed if not smack on Cohen's thick lamb chop, at least on the table, close by. The frozen foods salesman was sitting at supper with his wife and young son on a hot August evening a year ago. Cohen, a heavy man with hairy chest and beefy shorts; Edie, in skinny yellow shorts and red halter; and their ten-year-old Morris (after her father—Maurie, they called him, a nice kid though not overly bright—were all in the city after two weeks out, because Cohen's mother was dying. They had been enjoying Kingston, New York, but drove back when Mama got sick in her flat in the Bronx.

"Right on the table," said Cohen, putting down his beer glass and swatting at the bird. "Son of a bitch."

"Harry, take care with your language," Edie said, looking at Maurie, who watched every move.

The bird cawed hoarsely and with a flap of its bedraggled wings—feathers tufted this way and that—rose heavily to the top of the open kitchen door, where it perched staring down.

"Gevalt, a pogrom!"

"It's a talking bird," said Edie in astonishment.

"In Jewish," said Maurie.

"Wise guy," muttered Cohen. He gnawed on his chop, then put down the bone. "So if you can talk, say what's your business. What do you want here?"

"If you can't spare a lamb chop," said the bird, "I'll settle for a piece of herring with a crust of bread. You can't live on your nerve forever."

"This ain't a restaurant," Cohen replied. "All I'm asking is what brings you to this address?"

"The window was open," the bird sighed; adding after a moment, "I'm running. I'm flying but I'm also running."

"From whom?" asked Edie with interest.

"Anti-Semeets."

"Anti-Semites?" they all said.

"That's from who."

"What kind of anti-Semites bother a bird?" Edie asked.

"Any kind," said the bird, "also including eagles, vultures, and hawks. And once in a while some crows will take your eyes out."

"But aren't you a crow?"

"Me? I'm a Jewbird."

Cohen laughed heartily. "What do you mean by that?"

The bird began dovening. He prayed without Book or tallith, but with passion. Edie bowed her head though not Cohen. And Maurie rocked back and forth with the prayer, looking up with one wide-open eye.

When the prayer was done Cohen remarked, "No hat, no phylacteries?"

"I'm an old radical."

"You're sure you're not some kind of a ghost or dybbuk?"

"Not a dybbuk," answered the bird, "though one of my relatives had such an experience once. It's all over now, thanks God. They freed her from a former lover, a crazy jealous man. She's now the mother of two wonderful children."

"Birds?" Cohen asked slyly.

"Why not?"

"What kind of birds?"

"Like me. Jewbirds."

Cohen tipped back in his chair and guffawed. "That's a big laugh. I've heard of a Jewfish but not a Jewbird."

"We're once removed." The bird rested on one skinny leg, then on the other. "Please, could you spare maybe a piece of herring with a small crust of bread?"

Edie got up from the table.

"What are you doing?" Cohen asked her.

"I'll clear the dishes."

Cohen turned to the bird. "So what's your name, if you don't mind saying?"

"Call me Schwartz."

"He might be an old Jew changed into a bird by somebody," said Edie, removing a plate.

"Are you?" asked Harry, lighting a cigar.

"Who knows?" answered Schwartz. "Does God tell us everything?"

Maurie got up on his chair. "What kind of herring?" he asked the bird in excitement.

"Get down, Maurie, or you'll fall," ordered Cohen.

"If you haven't got matjes, I'll take schmaltz," said Schwartz.

"All we have is marinated, with slices of onion—in a jar," said Edie.

"If you'll open for me the jar I'll eat marinated. Do you have also, if you don't mind, a piece of rye bread—the spitz?"

Edie thought she had.

"Feed him out on the balcony," Cohen said. He spoke to the bird. "After that take off."

Schwartz closed both bird eyes. "I'm tired and it's a long way."

"Which direction are you headed, north or south?"

Schwartz, barely lifting his wings, shrugged.

"You don't know where you're going?"

"Where there's charity I'll go."

"Let him stay, papa," said Maurie. "He's only a bird."

"So stay the night," Cohen said, "but no longer."

In the morning Cohen ordered the bird out of the house but Maurie cried, so Schwartz stayed for a while. Maurie was still on vacation from school and his friends were away. He was lonely and Edie enjoyed the fun he had, playing with the bird.

"He's no trouble at all," she told Cohen, "and besides his appetite is very small."

"What'll you do when he makes dirty?"

"He flies across the street in a tree when he makes dirty, and if nobody passes below, who notices?"

"So all right," said Cohen, "but I'm dead set against it. I warn you he ain't gonna stay here long."

"What have you got against the poor bird?"

"Poor bird, my ass. He's a foxy bastard. He thinks he's a Jew."

"What difference does it make what he thinks?"

"A Jewbird, what a chuzpah. One false move and he's out on his drumsticks."

At Cohen's insistence Schwartz lived out on the balcony in a new wooden birdhouse Edie had bought him.

"With many thanks," said Schwartz, "though I would rather have a human roof over my head. You know how it is at my age. I like the warm, the windows, the smell of cooking. I would also be glad to see once in a while the *Jewish Morning Journal* and have now and then a schnapps because it helps my breathing, thanks God. But whatever you give me, you won't hear complaints."

However, when Cohen brought home a bird feeder full of dried corn, Schwartz said, "Impossible."

Cohen was annoyed. "What's the matter, crosseyes, is your life getting too good for you? Are you forgetting what it means to be migratory? I'll bet a helluva lot of crows you happen to be acquainted with, Jews or otherwise, would give their eyeteeth to eat this corn."

Schwartz did not answer. What can you say to a grubber yung?

"Not for my digestion," he later explained to Edie. "Cramps. Herring is better even if it makes you thirsty. At least rainwater don't cost anything." He laughed sadly in breathy caws.

And herring, thanks to Edie, who knew where to shop, was what Schwartz got, with an occasional piece of potato pancake, and even a bit of soupmeat when Cohen wasn't looking.

When school began in September, before Cohen would once again suggest giving the bird the boot, Edie prevailed on him to wait a little while until Maurie adjusted.

"To deprive him right now might hurt his school work, and you know what trouble we had last year."

"So okay, but sooner or later the bird goes. That I promise you."

Schwartz, though nobody had asked him, took on full responsibility for Maurie's performance in school. In return for favors granted, when he was let in for an hour or two at night, he spent most of his time overseeing the boy's lessons. He sat on top of the dresser near Maurie's desk as he laboriously wrote out his homework. Maurie was a restless type and Schwartz gently kept him to his studies. He also listened to him practice his screechy violin, taking a few minutes off now and then to rest his ears in the bathroom. And they afterwards played dominoes. The boy was an indifferent checker player and it was impossible to teach him chess. When he was sick, Schwartz read him comic books though he personally disliked them. But Maurie's work improved in school and even his violin teacher admitted his playing was better. Edie gave Schwartz credit for these improvements though the bird pooh-poohed them.

Yet he was proud there was nothing lower than C minuses on

Maurie's report card, and on Edie's insistence celebrated with a little schnapps.

"If he keeps up like this," Cohen said, "I'll get him in an Ivy League college for sure."

"Oh I hope so," sighed Edie.

But Schwartz shook his head. "He's a good boy—you don't have to worry. He won't be a shicker or a wifebeater, God forbid, but a scholar he'll never be, if you know what I mean, although maybe a good mechanic. It's no disgrace in these times."

"If I were you," Cohen said, angered, "I'd keep my big snoot out of other people's private business."

"Harry, please," said Edie.

"My goddamn patience is wearing out. That crosseyes butts into everything."

Though he wasn't exactly a welcome guest in the house, Schwartz gained a few ounces although he did not improve in appearance. He looked bedraggled as ever, his feathers unkempt, as though he had just flown out of a snowstorm. He spent, he admitted, little time taking care of himself. Too much to think about. "Also outside plumbing," he told Edie. Still there was more glow to his eyes so that though Cohen went on calling him crosseyes he said it less emphatically.

Liking his situation, Schwartz tried tactfully to stay out of Cohen's way, but one night when Edie was at the movies and Maurie was taking a hot shower, the frozen foods salesman began a quarrel with the bird.

"For Christ sake, why don't you wash yourself sometimes? Why must you always stink like a dead fish?"

"Mr. Cohen, if you'll pardon me, if somebody eats garlic he will smell from garlic. I eat herring three times a day. Feed me flowers and I will smell like flowers."

"Who's obligated to feed you anything at all? You're lucky to get herring."

"Excuse me, I'm not complaining," said the bird. "You're complaining."

"What's more," said Cohen, "even from out on the balcony I can hear you snoring away like a pig. It keeps me awake at night."

"Snoring," said Schwartz, "isn't a crime, thanks God."

"All in all you are a goddamn pest and free loader. Next thing you'll want to sleep in bed next to my wife."

"Mr. Cohen," said Schwartz, "on this rest assured. A bird is a bird."

"So you say, but how do I know you're a bird and not some kind of a goddamn devil?"

"If I was a devil you would know already. And I don't mean because your son's good marks."

"Shut up, you bastard bird," shouted Cohen.

"Grubber yung," cawed Schwartz, rising to the tips of his talons, his long wings outstretched.

Cohen was about to lunge for the bird's scrawny neck but Maurie came out of the bathroom, and for the rest of the evening until Schwartz's bedtime on the balcony, there was pretended peace.

But the quarrel had deeply disturbed Schwartz and he slept badly. His snoring woke him, and awake, he was fearful of what would become of him. Wanting to stay out of Cohen's way, he kept to the birdhouse as much as possible. Cramped by it, he paced back and forth on the balcony ledge, or sat on the birdhouse roof, staring into space. In the evenings, while overseeing Maurie's lessons, he often fell asleep. Awakening, he nervously hopped around exploring the four corners of the room. He spent much time in Maurie's closet, and carefully examined his bureau drawers when they were left open. And once when he found a large paper bag on the floor, Schwartz poked his way into it to investigate what possibilities were. The boy was amused to see the bird in the paper bag.

"He wants to build a nest," he said to his mother.

Edie, sensing Schwartz's unhappiness, spoke to him quietly.

"Maybe if you did some of the things my husband wants you, you would get along better with him."

"Give me a for instance," Schwartz said.

"Like take a bath, for instance."

"I'm too old for baths," said the bird. "My feathers fall out without baths."

"He says you have a bad smell."

"Everybody smells. Some people smell because of their thoughts or because who they are. My bad smell comes from the food I eat. What does his come from?"

"I better not ask him or it might make him mad," said Edie.

In late November Schwartz froze on the balcony in the fog and cold, and especially on rainy days he woke with stiff joints and could barely move his wings. Already he felt twinges of rheumatism. He would have liked to spend more time in the warm house, particularly when Maurie was in school and Cohen at work. But though Edie was good-hearted and might have sneaked him in in the morning, just to thaw out, he was afraid to ask her. In the meantime Cohen, who had been reading articles about the migration of birds, came out on the balcony one night after work when Edie was in the kitchen preparing pot roast, and peeking into the birdhouse, warned Schwartz to be on his way soon if he knew what was good for him. "Time to hit the flyways."

"Mr. Cohen, why do you hate me so much?" asked the bird. "What did I do to you?"

"Because you're an A-number-one trouble maker, that's why. What's more, whoever heard of a Jewbird? Now scat or it's open war."

But Schwartz stubbornly refused to depart so Cohen embarked on a campaign of harassing him, meanwhile hiding it from Edie and Maurie. Maurie hated violence and Cohen didn't want to leave a bad impression. He thought maybe if he played dirty tricks on the bird he would fly off without being physically kicked out. The vacation was over, let him make his easy living off the fat of somebody else's land. Cohen worried about the effect of the bird's departure on Maurie's schooling but decided to take the chance, first, because the boy now seemed to have the knack of studying—give the black bird-bastard credit—and second, because Schwartz was driving him bats by being there always, even in his dreams.

The frozen foods salesman began his campaign against the bird by mixing watery cat food with the herring slices in Schwartz's dish. He also blew up and popped numerous paper bags outside the birdhouse as the bird slept, and when he had got Schwartz good and nervous, though not enough to leave, he brought a full-grown cat into the house, supposedly a gift for little Maurie, who had always wanted a pussy. The cat never stopped springing up at Schwartz whenever he saw him, one day managing to claw out several of his tailfeathers. And even at lesson time, when the cat was usually excluded from Maurie's room, though somehow or other he quickly found his way in at the end of the lesson, Schwartz was desperately fearful of his life and flew from pinnacle to pinnacle—light fixture to clothestree to door-top—in order to elude the beast's wet jaws.

Once when the bird complained to Edie how hazardous his existence was, she said, "Be patient, Mr. Schwartz. When the cat gets to know you better he won't try to catch you any more."

"When he stops trying we will both be in Paradise," Schwartz answered. "Do me a favor and get rid of him. He makes my whole life worry. I'm losing feathers like a tree loses leaves."

"I'm awfully sorry but Maurie likes the pussy and sleeps with it."

What could Schwartz do? He worried but came to no decision, being afraid to leave. So he ate the herring garnished with cat food, tried hard not to hear the paper bags bursting like fire crackers outside the birdhouse at night, and lived terror-stricken closer to the ceiling than the floor, as the cat, his tail flicking, endlessly watched him.

Weeks went by. Then on the day after Cohen's mother had died in her flat in the Bronx, when Maurie came home with a zero on an arithmetic test, Cohen, enraged, waited until Edie had taken the boy to his violin lesson, then openly attacked the bird. He chased him with a broom on the balcony and Schwartz frantically flew back and forth, finally escaping into his birdhouse. Cohen triumphantly reached in and grabbing both skinny legs, dragged the bird out, cawing loudly, his wings wildly beating. He whirled the bird around and around his head. But Schwartz, as he moved in circles, managed to swoop down and catch Cohen's nose in his beak, and hung on for dear life. Cohen cried out in great pain, punched the bird with his fist, and, tugging at its legs with all his might, pulled his nose free. Again he swung the yawking Schwartz around until the bird grew dizzy, then with a furious heave, flung him into the night. Schwartz sank like stone into the street. Cohen then tossed the birdhouse and feeder after him, listening at the ledge until they crashed on the sidewalk below. For a full hour, broom in hand, his heart palpitating and nose throbbing with pain, Cohen waited for Schwartz to return but the broken-hearted bird didn't.

That's the end of that dirty bastard, the salesman thought and went in. Edie and Maurie had come home.

"Look," said Cohen, pointing to his bloody nose swollen three times its normal size, "what that sonofabitchy bird did. It's a permanent scar."

"Where is he now?" Edie asked, frightened.

"I threw him out and he flew away. Good riddance."

Nobody said no, though Edie touched a handkerchief to her eyes and Maurie rapidly tried the nine times table and found he knew approximately half.

In the spring when the winter's snow had melted, the boy, moved by a memory, wandered in the neighborhood, looking for Schwartz. He found a dead black bird in a small lot near the river, his two wings broken, neck twisted, and both bird-eyes plucked clean.

"Who did it to you, Mr. Schwartz?" Maurie wept.

"Anti-Semeets," Edie said later.

Donald Barthelme
1933-

It has been said that Barthelme's experimental work in fiction may have influenced more younger writers than the work of any other living American author. Whether or not this claim is valid is perhaps unimportant, but it does seem true that Barthelme represents an important force in contemporary fiction. In this story, the main character is a man writing a letter to his unborn son. He appears to be insane, but as we come to know him through what he writes, we may begin to wonder if he is not after all quite sane and the rest of the world insane. Such an idea is not uncommon to American literature, particularly as it is evidenced in recent novels like *Catch 22* and *One Flew Over The Cuckoo's Nest*; but Barthelme's unusual technique here and the sense of compassion evoked between father and son in the face of the commercial and atomic age make this a memorable story. The story is not entirely tragic, of course, and the humor displayed in the father's thinking modes is another important element. Suggested readings: *Come Back, Dr. Caligari* and *Unspeakable Practices, Unnatural Acts.*

SEE THE MOON?

I know you think I'm wasting my time. You've made that perfectly clear. But I'm conducting these very important lunar hostility studies. And it's not you who'll have to leave the warm safe capsule. And dip a toe into the threatening lunar surround.

I am still wearing my yellow flower which has lasted wonderfully.

My methods may seem a touch irregular. Have to do chiefly with folded paper airplanes at present. But the paper must be folded *in the right way.* Lots of calculations and worrying about edges.

Show me a man who worries about edges and I'll show you a natural-born winner. Cardinal Y agrees. Columbus himself worried, the Admiral of the Ocean Sea. But he kept it quiet.

The sun so warm on this screened porch, it reminds me of my grandmother's place in Tampa. The same rusty creaky green glider and the same faded colored canvas cushions. And at night the moon graphed by the screen wire, if you squint. The Sea of Tranquillity occupying squares 47 through 108.

See the moon? It hates us.

My methods are homely but remember Newton and the apple. And when Rutherford started out he didn't even have a decently heated laboratory. And then there's the matter of my security check—I'm waiting for the government. Somebody told it I'm insecure. *That's true.*

I suffer from a frightful illness of the mind, light-mindedness. It's not catching. You needn't shrink.

You've noticed the wall? I pin things on it, souvenirs. There is the red hat, there the book of instructions for the Ant Farm. And this is a traffic ticket written on a saint's day (which saint? I don't remember) in 1954 just outside a fat little town (which town? I don't remember) in Ohio by a cop who asked me what I did. I said I wrote poppycock for the president of a university, true then.

You can see how far I've come. Lunar hostility studies aren't for everyone.

It's my hope that these . . . souvenirs . . . will someday merge, blur—cohere is the word, maybe—into something meaningful. A grand word, meaningful. What do I look for? A work of art, I'll not accept anything less. Yes I know it's shatteringly ingenuous but I wanted to be a painter. They get away with murder in my view; Mr. X. on the *Times* agrees with me. You don't know how I envy them. They can pick up a Baby Ruth wrapper on the street, glue it to the canvas (in the *right place,* of course, there's that), and lo! people crowd about and cry, "A real Baby Ruth wrapper, by God, what could be realer than that!" Fantastic metaphysical advantage. You hate them, if you're ambitious.

The Ant Farm instructions are a souvenir of Sylvia. The red hat came from Cardinal Y. We're friends, in a way.

I wanted to be one, when I was young, a painter. But I couldn't stand stretching the canvas. Does things to the fingernails. And that's the first place people look.

Fragments are the only forms I trust.

Light-minded or no, I'm . . . riotous with mental health. I measure myself against the Russians, that's fair. I have here a clipping datelined Moscow, four young people apprehended strangling a swan. *That's* boredom. The swan's name, Borka. The sentences as follows: Tsarev, metalworker, served time previously for stealing public property, four years in a labor camp, strict regime. Roslavtsev, electrician, jailed previously for taking a car on a joyride, three years and four months in a labor camp, semi-strict regime. Tatyana Voblikova (only nineteen and a Komsomol member too), technician, one and a half years in a labor camp, degree of strictness unspecified. Anna G. Kirushina, technical worker, fine of twenty per cent of salary for one year. Anna objected to the strangulation, but softly: she helped stuff the carcass in a bag.

The clipping is tacked up on my wall. I inspect it from time to time, drawing the moral. Strangling swans is wrong.

My brother who is a very distinguished pianist . . . has no fingernails at all. Don't look it's horrible. He plays under another name. And tunes his piano peculiarly, some call it sour. And renders *ragas* he wrote himself. A night *raga* played at noon can cause darkness, did you know that? It's extraordinary.

He wanted to be an Untouchable, Paul did. That was his idea of a contemporary career. But then a girl walked up and touched him (slapped him, actually; it's a complicated story). And he joined us, here in the imbroglio.

My father on the other hand is perfectly comfortable, and that's not a criticism. He makes flags, banners, bunting (sometimes runs me up a shirt). There was never any question of letting my father drink from the public well. He was on the Well Committee, he decided who dipped and who didn't. That's not a criticism. Exercises his creativity, nowadays, courtesy the emerging nations. Green for the veldt that nourishes the gracile Grant's gazelle, white for the purity of our revolutionary aspirations. The red for blood is understood. That's not a criticism. It's what they all ask for.

A call tonight from Gregory, my son by my first wife. Seventeen and at M.I.T. already. Recently he's been asking questions. Suddenly he's conscious of himself as a being with a history.

The telephone rings. Then, without a greeting: *Why did I have to take those little pills?* What little pills? *Little white pills with a "W" on them.* Oh. Oh yes. You had some kind of a nervous disorder, for a while. *How old was I?* Eight. Eight or nine. *What was it? Was it epilepsy?* Good God no, nothing so fancy. We never found out what it was. It went away. *What did I do? Did I fall down?* No no. Your mouth trembled, that was all. You couldn't control it. *Oh, O.K. See you.*

The receiver clicks.

Or: *What did my great-grandfather do? For a living I mean?* He was a ballplayer, semi-pro ballplayer, for a while. Then went into the building business. *Who'd he play for?* A team called the St. Augustine Rowdies, I think it was. *Never heard of them.* Well . . . *Did he make any money? In the building business?* Quite a bit. *Did your father inherit it?* No, it was tied up in a lawsuit. When the suit was over there wasn't anything left. *Oh. What was the lawsuit?* Great-grandfather diddled a man in a land deal. So the story goes. *Oh. When did he die?* Let's see, 1938 I think. *What of?* Heart attack. *Oh. O.K. See you.*

End of conversation.

Gregory, you didn't listen to my advice. I said try the Vernacular Isles. Where fish are two for a penny and women two for a fish. But you wanted m.i.t. and electron-spin-resonance spectroscopy. You didn't even crack a smile in your six-ply heather hopsacking.

Gregory you're going to have a half brother now. You'll like that, won't you? will you half like it?

We talked about the size of the baby, Ann and I. What could be deduced from the outside.

I said it doesn't look very big to me. She said it's big enough for *us.* I said we don't need such a great roaring big one after all. She said they cost the earth, those extra-large sizes. Our holdings in Johnson's Baby powder to be considered too. We'd need acres and acres. I said we'll put it in a Skinner box maybe. She said no child of hers. Displayed under glass like a rump roast. I said you haven't wept lately. She said I keep getting bigger whether I laugh or cry.

Dear Ann. I don't think you've quite . . .

What you don't understand is, it's like somebody walks up to you and says, I have a battleship I can't use, would you like to have a battleship. And you say, yes yes, I've never had a battleship, I've always wanted one. And he says, it has four sixteen-inch guns forward, and a catapult for launching scout planes. And you say, I've always wanted to launch scout planes. And he says, *it's yours,* and then you have this battleship. And then you have to paint it, because it's rusting, and clean it, because it's dirty, and anchor it somewhere, because the Police Department wants you to get it off the streets. And the crew is crying, and there are silverfish in the chartroom and a funny knocking noise in Fire Control, water rising in the No. 2 hold, and the chaplain can't find the Palestrina tapes for the Sunday service. And you can't get anybody to sit with it. And finally you discover that what you have here is this great, big, pink-and-blue rockabye *battleship.*

Ann. I'm going to keep her ghostly. Just the odd bit of dialogue:

"What is little Gog doing."

"Kicking."

I don't want her bursting in on us with the freshness and originality of her observations. What we need here is *perspective.* She's good with Gregory though. I think he half likes her.

Don't go. The greased-pig chase and balloon launchings come next.

I was promising once. After the Elgar, a *summa cum laude.* The university was proud of me. It was a bright shy white new university on the

Gulf Coast. Gulls and oleanders and quick howling hurricanes. The teachers brown burly men with power boats and beer cans. The president a retired admiral who'd done beautiful things in the Coral Sea.

"You will be a credit to us, George," the admiral said. That's not my name. I'm protecting my identity, what there is of it.

Applause from the stands filled with mothers and brothers. Then following the mace in a long line back to the field house to ungown. Ready to take my place at the top.

But a pause at Pusan, and the toy train to the Chorwon Valley. Walking down a road wearing green clothes. Korea green and black and silent. The truce had been signed. I had a carbine to carry. My buddy Bo Tagliabue the bonus baby, for whom the Yanks had paid thirty thousand. We whitewashed rocks to enhance our area. Colonels came crowding to feel Bo's hurling arm. Mine the whitest rocks.

I lunched with Thais from Thailand, hot curry from great galvanized washtubs. Engineers banging down the road in six-by-sixes raising red dust. My friend Gib Mandell calling Elko, Nevada on his canvas-covered field telephone. "Operator I crave Elko, Nevada."

Then I was a sergeant with stripes, getting the troops out of the sun. Tagliabue a sergeant too. *Triste* in the Tennessee Tea Room in Tokyo, yakking it up in Yokohama. Then back to our little tent town on the side of a hill, boosting fifty-gallon drums of heating oil tentward in the snow.

Ozzie the jeep driver waking me in the middle of the night. "They got Julian in the Tango Tank." And up and alert as they taught us in Leadership School, over the hills to Tango, seventy miles away. Whizzing through Teapot, Tempest, Toreador, with the jeep's canvas top flapping. Pfc. Julian drunk and disorderly and beaten up. The M.P. sergeant held out a receipt book. I signed for the bawdy remains.

Back over the pearly Pacific in a great vessel decorated with oranges. A trail of orange peel on the plangent surface. Sitting in the bow fifty miles out of San Francisco, listening to the Stateside disc jockeys chattering cha cha cha. Ready to grab my spot at the top.

My clothes looked old and wrong. The city looked new with tall buildings raised while my back was turned. I rushed here and there visiting friends. They were burning beef in their back yards, brown burly men with beer cans. The beef black on the outside, red on the inside. My friend Horace had fidelity. "Listen to that bass. That's sixty watts worth of bass, boy."

I spoke to my father. "How is business?" "If Alaska makes it," he said, "I can buy a Hasselblad. And we're keeping an eye on Hawaii." Then he photographed my veteran face, f.6 at 300. My father once a cheerleader at a great Eastern school. Jumping in the air and making fierce angry down-the-field gestures at the top of his leap.

That's not a criticism. We have to have cheerleaders.

I presented myself at the Placement Office. I was on file. My percentile was the percentile of choice.

"How come you were headman of only one student organization, George?" the Placement Officer asked. Many hats for top folk was the fashion then.

I said I was rounded, and showed him my slash. From the Fencing Club.

"But you served your country in an overseas post."

"And regard my career plan on neatly typed pages with wide margins."

"Exemplary," the Placement Officer said. "You seem married, mature, malleable, how would you like to affiliate yourself with us here at the old school? We have a spot for a poppycock man, to write the admiral's speeches. Have you ever done poppycock?"

I said no but maybe I could fake it.

"Excellent, excellent," the Placement Officer said. "I see you have grasp. And you can sup at the Faculty Club. And there is a ten-per-cent discount on tickets for all home games."

The admiral shook my hand. "You will be a credit to us, George," he said. I wrote poppycock, sometimes cockypap. At four o'clock the faculty hoisted the cocktail flag. We drank Daiquiris on each other's sterns. I had equipped myself—a fibre-glass runabout, someplace to think. In the stadia of friendly shy new universities we went down the field on Gulf Coast afternoons with gulls, or exciting nights under the tall toothpick lights. The crowd roared. Sylvia roared. Gregory grew.

There was no particular point at which I stopped being promising.

Moonstruck I was, after a fashion. Sitting on a bench by the practice field, where the jocks chanted secret signals in their underwear behind tall canvas blinds. Lay-about babies loafing on blankets, some staked out on twelve-foot dog chains. Brown mothers squatting knee to knee in shifts of scarlet and green. I stared at the moon's pale daytime presence. It seemed . . . inimical.

Moonstruck.

We're playing Flinch. You flinched.

The simplest things are the most difficult to explain, all authorities agree. Say I was tired of p***yc**k, if that pleases you. It's true enough.

Sylvia went up in a puff of smoke. She didn't like unsalaried life. And couldn't bear a male acquaintance moon-staring in the light of day. Decent people look at night.

We had trouble with Gregory: who would get which part. She settled for three-fifths, and got I think the worst of it, the dreaming raffish

Romany part that thinks science will save us. I get matter-of-fact midnight telephone calls: *My E.E. instructor shot me down.* What happened? *I don't know, he's an ass anyhow.* Well that may be but still— *When's the baby due?* January, I told you. *Yeah, can I go to Mexico City for the holidays?* Ask your mother, you know she— *There's this guy, his old man has a villa . . .* Well, we can talk about it. *Yeah, was grandmother a Communist?* Nothing so distinguished, she— *You said she was kicked out of Germany.* Her family was anti-Nazi. *Adler means eagle in German.* That's true. There was something called the Weimar Republic, her father—*I read about it.*

We had trouble with Gregory, we wanted to be scientific. Toys from Procreative Playthings of Princeton. O Gregory, that Princeton crowd got you coming and going. Procreative Playthings at one end and the Educational Testing Service at the other. And that serious-minded co-op nursery, that was a mistake. "A growing understanding between parent and child through shared group experience." I still remember poor Henry Harding III. Under "Sibs" on the membership roll they listed his, by age:

26
25
23
20
19
15
10
9
8
6

O Mrs. Harding, haven't you heard? They have these little Christmas-tree ornaments for the womb now, they work wonders.

Did we do "badly" by Gregory? Will we do "better" with Gog? Such questions curl the hair. It's wiser not to ask.

I mentioned Cardinal Y (the red hat). He's a friend, in a way. Or rather, the subject of one of my little projects.

I set out to study cardinals, about whom science knows nothing. It seemed to me that cardinals could be known in the same way we know fishes or roses, by classification and enumeration. A perverse project, perhaps, but who else has embraced this point of view? Difficult nowadays to find a point of view kinky enough to call one's own, with Sade himself being carried through the streets on the shoulders of sociologists, cheers and shouting, ticker tape unwinding from high windows . . .

The why of Cardinal Y. You're entitled to an explanation.

The Cardinal rushed from the Residence waving in the air his hands, gloved in yellow pigskin it appeared, I grasped a hand, "Yes, yellow pigskin!" the Cardinal cried. I wrote in my book, *yellow pigskin.*

Significant detail. The pectoral cross contains nine diamonds, the scarlet soutane is laundered right on the premises.

I asked the Cardinal questions, we had a conversation.

"I am thinking of a happy island more beautiful than can be imagined," I said.

"I am thinking of a golden mountain which does not exist," he said.

"Upon what does the world rest?" I asked.

"Upon an elephant," he said.

"Upon what does the elephant rest?"

"Upon a tortoise."

"Upon what does the tortoise rest?"

"Upon a red lawnmower."

I wrote in my book, *playful.*

"Is there any value that has value?" I asked.

"If there is any value that has value, then it must lie outside the whole sphere of what happens and is the case, for all that happens and is the case is accidental," he said. He was not serious. I wrote in my book, *knows the drill.*

(*Oh I had heard reports, how he slunk about in the snow telling children he was Santa Claus, how he disbursed funds in unauthorized disbursements to unshaven men who came to the kitchen door, how his housekeeper pointedly rolled his red socks together and black socks together hinting red with red and black with black, the Cardinal patiently unrolling a red ball to get a red sock and a black ball to get a black sock, which he then wore together. . . .*)

Cardinal Y. He's sly.

I was thorough. I popped the Cardinal on the patella with a little hammer, and looked into his eyes with a little light. I tested the Cardinal's stomach acidity using Universal Indicator Paper, a scale of one to ten, a spectrum of red to blue. The pH value was 1 indicating high acidity. I measured the Cardinal's ego strength using the Minnesota Multiphasic Muzzle Map, he had an M.M.M.M. of four over three. I sang to the Cardinal, the song was "Stella by Starlight," he did not react in any way. I calculated the number of gallons needed to fill the Cardinal's bath to a depth of ten inches (beyond which depth, the Cardinal said, he never ventured). I took the Cardinal to the ballet, the ballet was "The Conservatory." The Cardinal applauded at fifty-seven points. Afterward, backstage, the Cardinal danced with Plenosova, holding her at arm's length with a good will and an ill grace. The skirts of the scarlet soutane stood out to reveal high-button shoes, and the stagehands clapped.

I asked the Cardinal his views on the moon, he said they were the conventional ones, and that is how I know all I know about cardinals. Not enough perhaps to rear a science of cardinalogy upon, but enough perhaps to form a basis for the investigations of other investigators. My report is over there, in the blue binding, next to my copy of *La Géomancie et la Néomancie des Anciens* by the Seigneur of Salerno.

Cardinal Y. One can measure and measure and miss the most essential thing. I liked him. I still get the odd blessing in the mail now and then.

Too, maybe I was trying on the role. Not for myself. When a child is born, the locus of one's hopes . . . shifts, slightly. Not altogether, not all at once. But you feel it, this displacement. You speak up, strike attitudes, like the mother of a tiny Lollobrigida. Drunk with possibility once more.

I am still wearing my yellow flower which has lasted wonderfully.

"What is Gog doing."

"Sleeping."

You see, Gog of mine, Gog o' my heart, I'm just trying to give you a little briefing here. I don't want you unpleasantly surprised. I can't stand a startled look. Regard me as a sort of Distant Early Warning System. Here is the world and here are the knowledgeable knowers knowing. What can I tell you? What has been pieced together from the reports of travellers.

Fragments are the only forms I trust.

Look at my wall, it's all there. That's a leaf, Gog, stuck up with Scotch Tape. No no, the Scotch Tape is the shiny transparent stuff, the leaf the veined irregularly shaped . . .

There are several sides to this axe, Gog, consider the photostat, "Mr. W. B. Yeats Presenting Mr. George Moore to the Queen of the Fairies." That's a civilized gesture, I mean Beerbohm's. And when the sculptor Aristide Maillol went into the printing business he made the paper by *chewing the fibers himself.* That's dedication. And here is a Polaroid photo, shows your Aunt Sylvia and me putting an Ant Farm together. That's how close we were in those days. Just an Ant Farm apart.

See the moon? It hates us.

And now comes J. J. Sullivan's orange-and-blue Gulf Oil truck to throw kerosene into the space heater. Driver in green siren suit, red face, blond shaved head, the following rich verbal transaction:

"Beautiful day."

"Certainly is."

And now settling back in this green glider with a copy of *Man.* Dear Ann when I look at *Man* I don't want you. Unfolded Ursala Thigpen seems eversomuchmore desirable. A clean girl too and with interests, cooking, botany, pornographic novels. Someone new to show my slash to.

In another month Gog leaps fully armed from the womb. What can I do for him? I can get him into A.A., I have influence. And make sure no harsh moonlight falls on his new soft head.

Hello there Gog. We hope you'll be very happy here.

LOVE: WOMEN

John Steinbeck
1902-1968

Salinas, California was Steinbeck's birthplace, and the town and surrounding area became the setting for many of his books and stories. Like Faulkner, he was the recipient of both the Nobel Prize and the Pulitzer Prize. His most famous novel, *Grapes of Wrath,* is still widely taught and read, but his short stories are not read as much now as they once were, which is saddening, since many of them are quite fine. "The Chrysanthemums," perhaps the most well known of his short stories, has a place here for its honest, poignant depiction of a woman, a "good" woman, who is allowed a brief, romantic glimpse of the freedom of the road. Her conversation with her husband later eloquently bespeaks her feelings and brings the reader to share her unfulfilment, her loss. Suggested readings: *Cannery Row* and *The Long Valley And Other Stories.*

THE CHRYSANTHEMUMS

The high grey-flannel fog of winter closed off the Salinas Valley from the sky and from all the rest of the world. On every side it sat like a lid on the mountains and made of the great valley a closed pot. On the broad, level land floor the gang ploughs bit deep and left the black earth shining like metal where the shares had cut. On the foot-hill ranches across the Salinas River, the yellow stubble fields seemed to be bathed in pale cold sunshine, but there was no sunshine in the valley now in December. The thick willow scrub along the river flamed with sharp and positive yellow leaves.

It was a time of quiet and of waiting. The air was cold and tender. A light wind blew up from the southwest so that the farmers were mildly hopeful of a good rain before long; but fog and rain do not go together.

Across the river, on Henry Allen's foothill ranch there was little work to be done, for the hay was cut and stored and the orchards were ploughed up to receive the rain deeply when it should come. The cattle on the higher slopes were becoming shaggy and rough-coated.

Elisa Allen, working in her flower garden, looked down across the yard and saw Henry, her husband, talking to two men in business suits. The three of them stood by the tractor shed, each man with one foot on the side of the little Fordson. They smoked cigarettes and studied the machine as they talked.

Elisa watched them for a moment and then went back to her work. She was thirty-five. Her face was lean and strong and her eyes were as clear as water. Her figure looked blocked and heavy in her gardening costume, a man's black hat pulled low down over her eyes, clod-hopper shoes, a figured print dress almost completely covered by a big corduroy apron with four big pockets to hold the snips, the trowel and scratcher, the seeds and the knife she worked with. She wore heavy leather gloves to protect her hands while she worked.

She was cutting down the old year's chrysanthemum stalks with a pair of short and powerful scissors. She looked down toward the men by the tractor shed now and then. Her face was eager and mature and handsome; even her work with the scissors was over-eager, over-powerful. The chrysanthemum stems seemed too small and easy for her energy.

She brushed a cloud of hair out of her eyes with the back of her glove, and left a smudge of earth on her cheek in doing it. Behind her stood the neat white farm house with red geraniums close-banked around it as high as the windows. It was a hard-swept-looking little house, with hard-polished windows, and a clean mud-mat on the front steps.

Elisa cast another glance toward the tractor shed. The strangers were getting into their Ford coupé. She took off a glove and put her strong fingers down into the forest of new green chrysanthemum sprouts that were growing around the old roots. She spread the leaves and looked down among the close-growing stems. No aphids were there, no sow bugs or snails or cutworms. Her terrier fingers destroyed such pests before they could get started.

Elisa started at the sound of her husband's voice. He had come near quietly, and he leaned over the wire fence that protected her flower garden from cattle and dogs and chickens.

"At it again," he said. "You've got a strong new crop coming."

Elisa straightened her back and pulled on the gardening glove again. "Yes. They'll be strong this coming year." In her tone and on her face there was a little smugness.

"You've got a gift with things," Henry observed. "Some of those yellow chrysanthemums you had this year were ten inches across. I wish you'd work out in the orchard and raise some apples that big."

Her eyes sharpened. "Maybe I could do it, too. I've a gift with things, all right. My mother had it. She could stick anything in the ground and make it grow. She said it was having planters' hands that knew how to do it."

"Well, it sure works with flowers," he said.

"Henry, who were those men you were talking to?"

"Why, sure, that's what I came to tell you. They were from the Western Meat Company. I sold those thirty head of three-year-old steers. Got nearly my own price, too."

"Good," she said. "Good for you."

"And I thought," he continued, "I thought how it's Saturday afternoon, and we might go into Salinas for dinner at a restaurant, and then to a picture show—to celebrate, you see."

"Good," she repeated. "Oh, yes. That will be good."

Henry put on his joking tone. "There's fights tonight. How'd you like to go to the fights?"

"Oh, no," she said breathlessly. "No, I wouldn't like fights."

"Just fooling, Elisa. We'll go to a movie. Let's see. It's two now. I'm going to take Scotty and bring down those steers from the hill. It'll take us maybe two hours. We'll go in town about five and have dinner at the Cominos Hotel. Like that?"

"Of course I'll like it. It's good to eat away from home."

"All right, then. I'll go get up a couple of horses."

She said: "I'll have plenty of time to transplant some of these sets, I guess."

She heard her husband calling Scotty down by the barn. And a little later she saw the two men ride up the pale yellow hillside in search of the steers.

There was a little square sandy bed kept for rooting the chrysanthemums. With her trowel she turned the soil over and over, and smoothed it and patted it firm. Then she dug ten parallel trenches to receive the sets. Back at the chrysanthemum bed she pulled out the little crisp shoots, trimmed off the leaves of each one with her scissors and laid it on a small orderly pile.

A squeak of wheels and plod of hoofs came from the road. Elisa looked up. The country road ran along the dense bank of willows and cottonwoods that bordered the river, and up this road came a curious vehicle, curiously drawn. It was an old spring-wagon, with a round canvas top on it like the cover of a prairie schooner. It was drawn by an old bay horse and a little grey-and-white burro. A big stubble-bearded man sat between the cover flaps and drove the crawling team. Underneath the wagon, between the hind wheels, a lean and rangy mongrel dog walked sedately. Words were painted on the canvas, in clumsy, crooked letters. "Pots, pans, knives, sisors, lawn mores, Fixed." Two rows of articles and the triumphantly definite "Fixed" below. The black paint had run down in little sharp points beneath each letter.

Elisa, squatting on the ground, watched to see the crazy, loose-jointed wagon pass by. But it didn't pass. It turned into the farm road in front of her house, crooked old wheels skirling and squeaking. The rangy dog darted from between the wheels and ran ahead. Instantly the two ranch shepherds flew out at him. Then all three stopped, and with stiff and quivering tails, with taut straight legs, with ambassadorial dignity, they slowly circled, sniffing daintily. The caravan pulled up to Elisa's wire fence and stopped. Now the newcomer dog, feeling out-numbered, lowered his tail and retired under the wagon with raised hackles and bared teeth.

The man on the wagon seat called out: "That's a bad dog ina fight when he gets started."

Elisa laughed. "I see he is. How soon does he generally get started?"

The man caught up her laughter and echoed it heartily. "Sometimes not for weeks and weeks," he said. He climbed stiffly down, over the wheel. The horse and the donkey drooped like unwatered flowers.

Elisa saw that he was a very big man. Although his hair and beard were greying, he did not look old. His worn black suit was wrinkled and spotted with grease. The laughter had disappeared from his face and eyes the moment his laughing voice ceased. His eyes were dark, and they were full of the brooding that gets in the eyes of teamsters and of sailors. The calloused hands he rested on the wire fence were cracked, and every crack was a black line. He took off his battered hat.

"I'm off my general road, ma'am," he said. "Does this dirt road cut over across the river to the Los Angeles highway?"

Elisa stood up and shoved the thick scissors in her apron pocket. "Well, yes, it does, but it winds around and then fords the river. I don't think your team could pull through the sand."

He replied with some asperity: "It might surprise you what them beasts can pull through."

"When they get started?" she asked.

He smiled for a second. "Yes. When they get started."

"Well," said Elisa, "I think you'll save time if you go back to the Salinas road and pick up the highway there."

He drew a big finger down the chicken wire and made it sing. "I ain't in any hurry, ma'am. I go from Seattle to San Diego and back every year. Takes all my time. About six months each way. I aim to follow nice weather."

Elisa took off her gloves and stuffed them in the apron pocket with the scissors. She touched the under edge of her man's hat, searching for fugitive hairs. "That sounds like a nice kind of a way to live," she said.

He leaned confidentially over the fence. "Maybe you noticed the writing on my wagon. I mend pots and sharpen knives and scissors. You got any of them things to do?"

"Oh, no," she said quickly. "Nothing like that." Her eyes hardened with resistance.

"Scissors is the worst thing," he explained. "Most people just ruin scissors trying to sharpen 'em, but I know how. I got a special tool. It's a little bobbit kind of thing, and patented. But it sure does the trick."

"No. My scissors are all sharp."

"All right, then. Take a pot," he continued earnestly, "a bent pot, or a pot with a hole. I can make it like new so you don't have to buy no new ones. That's a saving for you."

"No," she said shortly. "I tell you I have nothing like that for you to do."

His face fell to an exaggerated sadness. His voice took on a whining undertone. "I ain't had a thing to do today. Maybe I won't have no supper tonight. You see I'm off my regular road. I know folks on the highway clear from Seattle to San Diego. They save their things for me to sharpen up because they know I do it so good and save them money."

"I'm sorry," Elisa said irritably. "I haven't anything for you to do."

His eyes left her face and fell to searching the ground. They roamed about until they came to the chrysanthemum bed where she had been working. "What's them plants, ma'am?"

The irritation and resistance melted from Elisa's face. "Oh, those are chrysanthemums, giant whites and yellows. I raise them every year, bigger than anybody around here."

"Kind of a long-stemmed flower? Looks like a quick puff of coloured smoke?" he asked.

"That's it. What a nice way to describe them."

"They smell kind of nasty till you get used to them," he said.

"It's a good bitter smell," she retorted, "not nasty at all."

He changed his tone quickly. "I like the smell myself."

"I had ten-inch blooms this year," she said.

The man leaned farther over the fence. "Look. I know a lady down the road a piece, has got the nicest garden you ever seen. Got nearly every kind of flower but no chrysanthemums. Last time I was mending a copper-bottom washtub for her (that's a hard job but I do it good), she said to me: 'If you ever run acrost some nice chrysanthemums I wish you'd try to get me a few seeds.' That's what she told me."

Elisa's eyes grew alert and eager. "She couldn't have known much about chrysanthemums. You *can* raise them from seed, but it's much easier to root the little sprouts you see there."

"Oh," he said. "I s'pose I can't take none to her, then."

"Why yes you can," Elisa cried. "I can put some in damp sand, and you can carry them right along with you. They'll take root in the pot if you keep them damp. And then she can transplant them."

"She'd sure like to have some, ma'am. You say they're nice ones?"

"Beautiful," she said. "Oh, beautiful." Her eyes shone. She tore off the battered hat and shook out her dark pretty hair. "I'll put them in a flower-pot, and you can take them right with you. Come into the yard."

While the man came through the picket gate Elisa ran excitedly along the geranium-bordered path to the back of the house. And she returned carrying a big red flower-pot. The gloves were forgotten now. She kneeled on the ground by the starting bed and dug up the sandy soil with her fingers and scooped it into the bright new flower-pot. Then she picked up the little pile of shoots she had prepared. With her strong fingers she pressed them into the sand and tamped around them with her knuckles. The man stood over her. "I'll tell you what to do," she said. "You remember so you can tell the lady."

"Yes, I'll try to remember."

"Well, look. These will take root in about a month. Then she must set them out, about a foot apart in good rich earth like this, see?" She lifted a handful of dark soil for him to look at. "They'll grow fast and tall. Now remember this: In July tell her to cut them down, about eight inches from the ground."

"Before they bloom?" he asked.

"Yes, before they bloom." Her face was tight with eagerness. "They'll grow right up again. About the last of September the buds will start."

She stopped and seemed perplexed. "It's the budding that takes the most care," she said hesitantly. "I don't know how to tell you." She looked deep into his eyes, searchingly. Her mouth opened a little, and she seemed to be listening. "I'll try to tell you," she said. "Did you ever hear of planting hands?"

"Can't say I have, ma'am."

"Well, I can only tell you what it feels like. It's when you're picking off the buds you don't want. Everything goes right down into your fingertips. You watch your fingers work. They do it themselves. You can feel how it is. They pick and pick the buds. They never make a mistake. They're with the plant. Do you see? Your fingers and the plant. You can feel that, right up your arm. They know. They never make a mistake. You can feel it. When you're like that you can't do anything wrong. Do you see that? Can you understand that?"

She was kneeling on the ground looking up at him. Her breast swelled passionately.

The man's eyes narrowed. He looked away self-consciously. "Maybe I know," he said. "Sometimes in the night in the wagon there—"

Elisa's voice grew husky. She broke in on him: "I've never lived as you do, but I know what you mean. When the night is dark—why, the stars are sharp-pointed, and there's quiet. Why, you rise up and up! Every pointed star gets driven into your body. It's like that. Hot and sharp and—lovely."

Kneeling there, her hand went out toward his legs in the greasy black trousers. Her hesitant fingers almost touched the cloth. Then her hand dropped to the ground. She crouched low like a fawning dog.

He said: "It's nice, just like you say. Only when you don't have no dinner, it ain't."

She stood up then, very straight, and her face was ashamed. She held the flower-pot out to him and placed it gently in his arms. "Here. Put it in your wagon, on the seat, where you can watch it. Maybe I can find something for you to do."

At the back of the house she dug in the can pile and found two old and battered aluminum saucepans. She carried them back and gave them to him. "Here, maybe you can fix these."

His manner changed. He became professional. "Good as new I can fix them." At the back of his wagon he set a little anvil, and out of an oily tool-box dug a small machine hammer. Elisa came through the gate to watch him while he pounded out the dents in the kettles. His mouth grew sure and knowing. At a difficult part of the work he sucked his underlip.

"You sleep right in the wagon?" Elisa asked.

"Right in the wagon, ma'am. Rain or shine I'm dry as a cow in there."

"It must be nice," she said. "It must be very nice. I wish women could do such things."

"It ain't the right kind of a life for a woman."

Her upper lip raised a little, showing her teeth. "How do you know? How can you tell?" she said.

"I don't know, ma'am," he protested. "Of course I don't know. Now here's your kettles, done. You don't have to buy no new ones."

"How much?"

"Oh, fifty cents'll do. I keep my prices down and my work good. That's why I have all them satisfied customers up and down the highway."

Elisa brought him a fifty-cent piece from the house and dropped it in his hand. "You might be surprised to have a rival some time. I can sharpen scissors, too. And I can beat the dents out of little pots. I could show you what a woman might do."

He put his hammer back in the oily box and shoved the little anvil out of sight. "It would be a lonely life for a woman, ma'am, and a scarey life, too, with animals creeping under the wagon all night." He climbed over the single-tree, steadying himself with a hand on the burro's white rump. He settled himself in the seat, picked up the lines. "Thank you kindly, ma'am," he said. "I'll do like you told me; I'll go back and catch the Salinas road."

"Mind," she called, "if you're long in getting there, keep the sand damp."

"Sand, ma'am? . . . Sand? Oh, sure. You mean around the chrysanthemums. Sure I will." He clucked his tongue. The beasts leaned luxuriously into their collars. The mongrel dog took his place between the back wheels. The wagon turned and crawled out the entrance road and back the way it had come, along the river.

Elisa stood in front of her wire fence watching the slow progress of the caravan. Her shoulders were straight, her head thrown back, her eyes half-closed, so that the scene came vaguely into them. Her lips moved silently, forming the words "Good-bye—good-bye." Then she whispered: "That's a bright direction. There's a glowing there." The sound of her whisper startled her. She shook herself free and looked about to see whether anyone had been listening. Only the dogs had heard. They lifted their heads toward her from their sleeping in the dust, and then stretched out their chins and settled asleep again. Elisa turned and ran hurriedly into the house.

In the kitchen she reached behind the stove and felt the water tank. It was full of hot water from the noonday cooking. In the bathroom she tore off her soiled clothes and flung them into the corner. And then she scrubbed herself with a little block of pumice, legs and thighs, loins and chest and arms, until her skin was scratched and red. When she had dried herself she stood in front of a mirror in her bedroom and looked at her body. She tightened her stomach and threw out her chest. She turned and looked over her shoulder at her back.

After a while she began to dress, slowly. She put on her newest underclothing and her nicest stockings and the dress which was the symbol of her prettiness. She worked carefully on her hair, pencilled her eyebrows and roughed her lips.

Before she was finished she heard the little thunder of hoofs and the shouts of Henry and his helper as they drove the red steers into the corral. She heard the gate bang shut and set herself for Henry's arrival.

His step sounded on the porch. He entered the house calling: "Elisa, where are you?"

"In my room, dressing. I'm not ready. There's hot water for your bath. Hurry up. It's getting late."

When she heard him splashing in the tub, Elisa laid his dark suit on the bed, and shirt and socks and tie beside it. She stood his polished shoes on the floor beside the bed. Then she went to the porch and sat primly and stiffly down. She looked toward the river road where the willow-line was still yellow with frosted leaves so that under the high grey fog they seemed a thin band of sunshine. This was the only colour

Roecker, William A *comp.*

Stories that count. Edited by William A. Roecker. New York, Holt, Rinehart and Winston [1971]

viii, 214 p. 23 cm.

CONTENTS.—The ledge, by L. S. Hall.—The waterfowl tree, by W. A. Kittredge.—Open winter, by H. L. Davis.—Something big is happening to me, by W. Eastlake.—Red leaves, by W. Faulkner.—A good man is hard to find, by F. O'Connor.—Defender of the faith, by P. Roth.—Jody rolled the bones, by R. Yates.—The Jewbird, by B. Malamud.—See the moon? By D. Barthelme.—The chrysanthemums, by J. Steinbeck.—Us he devours, by J. B. Hall.—A sense of shelter, by J. Updike.—Oh, the wonder! By J. Larner.

1. Short stories, American. I. Title.

PZ1.R613St 813'.008 78-126799
[PS659] MARC
ISBN 0-03-084146-1

Library of Congress 71 [4]

in the grey afternoon. She sat unmoving for a long time. Her eyes blinked rarely.

Henry came banging out of the door, shoving his tie inside his vest as he came. Elisa stiffened and her face grew tight. Henry stopped short and looked at her. "Why—why, Elisa. You look so nice!"

"Nice? You think I look nice? What do you mean by 'nice'?"

Henry blundered on. "I don't know. I mean you look different, strong and happy."

"I am strong? Yes, strong. What do you mean 'strong'?"

He looked bewildered. "You're playing some kind of a game," he said helplessly. "It's a kind of a play. You look strong enough to break a calf over your knee, happy enough to eat it like a watermelon."

For a second she lost her rigidity. "Henry! Don't talk like that. You didn't know what you said." She grew complete again. "I'm strong," she boasted. "I never knew before how strong."

Henry looked down toward the tractor shed, and when he brought his eyes back to her, they were his own again. "I'll get out the car. You can put on your coat while I'm starting."

Elisa went into the house. She heard him drive to the gate and idle down his motor, and then she took a long time to put on her hat. She pulled it here and pressed it there. When Henry turned the motor off she slipped into her coat and went out.

The little roadster bounced along on the dirt road by the river, raising the birds and driving the rabbits into the brush. Two cranes flapped heavily over the willow-line and dropped into the river-bed.

Far ahead on the road Elisa saw a dark speck. She knew.

She tried not to look as they passed it, but her eyes would not obey. She whispered to herself sadly: "He might have thrown them off the road. That wouldn't have been much trouble, not very much. But he kept the pot," she explained. "He had to keep the pot. That's why he couldn't get them off the road."

The roadster turned a bend and she saw the caravan ahead. She swung full around toward her husband so she could not see the little covered wagon and the mis-matched team as the car passed them.

In a moment it was over. The thing was done. She did not look back.

She said loudly, to be heard above the motor: "It will be good, tonight, a good dinner."

"Now you're changed again," Henry complained. He took one hand from the wheel and patted her knee. "I ought to take you in to dinner oftener. It would be good for both of us. We get so heavy out on the ranch."

"Henry," she asked, "could we have wine at dinner?"

"Sure we could. Say! That will be fine."

She was silent for a while; then she said: "Henry, at those prize-fights, do the men hurt each other very much?"

"Sometimes a little, not often. Why?"

"Well, I've read how they break noses, and blood runs down their chests. I've read how the fighting gloves get heavy and soggy with blood."

He looked around at her. "What's the matter, Elisa? I didn't know you read things like that." He brought the car to a stop, then turned to the right over the Salinas River bridge.

"Do any women ever go to the fights?" she asked.

"Oh, sure, some. What's the matter, Elisa? Do you want to go? I don't think you'd like it, but I'll take you if you really want to go."

She relaxed limply in the seat. "Oh, no. No. I don't want to go. I'm sure I don't." Her face was turned away from him. "It will be enough if we can have wine. It will be plenty." She turned up her coat collar so he could not see that she was crying weakly—like an old woman.

James B. Hall
1918-

Poet, novelist and short story writer, James B. Hall was born in Ohio. He taught and directed writing programs at the University of Oregon and the University of California at Irvine, and is presently provost of the College of Fine Arts at the University of California at Santa Cruz. Among other things, Hall was a soldier and a seaman in his youth. His stories have appeared in such diverse magazines as *San Francisco Review* and *Atlantic*, and he was a founding editor of *Northwest Review*. "Us He Devours" is a complex story that mingles real and mythic, Greek and Christian elements to make a probing statement about human, female emotion. It might be compared to the work of D. H. Lawrence or discussed in Freudian terms. Suggested readings: *Us He Devours* and *15 x 3*.

US HE DEVOURS

The goat coughed in the tree outside her window.

Oh she had waited so long to see the hoofs firm upon the lowest branches, the flanks slender, stretched upward among the catalpa leaves, the head half concealed, the backward curving horns erect, glistening in the moist light of the moon.

Miss Festner had thought all these times were past, forever, but now her branches rustled louder, and she stiffened in her bed. Stringy and coarse and rancid as a chicken house floor, the odor afloat in the catalpa tree came to her. She lay in her bed and she felt her back and her thighs harden. This time she was determined to wait.

From experience Miss Festner knew that to leap from her bed, to rush to the casement, to cry out, was useless. When younger she had cried out, in fear; later she knew she must wait without emotion. Not always did the goat leap with a terrible cracking of small branches, and scramble pawing across her window sill.

Sometimes it came—perhaps silently—then deserted her. Sometimes the cry of reed pipes swelled inside her room until her ears and heart and her hard breasts ached; sometimes, after the cry of the loon and after the last crackling noise of great weight among branches, it went away. If it awakened her, and then deserted her, she would go to her window and

"Us He Devours," from *Us He Devours* by James B. Hall, New Directions-San Francisco Review, New York, 1964. Reprinted by permission of James B. Hall.

stare out across the town, which fell away below her windows toward the river. Therefore she did not now dare look toward the window when the odor of stalls and rabbit hutches and stables came to her like smoke from the leaves of the shimmering tree.

For this it seemed she had been waiting a very long time. She had almost given up hope, but now she did what she could. Her quick money-counting fingers dug deeper into the little holes in the farthest edges of her mattress. The sheet across her knees and thighs and her dry belly made spasms of motion.

Some things she could not control, but some things she could do: always she left her window open, she used only the lightest of sheets, and always she was *clean, clean.* If she looked now the eyes she might see would flee into the kingdom of her dreams. But oh tonight she could not wait.

With her eyes still closed she threw the small sheet from her body. Exposed. Yes and on display and naked as the first day her quick money-counting fingers worked inside her Teller's cage. From Escrows in the bank, she had gone behind a Teller's window. Since then she had her window at the bank, with bars, and the businessmen of the town came to her with money and she handled each day the hard, hand-fitting, phallic rolls of dimes, nickels, and quarters. That night in spring, for the first time, the goat coughed in the catalpa tree in the yard of her small house and in her inexperience and her fear she had run too quickly to her bedroom window and the musk-scented thing had fled somewhere across the roiled shadows of her yard.

Finally she learned to wait motionless in her bed, for only then would the wool-soft yarn and the perfume and the polished mother-of-pearl horns and the soft resilient body—only then would it stay lovely as flowers unfolding beside and over her until the dawn humming awoke in her arms. Those mornings she telephoned Mr. Nelscot at the bank. She did not go down the hill to sit behind the window of her Teller's cage until after her lunch.

Louder now outside her bedroom window the small branches scattered. Was now the time, this night?

In the catalpa tree outside she heard it whet the saber of its horns against the topmost branches. Were the hoarse violent eyes staring at her now?

She resisted a moment, and then she no longer cared. To see, to glimpse it among branches seemed enough. She opened wide her eyes.

No. Not there. Gone.

The cry of the loon in the frozen trees chilled her. She had been terribly hot; now she was not hot. She felt more deserted, and more forlorn, than ever before. Yet she was not and never could be sinfully passive, for urgency even in her waking hours grew like a fuse somewhere inside her. She recognized, she even welcomed, the desperation that came galloping to her. She knew she must go out, must seek, must search once more.

Of late when the goat coughed in the branches outside her window and then deserted her, she had followed. Once she had been astonished at her own headlong urgency, but she had gone on because she believed that in frenzy was the hot little kernel of satisfaction. Now that restraint was somewhere far behind her she could think of nothing at all except a highway, twisting somewhere ahead.

II

Furiously she drove the country, limestone roads. Ahead on a curve the guardrails writhed in her headlight beams. At a crossroad she saw the shadow of a country mailbox lie back beside some farmer's lane, and as she passed the black check mark shadow seemed to fade, and then to become a check mark of flame in the corner of her headlong eye.

The constant search, it was, that vexed her. At one time the first place she stopped was always the right place. But as the years fled her, she found the right place was now always farther away, until now she was resigned to the longest drive of all: this night she knew without caring that she would go far beyond a familiar tilt-roofed, ramschackle barn that roosted in a pasture, reviled even by the shoat's moist farming nose.

One spring she had first gone outside. She had gone directly to a certain creek that divided two meadows, where a sand bar of supine luminous tissues of gravel lay exposed between rocks and the water. Later she found her sand bar was not the right place and she had to drive on to a field freshly harrowed, and then on still farther, in the fall, to a place of stubbles, of wheat lately under the sickle bars of harvest. From habit, or from some terrible wish, she still drove first to the sand bar and then to the fields, in the order of their discovery. Finally she came to a familiar bridge. Across this bridge was a grove of oaks that was lovely and dark and deep, a mat of green between two hills.

The planks of the bridge seemed to say this was the place that she must find. But she could accept no comfort from the mutter of planks. Always, until the final moment, there was uncertainty. Suppose the place now had to be still more remote, a place where she could never travel, a place so cleverly concealed in a shaggy-thighed wood that no one could ever find it. She could not think upon that ultimate possibility. As always, at this time, she knew with the Bible-black certainty of prayer that here was the place. Here nothing would be denied her.

The boxes and packages she kept locked in the car trunk. There were things she bought on impulse during her lunch hour or on Saturday, as though each purchase were for herself. She had not thought there were so many, but the oblong, white boxes and the largest flat box—all of them—seemed to leap into her arms. Without pausing she ran across a culvert and across a flat small meadow and into the first sentinel trees at the oak grove's edge.

Too late she realized the briers also guarded the grove. They had grown and had become heavy as barbed wire since the last time.

With the white boxes held high above her head, and with her robe open, flapping behind her, she leaped high and for a moment seemed to float above the caress of briers. She landed running. Her legs burned. But Miss Festner did not cry out.

Ahead she saw the smooth arena, in the center of her secret grove of oaks.

"Here, oh here," she said to the briers, which seemed to roll away in unbroken humps of light toward a creek beyond.

"Here. I am here, now," she said to the crossed branches of the trees overhead. "Here . . ."

She took off her robe.

She spread the robe near the boxes, at the edge of the clearing. Carefully in the moonlight she searched the clay ground, inch by inch; there was no dung, and no hair of cattle wedged in the bark of the oak trees. As she had imagined as she drove those limestone roads, the grove was clean, clean.

In the middle of the hoof-packed clay in the center of the grove of oaks, Miss Festner lay herself down upon the ground, which now seemed warm under the muscles of her flesh.

Nothing did come to her.

She was alone.

She listened but she heard only the mockery of silence among the trunks of trees. The intricate thunder of possibility shook her: was this the end, was she to be deserted like this at the final meeting place between two hills.

Then she heard it cough.

Nearby in the encircling brier she heard its jaws nibble the harsh vegetation. A small branch ripped under the plunge of a hoof. Then she heard it above her, high in the canopy of branches overhead; perhaps it was now looking down at the raised, white supplication of her arms.

She heard once more the cry of the loon: near, then far away. She heard something hoarse, and very close, in the ring of the briers. Held fast in the bondage of her desire, she lay with eyes closed in the moonlight, and still nothing came to her.

Over, she thought. Oh over and gone and never again to return to me. She realized a truth about herself: since the first time when the hair was sweet as a cloud of wool above her she had given more and more of herself. She had walked much, had driven farther and farther into strange woods. Then, like a reprieve, the coarse odor came to her. The lust of its eye rustled the briers.

The gifts. Yes, the boxes piled near her robe. Each time, with gifts, she also gave more and more. At first it was only a flower tossed lightly upon the sand bar. Then her gifts were only the green enticement, but finally she had to give the silks of reward, everything.

In a frenzy she opened her gifts.

Against rocks she broke the expensive, sullen perfumes. Each vial shattered and split and this enticement by odor overwhelmed even the trunks of the black trees.

Oh, come to me?

She paused, listened.

Somewhere beyond the shadows, somewhere in the forest of that night she felt something advance. She felt something come closer to her.

Her quick money-counting fingers clawed at the smaller boxes. She ripped tissue paper from all the jewels she had purchased at all the big jewelry stores all across the city. Tiaras and small rings and pearls in white strands, all these she tore into shreds of diamonds and single rubies and broken pearls, and these she threw into the encircling briers.

Oh, come to me?

The odor—so lurid, so near—seemed to stroke her thighs, and then in the old way it seemed to retreat beyond her farthest gifts.

Without her seeming to touch the hoof-packed clay she ran to the largest, final package. This she had saved, for the habit of frugality could also be with her, even in moments of extravagance.

She opened the box. The white, intense fleece of a lamb was what she held aloft. She waved the fleece in the light of the clearing. She held the fleece above her lowing mouth. She allowed the fleece to fall like a shower of myrrh and spice, to fall like the color of flowers around her, to cover her shoulders and her back with the incense of new wool.

Oh, come to me?

When nothing came to her, Miss Festner ran toward the thing she heard, toward a harsh plunging noise, in those final briers.

But she stopped. She knew it had deceived her, and therefore she stood weeping and ruined, fanned by the hot cry of the loon, in the center of briers and all her nights.

III

Escrow, Checking, Loans, and finally a Teller's cage: she had worked through each department, and now as the green floodgate doors of the bank opened, promptly at ten, she watched people swim into the bright hard marble pool of light, the interior of First National, Main.

In the hard security of a Teller's cage, she began this day by loosening the green drawstrings of green moneybags. Rolls of coins were what she found in each puffy little sack, rolls of dimes, and quarters, and half dollars, each roll made especially for her hand. In even rows the packets of bills, the twenties and fifties, fit precisely into each slot of her tray, and she felt the first smile of the morning hazard its first trial with the flesh of her own lips and cheeks as a customer snuffled just beyond the bars of her window.

From up the line, from Window Number One, Miss Festner heard the money-counting sound of laughter. The sound of the laughter made her see the two derby hats and the two false beards of the two men who were shaking hands with a Vice-President in the officers' enclosure, across the room. When she also saw the two beards rise and fall with the handshakes of the two men, she felt her own mouth pick up the laughter and pass it on to the next Teller in the long, money-counting line.

The State's Centennial Year, it was. The State Banking Inspectors were making believe. Across the room, in the officers' marble enclosure, two short men in make-believe beards began to laugh and laugh.

While her fingers counted out sixty-nine-sixty of the pensioner's check, which had snuffled under the bars of her window, she knew the ledgers and the adding machine tapes folded and held with paper clips and the dormant accounts and the Escrows were writhing, somewhere in the vaults or the storage rooms of First National, Main Branch.

Though the bills and the coins flowed through and around and over her fingers as water flows over and around a sand bar in some moonlit creek, the two derby hats and the beards of false gray hair seemed to float, seemed to become an echo, in the high corners of the main floor.

The edges of marble, the parallel shadows on the foot-trampled floor, the parallel lines of the brass-barred window before her, were the squares and the bars of a place she clearly remembered.

Across the bridge, beyond the village edge, was where the pens were. There in Ohio, beyond the edge of a limestone road, she had awakened from the sleepless dawns of girlhood to hear the cruel roosters cry *blood, blood, bloooood* across the sties and pens and across the hen yard's dusty wallows. Often she lay in her bed, listening to the sounds of animals already awake; the snigger of boars or somewhere in the corner of a pasture the dry dirt-pawing hoof of her father's bull. The dirt, the droppings of turkeys and pea fowl, and the dung of sparrows on a beam under the barn's eave were always there, or were seen in memory only as a brown composite of wind and random dust flapping across barnyards.

In that house the women swept floors, brushed crumbs from tables, rocked toward evening, waited for the odor of farm boots and the odor of work clothes, denim jackets, and old felt hats to walk through kitchen doors; waited until the warm odor of milk drifted into the fried heat of a kitchen in March.

In summer a tomcat lolled on the tendrils and the matted leaves of a grape arbor, and stared all day at the martin's box high on a curved, white pole.

Mostly she remembered the things maimed: a rabbit leaping from stubble into the light of her father's sickle bar; the cut-shoat's lyric scream; the pullet, headless toward noon, butting a post of her mother's clothesline. Or the hired men, their fingers aligned at the thresher's dinner table, each man with something clipped off, missing: a finger gone to the nibbling belt of a corn sheller, a toe left at a chopping block, a hand or a forearm shucked by the whirling, frost-wet picker rolls.

All of that was past. She had gone to school, though she had visited her old home out of sentiment at the change of each season. For three years she taught at a consolidated high school. Though she tried to beat them with a yardstick the hulking baseball and football and basketball players refused to obey her. Finally the principal said why after all the First National, Main, paid twice as much, and then she could really have a place of her own. Therefore she had gone to live at the edge of this town, where sometimes a goat coughed in the catalpa leaves, and the backward curve of horn was mother-of-pearl in the moist light of the moon.

The two Inspectors came back toward noon.

Finally they began to work. Because it really was the Centennial Year, they wore derby hats and gray, false whiskers while they walked in and out of the officers' marble enclosure, or in and out of the vaults. She heard them laughing as they worked, and from her window it seemed they walked through the glass partitions. Toward three o'clock they walked past, together, nibbling a candy bar with their white goat teeth; and then they were behind the row of Tellers, nibbling stacks and stacks of twenties and fifties with their money-counting fingers.

At four o'clock doors were locked and the blinds were drawn, and only the feet and the knees of people walked past in the disembodied street. When she saw the legs walking past, Miss Festner thought, Why yes, tomorrow or the next day some one of the officers will walk up behind me and will stare and will then walk away as though he had seen something different. Then she would say what she knew all the others like her always said to the press: For my friends, for my friends, I did it, because I wanted them to be as happy as I have always been. You see, I gave it all to my friends . . .

At check-out, in the steel-lined vault, she saw the other money trays, all in a row. She knew this might be her last night at home in her own bed, in the room where the catalpa leaves were sometimes perfume in the night.

For the last time, tonight, she knew she might hear the hoofs firm upon the lowest branches, might see the flanks slender, stretched upward among the leaves, and might see also that final, unwinking eye stare at her from the tenderness of leaves.

Without hesitation she opened her massive, over-the-shoulder purse. Into the wide unlatched maw she stuffed all the singles and bundles of twenties and bundles of fifty dollar bills that her country hands could gather. In case, oh, in case it was money that was wanted, after all.

As always, Mr. Nelscot was standing at the bank door.

He smiled and he bowed very slightly as he let Miss Festner and her valise of a purse out the door.

All over again she heard the click of the door of First National, Main, behind her. She knew he would never do more than smile, would never do more than bow ever so slightly as he opened the door for her to leave. Or had that been his voice, after all; had he said as she left, as the door shut and clicked somewhere in the past and also in the future of her days, had he said too late, "See you. Same time tomorrow?"

LOVE: MEN

John Updike
1926-

Updike was born in Shillington, Pennsylvania. His novels and stories have enjoyed considerable success, and his painstaking, sometimes ornate style has been the subject of critical discussion. In "A Sense Of Shelter" he displays his remarkable talent for detail, making the reader experience the "feel" of the classroom and school and the awkward, intense emotions of an intellectual, snobbish and sensitive high school boy. Perhaps surprisingly then, nostalgia and recognition of self are strong elements in the story. Suggested readings: *Rabbit, Run, Pigeon Feathers* and *The Same Door.*

A SENSE OF SHELTER

Snow fell against the high school all day, wet big-flaked snow that did not accumulate well. Sharpening two pencils, William looked down on a parking lot that was a blackboard in reverse, car tires had cut smooth arcs of black into the white, and wherever a school bus had backed around, it had left an autocratic signature of two *V*'s. The snow, though at moments it whirled opaquely, could not quite bleach these scars away. The temperature must be exactly 32°. The window was open a crack, and a canted pane of glass lifted outdoor air into his face, coating the cedarwood scent of pencil shavings with the transparent odor of the wet window sill. With each revolution of the handle his knuckles came within a fraction of an inch of the tilted glass, and the faint chill this proximity breathed on them sharpened his already acute sense of shelter.

The sky behind the shreds of snow was stone-colored. The murk inside the high classroom gave the air a solidity that limited the overhead radiance to its own vessels; six globes of dull incandescence floated on the top of a thin sea. The feeling the gloom gave him was not gloomy but joyous: he felt they were all sealed in, safe; the colors of cloth were dyed deeper, the sound of whispers was made more distinct, the smells of tablet paper and wet shoes and varnish and face powder pierced him with a vivid sense of possession. These were his classmates sealed in, his, the stupid as well as the clever, the plain as well as the lovely, his enemies as well as his friends, his. He felt like a king and seemed to move to his seat between the bowed heads of subjects that loved him less than he loved them. His seat was sanctioned by tradition; for twelve years he had sat at the rear of classrooms, William Young, flanked by Marsha Wyckoff and Andy Zimmerman. Once there had been two Zimmermans, but one went to work in his father's greenhouse, and in some classes—Latin and Trig—there were none, and William sat at the edge of the class as if on the lip of a cliff, and Marsha Wyckoff became Marvin Wolf or Sandra Wade, but it was always the same desk, whose surface altered from hour to hour but from whose blue-stained ink-hole his mind could extract, like a chain of magicians' handkerchiefs, a continuity of years. As a senior he was a kind of king, and as a teacher's pet another kind, a puppet king, who gathered in appointive posts and even, when the moron vote split between two football heroes, some elective ones. He was not popular, he had never had a girl, his intense friends of childhood had drifted off into teams and gangs, and in large groups—when the whole school, for instance, went in the fall to the beautiful, dung-and-cotton-candy-smelling county fair—he was always an odd man, without a seat on the bus home. But exclusion is itself a form of inclusion. He even had a nickname: Mip, because he stuttered. Taunts no longer much frightened him; he had come late into his physical inheritance, but this summer it had arrived, and he at last stood equal with his enormous, boisterous parents, and had to unbutton his shirt cuffs to get his wrists through them, and discovered he could pick up a basketball with one hand. So, his long legs blocking two aisles, he felt regal even in size and, almost trembling with happiness under the high globes of light beyond whose lunar glow invisible snowflakes were drowning on the gravel roof of his castle, believed that the long delay of unpopularity had been merely a consolidation, that he was at last strong enough to make his move. Today he would tell Mary Landis he loved her.

He had loved her ever since, a fat-faced tomboy with freckles and green eyes, she deftly stole his rubber-lined schoolbag on the walk back from second grade along Jewett Street and outran him—simply had better legs. The superior speed a boy was supposed to have failed to come; his kidneys burned with panic. In front of the grocery store next to her home she stopped and turned. She was willing to have him catch up. This humiliation on top of the rest was too much to bear. Tears broke in his throat; he spun around and ran home and threw himself on the floor of the front parlor, where his grandfather, feet twiddling, perused the newspaper and soliloquized all morning. In time the letter slot rustled, and the doorbell rang, and Mary gave his mother the schoolbag and the two of them politely exchanged whispers. Their voices had been to him, lying there on the carpet with his head wrapped in his arms, indistinguishable. Mother had always liked Mary. From when she had been a tiny girl dancing along the hedge on the end of an older sister's arm, Mother had liked her. Out of all the children that flocked, similar as pigeons, through the neighborhood, Mother's heart had reached out with claws and fastened on Mary. He never took the schoolbag to school again, had refused to touch it. He supposed it was still in the attic, still faintly smelling of sweet pink rubber.

Fixed high on the plaster like a wren clinging to a barn wall, the buzzer sounded the two-minute signal. In the middle of the classroom Mary Landis stood up, a Monitor badge pinned to her belly. Her broad red belt was buckled with a brass bow and arrow. She wore a lavender sweater with the sleeves pushed up to expose her forearms, a delicately cheap effect. Wild stories were told about her; perhaps it was merely his knowledge of these that put the hardness in her face. Her eyes seemed braced for squinting and their green was frosted. Her freckles had faded. William thought she laughed less this year; now that she was in the Secretarial Course and he in the College Preparatory, he saw her in only one class a day, this one, English. She stood a second, eclipsed at the thighs by Jack Stephens' zebra-striped shoulders, and looked back at the class with a stiff worn glance, as if she had seen the same faces too many times before. Her habit of perfect posture emphasized the angularity she had grown into. There was a nervous edge, a boxiness in her bones, that must have been waiting all along under the childish fat. Her eye sockets were deeply indented and her chin had a prim square set that seemed in the murky air tremulous and defiant. Her skirt was cut square and straight. Below the waist she was lean; the legs that had outrun him were still athletic; she starred at hockey and cheerleading. Above, she was abundant: so stacked her spine curved backwards to keep her body balanced. She turned and in switching up the aisle encountered a boy's leg thrown into her path. She coolly looked down until it withdrew. She was used to such attentions. Her pronged chest poised, Mary proceeded out the door, and someone she saw in the hall made her smile, a wide smile full of warmth and short white teeth, and love scooped at William's heart. He would tell her.

In another minute, the second bell rasped. Shuffling through the perfumed crowds to his next class, he crooned to himself in the slow, over-enunciated manner of the Negro vocalist who had brought the song back this year:

> *Lah-vender blue, dilly dilly,*
> *Lavendih gree-heen;*
> Eef *I were king, dilly dilly,*
> *You would: be queen.*

The song gave him an exultant sliding sensation that intertwined with the pleasures of his day. He knew all the answers, he had done all the work, the teachers called upon him only to rebuke the ignorance of the others. In trig and Soc Sci both it was this way. In gym, the fourth hour of the morning, he, who was always picked near the last, startled his side by excelling at volleyball, leaping like a madman, shouting like a bully. The ball felt light as a feather against his big bones. His hair in wet quills from the shower, he walked in the icy air to Luke's Luncheonette, where he ate three hamburgers in a booth with three juniors. There was Barry Kruppman, a tall, thyroid-eyed boy who came on the school bus from the country town of Bowsville and who was an amateur hypnotist; he told the tale of a Portland, Oregon, businessman who under hypnosis had been taken back through sixteen reincarnations to the condition of an Egyptian concubine in the household of a high priest of Isis. There was his friend Lionel Griffin, a pudgy simp whose blond hair puffed out above his ears in two slick waxed wings. He was rumored to be a fairy, and in fact did seem most excited by the transvestite aspect of the soul's transmigration. And there was Lionel's girl Virginia, a drab little mystery who chain-smoked Herbert Tareytons and never said anything. She had sallow skin and smudged eyes and Lionel kept jabbing her and shrieking, making William wince. He would rather have sat with members of his own class, who filled the other booths, but he would have had to force himself on them. These juniors admired him and welcomed his company. He asked, "Wuh-well, was he ever a c-c-c-cockroach, like Archy?"

Kruppman's face grew intense; his furry lids dropped down over the bulge of his eyes, and when they drew back, his pupils were as small and hard as BBs. "That's the really interesting thing. There was this gap, see, between his being a knight under Charlemagne and then a sailor on a ship putting out from Macedonia—that's where Yugoslavia is now—in the time of Nero; there was this gap, when the only thing the guy would do was walk around the office snarling and growling, see, like this." Kruppman worked his blotched ferret face up into a snarl and Griffin shrieked. "He tried to bite one of the assistants and they think that for six hundred years"—the uncanny, unhealthy seriousness of his whisper hushed Griffin momentarily—"for six hundred years he just was a series of wolves. Probably in the German forests. You see, when he was in Macedonia"—his whisper barely audible—"he murdered a woman."

Griffin squealed in ecstasy and cried, "Oh, Kruppman! Kruppman, how you do go on!" and jabbed Virginia in the arm so hard a Herbert Tareyton jumped from her hand and bobbled across the Formica table. William gazed over their heads in pain.

The crowds at the soda counter had thinned so that when the door to the outside opened he saw Mary come in and hesitate there for a second where the smoke inside and the snow outside swirled together. The mixture made a kind of—Kruppman's ridiculous story had put the phrase in his head—wolf-weather, and she was just a gray shadow caught in it alone. She bought a pack of cigarettes from Luke and went out again, a kerchief around her head, the pneumatic thing above the door hissing behind her. For a long time, always in fact, she had been at the center of whatever gang was the one: in the second grade the one that walked home up Jewett Street together, and in the sixth grade the one that went bicycling as far away as the quarry and the Rentschler estate and played touch football Saturday afternoons, and in the ninth grade the one that went roller-skating at Candlebridge Park with the tenth-grade boys, and in the eleventh grade the one that held parties lasting past midnight and that on Sundays drove in caravans as far as Philadelphia and back. And all the while there had been a succession of boy friends, first Jack Stephens and Fritz March in their class and then boys a grade ahead and then Barrel Lord, who was a senior when they were sophomores and whose name was in the newspapers all football season, and then this last summer someone out of the school altogether, a man she met while working as a waitress in the city of Alton. So this year her weekends were taken up, and the party gang carried on as if she had never existed, and nobody saw her much except in school and when she stopped by in Luke's to buy a pack of cigarettes. Her silhouette against the big window had looked wan, her head hooded, her face nibbled by light, her fingers fiddling on the veined counter with her coins. He yearned to reach out, to comfort her, but he was wedged deep in the shrill booths, between the jingling guts of the pinball machine and the hillbilly joy of the jukebox. The impulse left him with a disagreeable feeling. He had loved her too long to want to pity her; it endangered the investment of worship on which he had not yet realized any return.

The two hours of the school afternoon held Latin and a study hall. In study hall, while the five people at the table with him played tic-tac-toe and sucked cough drops and yawned, he did all his homework for the next day. He prepared thirty lines of Vergil, Aeneas in the Underworld. The study hall was a huge low room in the basement of the building; its coziness crept into Tartarus. On the other side of the fudge-colored wall the circular saw in the woodworking shop whined and gasped and then whined again; it bit off pieces of wood with a rising, somehow terrorized inflection—*bzzzzzup!* He solved ten problems in trigonometry. His mind cut neatly through their knots and separated them, neat stiff squares of answer, one by one from the long but finite plank of problems that connected Plane Geometry with Solid. Lastly, as the snow on a ragged slant drifted down into the cement pits outside the steel-mullioned windows, he read a short story by Edgar Allan Poe. He closed the book softly on the pleasing sonority of its final note of horror, gazed at the red, wet, menthol-scented inner membrane of Judy Whipple's yawn, rimmed with flaking pink lipstick, and yielded his conscience to the snug sense of his work done, of the snow falling, of the warm minutes that walked through their shelter so slowly. The perforated acoustic tiling above his head seemed the lining of a long tube that would go all the way: high school merging into college, college into graduate school, graduate school into teaching at a college—section man, assistant, associate, *full* professor, possessor of a dozen languages and a thousand books, a man brilliant in his forties, wise in his fifties, renowned in his sixties, revered in his seventies, and then retired, sitting in the study lined with acoustical books until the time came for the last transition from silence to silence, and he would die, like Tennyson, with a copy of *Cymbeline* beside him on the moon-drenched bed.

After school he had to go to Room 101 and cut a sports cartoon into a stencil for the school paper. He liked the building best when it was nearly empty, when the casual residents—the rural commuters, the do-nothings, the trash—had cleared out. Then the janitors went down the halls sowing seeds of red wax and making an immaculate harvest with broad brooms, gathering all the fluff and hairpins and wrappers and powder that the animals had dropped that day. The basketball team thumped in the hollow gymnasium; the cheerleaders rehearsed behind drawn curtains on the stage. In Room 101 two empty-headed typists with stripes bleached into their hair banged away between giggles and mistakes. At her desk Mrs. Gregory, the faculty sponsor, wearily passed her pencil through misspelled news copy on tablet paper. William took the shadow box from the top of the filing cabinet and the styluses and little square plastic shading screens from their drawer and the stencil from the closet where the typed stencils hung, like fragile scarves, on hooks. B-BALLERS BOW, 57-42, was the headline. He drew a tall b-baller bowing to a stumpy pagan idol, labelled "W" for victorious Weiserton High, and traced it in the soft blue wax with the fine loop stylus. His careful breath grazed his knuckles. His eyebrows frowned while his heart bobbed happily on the giddy prattle of the typists. The shadow box was simply a black frame holding a pane of glass and lifted at one end by two legs so the light bulb, fitted in a tin tray, could slide under; it was like a primitive lean-to sheltering a fire. As he worked, his eyes smarting, he mixed himself up with the light bulb, felt himself burning under a slanting roof upon which a huge hand scratched. The glass grew hot; the danger in the job was pulling the softened wax with your damp hand, distorting or tearing the typed letters. Sometimes the center of an *o* struck to your skin like a bit of blue confetti. But he was expert and cautious. He returned the things to their places feeling airily tall, heightened by Mrs. Gregory's appreciation, which she expressed by keeping her back turned, in effect stating that other staff members were undependable but William did not need to be watched.

In the hall outside Room 101 only the shouts of a basketball scrimmage reverberated; the chant of the cheerleaders had been silenced. Though he had done everything, he felt reluctant to leave. Neither of his parents—both worked—would be home yet, and this building was as much his home. He knew all its nooks. On the second floor of the annex, beyond the art room, there was a strange, narrow boys' lavatory that no one ever seemed to use. It was here one time that Barry Kruppman tried to hypnotize him and cure his stuttering. Kruppman's voice purred and his irises turned tiny in the bulging whites and for a moment William felt himself lean backward involuntarily, but he was distracted by the bits of bloodshot pink in the corners of these portentous eyes; the folly of giving up his will to an intellectual inferior occurred to him; he refused to let go and go under, and perhaps therefore his stuttering had continued.

The frosted window at the end of the long room cast a watery light on the green floor and made the porcelain urinals shine like slices of moon. The semi-opacity of this window gave the room's air of secrecy great density. William washed his hands with exaggerated care, enjoying the lavish amount of powdered soap provided for him in this castle. He studied his face in the mirror, making infinitesimal adjustments to attain the absolutely most flattering angle, and then put his hands below his throat to get their strong, long-fingered beauty into the picture. As he walked toward the door he sang, closing his eyes and gasping as if he were a real Negro whose entire career depended upon this recording:

Who—told me so, dilly dilly,
Who told me soho?
Aii *told myself, dilly dilly,*
I told: me so.

When he emerged into the hall it was not empty; one girl walked down its varnished perspective toward him, Mary Landis, a scarf on her head and books in her arms. Her locker was up here, on the second floor of the annex. His own was in the annex basement. A tickling sensation that existed neither in the medium of sound nor of light crowded against his throat. She flipped the scarf back from her hair and in a conversational voice that carried well down the clean planes of the hall said, "Hi, Billy." The name came from way back, when they were both children, and made him feel small but brave.

"Hi. How are you?"

"Fine." Her smile broadened out from the *F* of this word.

What was so funny? Was she really, as it seemed, pleased to see him? "Du-did you just get through cheer-cheer-cheer-leading?"

"Yes. Thank God. *Oh* she's so awful. She makes us do the same stupid locomotives for every cheer; I told her, no wonder nobody cheers any more."

"This is M-M-Miss Potter?" He blushed, feeling that he made an ugly face in getting past the *M*. When he got caught in the middle of a sentence the constriction was somehow worse. He admired the way words poured up her throat, distinct and petulant.

"Yes, Potbottom Potter," she said, "she's just aching for a man and takes it out on us. I wish she would get one. Honestly, Billy, I have half a mind to quit. I'll be so glad when June comes, I'll never set foot in this idiotic building again."

Her lips, pale with the lipstick worn off, crinkled bitterly. Her face, foreshortened from the height of his eyes, looked cross as a cat's. It a little shocked him that poor Miss Potter and this kind, warm school stirred her to what he had to take as actual anger; this grittiness in her was the first abrasive texture he had struck today. Couldn't she see around teachers, into their fatigue, their poverty, their fear? It had been so long since he had spoken to her, he wasn't sure how coarse she had become. "Don't quit," he brought out of his mouth at last. "It'd be n-n-n-nuh—it'd be nothing without you."

He pushed open the door at the end of the hall for her and as she passed under his arm she looked up and said, "Why, aren't you sweet?"

The stairwell, all asphalt and iron, smelled of galoshes. It felt more secret than the hall, more specially theirs; there was something magical in its shifting multiplicity of planes as they descended that lifted the spell on his tongue, so that words came as quickly as his feet pattered on the steps.

"No I mean it," he said, "you're really a beautiful cheer-leader. But then you're beautiful period."

"I've skinny legs."

"Who told you that?"

"Somebody."

"Well *he* wasn't very sweet."

"No."

"Why do you hate this poor old school?"

"Now Billy. You know you don't care about this junky place any more than I do."

"I love it. It breaks my heart to hear you say you want to get out, because then I'll never see you again."

"You don't care, do you?"

"Why sure I care; you *know*"—their feet stopped; they had reached bottom, the first-floor landing, two brass-barred doors and a grimy radiator—"I've always li-loved you."

"You don't mean that."

"I do too. It's ridiculous but there it is. I wanted to tell you today and now I have."

He expected her to laugh and go out the door, but instead she showed an unforeseeable willingness to discuss this awkward matter. He should have realized before this that women enjoy being talked to. "It's a very silly thing to say," she asserted tentatively.

"I don't see why," he said, fairly bold now that he couldn't seem more ridiculous, and yet picking his words with a certain strategic care. "It's not *that* silly to love somebody, I mean what the hell. Probably what's silly is not to do anything about it for umpteen years but then I never had an opportunity, I thought."

He set his books down on the radiator and she set hers down beside his. "What kind of opportunity were you waiting for?"

"Well, see, that's it; I didn't know." He wished, in a way, she would go out the door. But she had propped herself against the wall and plainly awaited more talking. "Yuh-you were such a queen and I was such a nothing and I just didn't really want to presume." It wasn't very interesting; it puzzled him that she seemed to be interested. Her face had grown quite stern, the mouth very small and thoughtful, and he made a gesture with his hands intended to release her from the bother of thinking about it; after all, it was just a disposition of his heart, nothing permanent or expensive; perhaps it was just his mother's idea anyway. Half in impatience to close the account, he asked, "Will you marry me?"

"You don't want to marry me," she said. "You're going to go on and be a great man."

He blushed in pleasure; is this how she saw him, is this how they all saw him; as worthless now, but in time a great man? Had his hopes always been on view? He dissembled, saying, "No I'm not. But anyway, you're great now. You're so pretty, Mary."

"Oh, Billy," she said, "if you were me for just one day you'd hate it."

She said this rather blankly, watching his eyes; he wished her voice had shown more misery. In his world of closed surfaces a panel, carelessly pushed, had opened, and he hung in this openness paralyzed, unable to think what to say. Nothing he could think of quite fit the abruptly immense context. The radiator cleared its throat; its heat made, in the intimate volume just this side of the doors on whose windows the snow beat limply, a provocative snugness; he supposed he should try, and stepped forward, his hands lifting toward her shoulders. Mary sidestepped between him and the radiator and put the scarf back on. She lifted the cloth like a broad plaid halo above her head and then wrapped it around her chin and knotted it so she looked, in her red galoshes and bulky coat, like a peasant woman in a movie of Europe. With her thick hair swathed, her face seemed pale and chunky, and when she recradled the books in her arms her back bent humbly under the point of the kerchief. "It's too hot in here," she said. "I've got to wait for somebody." The disconnectedness of the two statements seemed natural in the fragmented atmosphere his stops and starts had produced. She bucked the brass bar with her shoulder and the door slammed open; he followed her into the weather.

"For the person who thinks your legs are too skinny?"

"Uh-huh." As she looked up at him a snowflake caught on the lashes of one eye. She jerkily rubbed that cheek on the shoulder of her coat and stamped a foot, splashing slush. Cold water gathered on the back of his thin shirt. He put his hands in his pockets and pressed his arms against his sides to keep from shivering.

"Thuh-then you wo-won't marry me?" His wise instinct told him the only way back was by going forward, through absurdity.

"We don't know each other," she said.

"My God," he said. "Why not? I've known you since I was two."

"What do you know about me?"

This awful seriousness of hers; he must dissolve it. "That you're not a virgin." But instead of making her laugh this made her face go dead and turned it away. Like beginning to kiss her, it was a mistake; in part, he felt grateful for his mistakes. They were like loyal friends who are nevertheless embarrassing. "What do you know about *me*?" he asked, setting himself up for a finishing insult but dreading it. He hated the stiff feel of his smile between his cheeks; glimpsed, as if the snow were a mirror, how hateful he looked.

"That you're basically very nice."

Her returning good for evil blinded him to his physical discomfort, set him burning with regret. "Listen," he said, "I did love you. Let's at least get that straight."

"You never loved anybody," she said. "You don't know what it is."

"O.K." he said. "Pardon me."

"You're excused."

"You better wait in the school," he told her. "He's-eez-eez going to be a long time."

She didn't answer and walked a little distance, toeing out in the childish Dutch way common to the women in this county, along the slack cable that divided the parking lot from the softball field. One bicycle, rusted as if it had been there for years, leaned in the rack, its fenders supporting airy crescents of white.

The warmth inside the door felt heavy. William picked up his books and ran his pencil along the black ribs of the radiator before going down the stairs to his locker in the annex basement. The shadows were thick at the foot of the steps; suddenly it felt late, he must hurry and get home. He was seized by the irrational fear that they were going to lock him in. The cloistered odors of paper, sweat, and, from the woodshop at the far end of the basement hall, sawdust no longer flattered him. The tall green double lockers appeared to study him critically through the three air slits near their tops. When he opened his locker, and put his books on his shelf, below Marvin Wolf's, and removed his coat from his hook, his self seemed to crawl into the long dark space thus made vacant, the humiliated ugly, educable self. In answer to a flick of his great hand the steel door weightlessly floated shut and through the length of his body he felt so clean and free he smiled. Between now and the happy future predicted for him he had nothing, almost literally nothing, to do.

Jeremy Larner
1937-

Jeremy Larner lives in Los Angeles, where he writes articles of contemporary concern as well as fiction. He was educated at Brandeis and the University of California at Berkeley, and his novel *Drive, He Said* won the Delta Prize in 1964. "Oh, the Wonder" is the bright, sad, insightful story of a young graduate student, an ex-amateur boxer, who feels the heavy social and academic pressures of his generation. Much of the story's beauty comes from Larner's ability to show Willie and his girl Sarah from more than one point of view; for instance, Willie as he sees himself, and Willie as Sarah sees him. These awarenesses are increasing, so the characters can come to their own realizations; through what they feel, the reader, without having to "choose sides," can also feel, and this adds greatly to the power of the work. A second story about Willie appeared in the October 1968 issue of *Harper's*.

OH, THE WONDER!

I

On a warm evening in May, Willie McBain telephoned his friend Lickens, who lived not far away on the Lower East Side of New York City.

"For me the worst time is after supper," he told Lickens. "It gets worse every minute. I try to keep from sleeping so I won't dream. I make sure that even if I do fall out I've got the lights and the radio on."

"But just what is it?" Lickens wanted to know.

"That's it, that's it: I don't know. Nothing! I'm going out of my box!"

"Afraid of getting married?"

"Of course! I'm afraid of everything. Oh the wonder of it, Lickens! Oh the wonder of it all. Life is unbearable. How can you be alive without going out of your box?"

"There are ways," Lickens said.

"Not with my stomach. I can't keep anything inside me, Lickens. I vomit before dinner and I vomit after dinner. I'm even afraid to go to the docaroony."

"Then that's what you're afraid of."

"Sure! But the reason I'm afraid is that if I keep talking to him I might really find out what I'm afraid of."

"So you're not only afraid, you're afraid of finding out what you're afraid of?"

"Oh the wonder of it all!"

"Me, too." Lickens sighed.

"Lickens!"

"Um?"

"Come over here and go me sock for sock!"

Lickens demurred. His arms had not yet recovered from the last time. He suggested they go for a beer.

"Can't," said Willie. "I've got to work."

"But you won't work. You know that. Take a break and then maybe things will be better."

"Then maybe things will be tomorrow, that's all! But why not? No, fuck it, Lickens, this has got to be done tonight, so get thee the hell away from me. I've got to hang up."

"Good luck."

Willie McBain was a graduate student in Philosophy at Columbia University. He had set aside that night—just as he had set aside the eleven nights previous—to finish a paper that had been due in January. Within a week his extensions would be up on two more papers from the Fall semester, and he had not even begun research on one of them. When those were finished, he would have three fun-packed weeks in which to write his Master's paper and pass his language examinations. He complied with the mickeymouse because he wanted to teach; he thought he had a new way of teaching. Willie wanted to account for man's unpleasant psychology in philosophic terms. Specifically, he was impressed by the problem of aggression. From all that he felt and saw, he knew that to live was to hurt oneself. Could the pattern be undone? Could men come to know the score and do what they could for themselves? Or were his thoughts merely personal? These were the questions he would make his students answer, the very questions that had been neatly avoided by the spinners of spiritual and political systems. Because they were afraid: it's always so much easier to write things out neatly when you don't have to care how they really are. Willie was going to make them see. He would hunt them down remorselessly, cutting off every avenue of transcendental escape. He didn't have the answers, he knew; but he could make a start by insisting on the real questions.

But sooner or later he would have to write a book, and for the moment Willie McBain could not even manage to read a book. He would plot his time and settle carefully in the rubble of his railroad flat, only to find himself staring for hours at a single page. He could concentrate for a paragraph or two, then twenty minutes would disappear and he would come back to himself with a start, furious, without the slightest idea where he had been. The psychiatrist agreed that it was more than a matter of willpower. But still it made Willie angry. No matter what the doctor said, sooner or later he had to control himself, that was what it boiled down to, or else they might as well start padding the walls and removing sharp objects.

He pawed for the phone, and called Philadelphia where his fiancee was finishing her last year at college.

"I can't work," he told her. "I'm like that machine that turns itself off. Why don't you go out and find someone worthwhile?"

"Because I've got someone," she said. "Someone who turns *me* on. Willie, if you could only relax for a while. It doesn't make any difference if you can't do what you want right this minute. You'll do your work when you're really and truly ready, and tearing at yourself won't help."

"Sure I'll do my work! What if I don't? There's no law says I will. What's the difference between me and thousands of pretentious half-wits in this city who gas about what they are going to do some day?"

"There is a difference; I can't prove it to you but there is. I know it and so does everyone who ever met you."

Willie laughed. "Don't be a goddam girl-friend!"

She didn't answer. "What's the matter?" he said. "Are you hurt?"

"I guess so," she said. "I'm sorry."

"Look," he said. "I'm going to flunk out of school. I'll be drafted and you'll never see me again."

"I wouldn't like that. I'd go to the Army and make them give you back."

"What are you doing?" he asked her. "Get anything done tonight?"

She giggled. "Oh, I'm supposed to be studying for my Sosh finals tomorrow. But I think I know the material pretty well—I've just been sitting up talking with Francine . . ."

"Francine! That flaccid ass!"

"Shhhhhhhhh."

"Don't shhh me! I thought you promised not to see her anymore."

"I didn't promise."

"Oh, I get it, you just let me *think* you promised!"

"I can't talk about it now."

"Why not, 'cause she'll hear? Screw that! Who's more important to you anyway, me or her! Are you going to waste your whole life on namby-pamby gushing fawning half-wits? People who might challenge you you avoid like the plague! What's going to become of you, goddammit?"

He was nearly out of his box with rage. He shouted at her until she cried. When it was over he felt worse than ever. She promised to send Francine away and go back to studying, and he said, choking, that if it didn't really matter what she did. He said if only he had her in his bed right that very instant—that was all that could make any difference. When he hung up he took a dish and slammed it against the wall.

Sarah was really not the girl for him. Perhaps he only loved her because she loved him. She was so utterly dependent on him, couldn't make a move without him, no plans, no ambitions, no nothing of her own . . . She wanted to be pregnant: he had to make damn sure every time that she got her diaphragm in. The ready-made identity! She would marry him and attach her life to his like a leech. But wasn't that what a woman was supposed to do? Was it wrong for a bright young girl to think of nothing but babies? Or was he so far out of his box he couldn't see straight?

But how would she become a person? Sarah wanted to think their life together was a lovely-dovey-ducky-wucky dreamaroony, and that wasn't what life was like! Life was too goddam unbearable, you had to be ready to fight! He, at least, had the guts to go to the doctor.

He paced the room thinking of his prize-fighting days. Maybe he should have turned pro. The new light-heavy-weight champ was a punk. Willie had a theory about how he could be set up. He cracked his fists into the porcelain of the fridgaroony, feeling it dent and spring out again. Neighbors pounded on the thin wall, loosening bits of plaster, and Willie pounded back, pound for pound, till the ceiling shook and he heard crashes on the other side.

He heard someone running down the stairs. Maybe the cops would come. Willie had never quite hit a cop. He coveted that pleasure: to sink a fist in one's massive blue frontage. He didn't care if they killed him.

He sat on the bed to watch a movie he had started in his mind. He was putting the slug to one cop after another while they pumped bullets into him and the whole block poured out to watch in love and fascination. Everyone loved him, he knew it—no matter if he brought the roach-infested house down. Even Sarah, whose teary face in the movie gave him a laugh. No babies now. No comfy for Sarah. Bitterly he thought how she would be the only one to miss the splendour of his gesture. She would feel cheated, and even think him foolish.

The hell with her, he would be dead. He laughed out loud and shook his head. He couldn't understand why when he was depressed he thought so little of dying. Normally the fear of death overtook him in every happiness, ran him down like a wolfhound. He was pondering this when the phone rang . . .

Ten minutes later he phoned Lickens.

"Luscious Louise called," he reported.

"Um," said Lickens.

"She wants me to come over. She's lonely. She wants me to talk to her. Let's be friends, she says."

"You going?"

"I shouldn't. But I was thinking what the hell I can't work anyway, maybe after this I'll come back, take a benny, stay up all night and it will be all out of my system, see?"

"So why call me?"

"You're supposed to talk me out of it."

"That's not fair. . . . But if you want, I'll go in your place."

"No," answered Willie, still sad, though the fact was that Lickens' offer had clinched it for him. "I'm going. Trouble is, I've got this itch in the old groinaroony . . ."

". . . and when Ah itches, Ah scratches!" Lickens drawled.

Luscious Louise made it difficult for about half an hour. She really did want to talk. She didn't know what to do with herself. She was too bright; she was tired of being a secretary. She had this idea that she would go to law school and she wanted Willie McBain to love her for it. Willie knew what her trouble was.

"I know what your trouble is," he said. "You want a penis. But you can't get one by going to law school. The only way is to use mine while you have a chance."

She tried to get on her high horse, but he wouldn't let her. He knew she wanted to.

"You know you want to," Willie said.

She sighed.

Making love to Louise was like riding the white horse in the circus. Where was she taking him, slick nervous antelope with such strange interior muscles?! She could play a tune on him like a piccolo. Sarah was tamer and didn't shriek so much—well, why should she? He loved her, she knew it . . . he wasn't even thinking of Luscious Louise except when she . . . wow! . . . she was going out of her box . . . he had never . . . now why couldn't Sarah be more like

this!

?

When she saw it was all up with him she snuggled close and closed her eyes in contentment. But Willie lay with his fists clenched and teeth jammed together like nails. He couldn't stand it; he wanted to get up and rush out on the fire escape and throw himself over. If he relaxed a single muscle he would plunge headfirst down the brickface wall and crunch powerfully through the sidewalk miles deep beneath the candy store.

Louise was clutching at his arms. "Willie, Willie-baby . . ."

"Let me go!"

He stood facing her, pathetic in his undershirt, his back against the wall while she made absurd calming motions.

"Get out of bed and I'll slam you one!"

She lay where she was. As he pulled on his clothes he heard her sniffling. Only when he was safely down in the street and running did he realize he had been tearing his hair and ears.

He ran six blocks down Avenue B and thumped three-at-a-time up the wooden steps of Lickens' tenement.

He knocked and from within heard the sounds of Lickens grumbling and rolling out of bed. Then the striking of a match.

"You!" said Lickens. "G'morning, silly bastard!"

Willie saw that Lickens' eyes were not quite open.

"Now Lickens, sorry to wake you, man, just get back in bed, fall out, land of nod, forget and forgive, Lickens, that's it, easy there . . ."

"Peckerhead!" Lickens mumbled, as Willie eased him back onto his mattress. The keys were on the night table where Willie could palm them without any trouble. He stood for a while watching Lickens drop back to sleep and right next to him Lickens' beautiful wife sleeping in a band of moonlight, her face calm and womanly, her long hair strewn lightly on the pillow. Her features were more relaxed than in her waking hours. And her mouth closed. He bent close to admire her full lips and long dark lashes. She breathed sweetly as a doe. And look at Lickens lying there, snorting and twisting! What a jackass to be thumping himself around so and sticking his silly head under the pillow! Lickens didn't have any problems. His only problem was he thought he had problems. Lucky Lickens!

But no luckier than he, Willie McBain, might be! He had no debts, no job, no cancer. Nothing to lose but worry and time.

The junkpiley Lickensmobile sat right around the corner. Willie unlocked it, started it up and set off for Philadelphia.

He bit his nails at eighty miles an hour down the New Jersey turnpike. He didn't know it, but he was worried that he would arrive to find Sarah gone. Hung around his mind like an albatross was a picture of her with Roger Stennis. Stennis was the most respected student in Sarah's graduating class—an alert young man with quick lips and clean eyes. Stennis was going to be an historian, and one of the best: he had won a fellowship to Oxford and Willie was certain that Roger would like nothing better than to take Willie's Sarah along with him. And it was logical—why shouldn't she go? Wouldn't a cottage on the green and a well-bordered life and a creative, productive, attentive husband be far, far preferable to a stinking slum-hole in New York and a hung-up, hateful husband off screwing with Luscious Louise and even when with her flailing and cursing, climbing up by tearing her down, desperately clutching and snapping at every weakness in sight in his last-ditch efforts to punish the world for his own shortcomings? A sweet, bright girl like her, so long abused? She should have been long gone already. Without seeing it he saw in his mind a bed with Sarah and Roger Stennis well-sheeted together.

He would never forget what had happened when he took off on his canoe trip the summer before. On principle he had insisted that Sarah not refuse dates with other men, but when she wrote him she had gone out with Roger Stennis he nearly went out of his box. Stennis had been in love with her a long time—no doubt about that. Sure, going out he didn't mind, but Stennis was a betrayal! He would kill the bastard. He would blast his head open with a hard right.

There was blood in his mouth from where he had chewed into his cheek. Glancing at his gas gauge, he saw the needle stuck on empty, and, dressed hurriedly as he was in workshirt and jeans, his rummagings produced a mere quarter. His headlights picked up a sign announcing a rest stop. He had to think of something. Fifteen minutes later he found himself sitting over an empty coffee cup in a Howard Johnson's. He tried to remember the waitress bringing him the coffee: had she been friendly? Perhaps he had gotten it himself. He was sitting alone at a little table, and the only other people in the place were a clutch of fifteen-sixteen-year-old boys at the counter.

Damned if they weren't giggling!

They were staring at him and trying to puzzle him out and giggling because they had never seen anything like him in their part of New Jersey.

Willie glared back with a vicious eyeblast intensity utterly unequal to their intentions and sending them into gales of laughter.

Willie's standing silenced them, until a brave one voiced the single word they knew for him: "Hey Mister, you a beatnik or sompin!"

Willie said, "No, are you?" A volcano of giggles.

"What's your name?" Willie said. "You!"

The boy was stumped for a second. "Puddentane!" he said triumphantly, and put his comrades in convulsions.

"Well look, Puddentane, you look like a beatnik to me, with all that acne and that grease on your hair. How about it?"

"I'm just a normal American boy," Puddentane replied. The laughter this time was uneasy; the boys poked each other, shifted, whispered.

"What do normal American boys do with themselves, Puddentane?

Hang around Howard Johnson's all night and stare at customers?"

"If we feel like it," said Puddentane. "We're not big-time like you."

"Don't you masturbate?"

The boys giggled in shock and broke out in very loud laughter and finally hoots. "Oh, brother!" said Puddentane. "You *are* a weird one!"

"It's weird to talk about sex, isn't it? You normal American boys don't like it, do you? It embarrasses you, huh?"

"Oh sure," someone said. No one was laughing.

"If it doesn't embarrass you, why are you turning red, Puddentane?"

Puddentane didn't know why he was turning red, but he did know, at last, that he had hated Willie's guts the moment he saw him. The boys shrunk back like snakes, their eyes fixed on Willie.

"Why don't you go back to Russia?" one of them inquired.

"You want to fight?" said Willie instantly.

He caught them unprepared. The five of them working together could have taken him, but separately they couldn't decide. Time out for consultation.

"I'll leave you normal American boys to your circle-jerk." Willie took his departure.

As he went out the door, he heard behind him the shout, "Goodbye, beatnik!"—and then a chorus of shouts: "Goodbye, Communist, Goodbye, orangoutang, Goodbye, pigpen!" The five trailed behind as he walked toward the Lickensmobile and came close as he started it, shouting, jeering, thumping on the fenders and windows.

A mile later Willie remembered his gas gauge. Since traffic was light he was able to back carefully up the turnpike till he reached the Howard Johnson's again. There was a souped-up Ford in back which obviously belonged to the blackhead set. Willie took Lickens' always-ready rubber tube from the back seat and siphoned off the gasoline from the jutting Fordaroony into the thirsty tank of the Lickensmobile. As he was finishing the boys came out and spotted him. The Ford gave hot pursuit and undoubtedly would have caught him had it not run out of gas in three minutes.

But Willie had forgotten his new-found enemies in two minutes. He was remembering Sarah: "Roger? Why, he's only a *boy!*"

"Did you kiss him?" he had asked.

"Yes," she had said, flaring up. "I think so. So what?" I *think so? So what!* How had he put up with her solid brass evasiveness? He was eating on his tongue. It was obvious she was gone; he knew it now. He was driving full speed ahead into a tunnel that receded as fast as he came. But if he could encounter anything at all in the tunnel he would destroy it, or destroy himself trying.

He swung into Philadelphia and drove straight to the apartment where Sarah lived with her roommate, charged up the stairs and knocked three hard knocks at the door. In a matter of seconds he expected to be back in the Lickensmobile, racing for every last inch of justice he could extract. There was no answer to his knock. But he had forgotten that it was six o'clock in the morning. He had stormed down two landings when he heard the door open; he rushed back up and there was the anxious, bewildered, asleep face of his Sarah peering out from behind the door. There was no question of her not being there; it did not even occur to him. They sat in the kitchen having breakfast, she delighted and asleep, he at last relaxed. He had not remembered the depth or the sureness of her brown eyes, the charming rumple of her cotton bathrobe, her little breasts peeping out at him like baby birds. Relaxed: the new sun rippled on the kitchen wall, toilets flushed, radios came on. The dread night had vanished and Willie might curl the warm day around him and sleep.

Sarah tucked him into her bed all odorous of woman and he tumbled down a well, his thoughts behind him. He was up by noon, before she got back from her last final exam, in time to shower and wash all the Lusciousness of Louise from his stomach, chest and groin. Sarah's roommate was up and made bacon-lettuce-and-tomato sandwiches smothered in mayonnaise and rye bread (because she loved Willie, too, naturally—it was a problem). Willie ate two huge BLT's, laughed, joked, drank his beer, pinched Sarah's ass and the roommate's too. After lunch he went into Sarah's room and into bed with Sarah, quickly, voraciously, because the instant he was through Willie jumped up and sat down at the typewriter and from memory resumed his paper at the point where he had left off and finished it without even stopping to hesitate. There was no doubt in his mind, nor of anything else at the moment. If he did not go out of his box at an early age, he was going to be quite a man.

In only an hour he was through, and out of steam anyway, and collapsed back in bed with Sarah, where for a full five minutes he watched her sweet, spirited eyes dart back and forth along the book she was reading. Then his watching was too much for her and she turned to him. Until suppertime they stuck close, each to the other's skin, and talked about what they would make of their life together. Willie stretched out as he talked, and watched the afternoon sun come bouncing off the upturned venetian blinds and sparkle slowly across the ceiling.

More than anything, Sarah wanted to be his and to bear his children. But she had decided to take a degree in Social Psychology; for she had to be a person in her own right, and this meant having work of her own to last her whole life long and keep her from bringing to her children that desperate clutch which her own mother even now could not relax. Willie nodded, basked in her completeness. There was nothing unbeautiful in her, she fitted together in every part and thought: when he was not out of his box he saw this truly and wondered at his incredible luck in having her. What had he done, he whispered, caressing her trim thigh, interrupting her, to deserve someone so perfect? Just being you, she answered to his most private ear, pulling him close and delighting him with a gesture they had never before dared or even imagined.

Their final plans, as the light wobbled orange on the ceiling: in the morning they would drive to New York, take out a license and get married by a justice of the peace. Or why get married at all? he wondered idly—but she shyly confessed it meant something to her, she still had that much of the middle class in her. Or maybe it really wasn't that at all, she insisted, growing more confident, but simply that she wanted to feel him hers, the full weight of their promise to each other. Promise? Willie laughed, but he was flattered, pleased, touched . . . She thought him capable of keeping a promise!

Even so her parents would be shocked, but never mind . . . they would get over it, and she would never in all eternity get over him. Her parents would say how can you live? But what did they know about living? Willie and Sarah would live all right, just watch them.

They did not need the things their parents had needed. They would be too alive for the buying-earning routine through which they were expected to stumble and excuse their lives away. They had no use for empty job-working. They would live simply in an old barn in the country, changing it over with the love of their own hands, making it belong to them and the pulsing life they would bring to it. Life was possible, really possible, for those who had the gift of loving.

II

Willie came back to himself like an object sucking into a vacuum. Without warning, the room was dark. Night had pushed the sun down out of the sky and crept over the land looking for Willie. It got worse every minute, as it had the day before and the day before that, as it did on days when he loved and days when he was removed from his love. Sarah was sleeping nestled in his shoulder; he looked at her, felt of her . . . and could not stand her breathing there. He stroked her hair, trying, trying—he thrust her roughly away. He did not wake her. She looked like a goddam child. What had she ever done in her life to make him believe she could be a woman? He couldn't have a woman, not him, not yet: he was too weak and too young. They made an absurd spectacle, Sarah and he—two overgrown babies hugging each other and playing big people in a dream world. Disgusting! She was so soft he could hardly fuck her. Why did he need this? His moment with Luscious Louise seemed infinitely more honest.

It was getting worse and he couldn't face it. Headlights shot into the room and raced across the ceiling. He lay petrified. He wanted to sleep, to conk out and stay out—but he was afraid of his dreams. His fists clamped tight to his groin, he tried grimly to focus on the hayloft in that mythical barn, where he would have rigged a punching-bag. Of course there would be no barn. No morning, either, nothing but a grubby, scroungy life of night after night. The doctor couldn't cure him—what nonsense for her to count on that! There was nothing to cure him of, his sickness was life. He was not out of his box; it was just that he could not fool himself. He was not a woman, he could not lie all warm and smelly and dream of babies and houses: the night was there and he saw it, and there was nothing he or anyone could do about it.

If he could not sleep he had to act, to move. Or else it would all be up. He must rise now and turn on the lights and the radio. Get up, get out of bed, turn on lights and radio. He strained against his body until he broke out in a violent sweat. Lying paralyzed and unblinking in the soaking sheets he saw himself pulled as if by a magnet, sucked to the window and through the slats of the venetian blinds, through the shivered glass and through the crusted streets like so many sheets of paper, cutting clean as a knife-blade into the grave.

He rose at last, lurching heavily, a landlubber coming on deck in a hurricane and stumbling for the rail . . . arms stiff as boards, he snapped on the lights, snapped on the radio.

Got to the bathroom as his insides came rushing out, and lay with his head in the toilet-bowl while his lungs and stomach heaved in dry spasms. He was dying, surely dying, oh merciful God, just let it be quick, he prayed to himself. Later he knew that Sarah must have woken up; she clung to his back, soothing him, still asleep and moaning for his hurt. With a twitch of his shoulders he shrugged her away, so that she banged her head on the sink and cried like a little girl. He threw up again, this time with relief; lay weak with his head in the toilet, purged, subsiding; and he loved her and everyone with all his heart, mixing his own happy tears with the vomit.

They went out to eat—showered, dressed up, holding hands and feeling large and good as an opera. It should have worked. The restaurant was something special: linen napkins, silver three-foot menus, two kinds of waiters, and so many plates there was no room for your elbows. Maybe it was too much for them. They ate extremely well, but there was nothing to say. Sarah simply sat there. Willie made a few remarks on his work, then hers, and she made routine answers, but she had nothing to say, nothing to start on her own. She was nervous and did not want to talk at all, just sit there and enjoy being with him. He saw she felt only for him; it was he who had to begin any thought that might connect them to the outside world, to life. She was competent to follow; it was up to him to begin and she would follow wherever he led. Willie saw more clearly than ever that his love for Sarah could bring him into no new relations with the world. Hardly! Difficult as it was to keep himself alive he would henceforth be expected to pull for two.

He sat on the back of his neck with his meat and potatoes, bread and tomatoes bombing him to his chair, while the chair itself sank slowly to the bottom of the ocean. As the depths closed over him he saw her smile, waveringly. Oh the tentativity of her; she could scarcely keep herself afloat! Her hand drifted toward him apologetically. Hardly daring to touch, she walked her fingers on the back of his hand.

"You have nothing to say for yourself, do you?"

She was hurt. "Am I on trial?"

He belched. "Oh what the hell!" he said.

"Look, it's been a long day," she said, biting her lip. If only she would lose her temper!

"And a hard day?" he needled hopefully.

"A hard day but a very good day," she said quietly. "Willie, I'm so tired. Please don't be hard on me."

He couldn't even bring himself to look at her. "I'm not being *hard* on you," he muttered. He ordered a globular heap of ice creams, which impacted themselves together about halfway down.

They walked down one of the streets bordering campus, where all the little stores were still open and brightly lit. Neat pressed suits could be had, and notebooks. He shoveled through a used-book stack while she looked on absently, as though all books were alike to her. He walked her rapidly down the street to one of the movie-houses. They were playing a sophisticated comedy with titillating risqué dialogue, the kind of picture he would see only in an emergency. He stopped with her in front of the posters.

"Well?" he said. She smiled, ready to go either way. "Do you want to see it?"

"If you do, Willie."

"The hell with whether I do! You're a person! This is a movie—either you want to see it, deep down *here* (poking her), or you don't. But don't do it just for me, baby—don't let yourself get away with that!"

She stuck her lip out and walked away. He ran after her, grabbed her roughly.

"No, goddammit! I'm not going to let you be hurt. That's too easy, Sarah. I just want to know a simple thing: do you or don't you want to see the movie? It's only a decision, baby, it's got nothing to do with me. You just say yes or no and it's all over."

She tried to jerk away, hatefully, but he held her fast. "You absolute bastard!" she cried. She began to weep. Willie relaxed. She was his small, tender girl, and he wanted only to love her and soothe her hurt. While he held her and caressed her she blubbered that she didn't know, didn't care about the movie—she knew he was nervous and would be happy doing anything that helped him relax, that's all, because she loved him. She didn't think of going to a harmless movie as a decision, she wasn't thinking of wasting her valuable time or building her valuable life. She was with him, and did it make much difference what they did?

Okay, okay, he said. Please don't cry. Here: he kissed away a tear. She cried happily now, with her head sniffling on his chest. People were looking. I feel so foolish, she said, standing like this in the middle of the sidewalk.

They walked on; he couldn't blame her. It was his twisted-up way of seeing things. But he had nothing left to say to her. Had they really said all they ever had to say in one afternoon? They walked on in silence past the little shops and the dressy college people, and Willie wanted desperately to be alone.

He felt like dashing up the street and around the corner. Just standing by himself in his own body would be so free and fine. No little one to tow along beside him. Just to be himself in his own skin, smelling the night air and doing whatever, moving wherever, his desires took him. Himself alone.

But that was not to be. They met some friends of Sarah's on the street and had to stand babbling. Willie said little—the people were schmucks as far as he was concerned. He watched Sarah; she was giggling of all things, like a teenager. That was because the people had joked about marriage, and she didn't know what to say: she was giggling and looking up at him. He scowled and saw her eyes fill up with hurt. The inquiring young man & woman, when they got no reply from Sarah and no attention from Willie, smiled as if to shrug, and moved on.

"Maybe next week!" he called after them, like a fool.

Once more in a pinch she had lapsed into girlishness and made him look the brute.

"I only want you to respect yourself," he said.

She turned in anger—"Must you *watch* me like that!"—but the anger soon faded into a kind of bewilderment that was exasperating but really, when he thought about it, did her credit. She knew what he meant, why he was forced to watch. She was not by any means dead or done.

She took his arm.

"I'm sorry," she said. "I don't know what gets into me. My poor Willie, you certainly have a lot to put up with . . ."

But it was too late, Roger Stennis was upon them, looking five years older, bolstered by two grinning sycophants, handsome as the devil and dressed like the Duke of Wales. "Sarah!" he announced, in his bulletin-board baritone. He shook Willie's hand with a single pump, European style. He introduced his entourage, who followed suit.

"Well, old man!" Roger said.

"Well, old man!" mocked Willie.

Roger took the mockery fondly. Good old basically lovable, irascible Willie. We know you.

"How are things down at Columbia? Department all right?"

Okay, Willie guessed.

"Be through in another year, I suppose?"

"Through?"

"Phd, I mean. The old union card."

"Well, I don't know," Willie said, though he knew very well and the answer was no. "Three years would be a pretty short trip."

But it seemed that Roger would have it in three. After his year at Oxford on the Fulbright, he would enter the new three-year program at Harvard. He had an understanding with the department there.

"Nice," Willie said.

"Yes, but it's just the externals," Roger confessed.

"What really matters is what you do with it."

"Yes."

There was a difficult pause, as though Roger had inquired what Willie had done with his two years since college, and Willie had not been able to answer. But Roger didn't have to ask. Willie would have been almost brilliant, if he were not so hopelessly hungup . . .

They all shook hands again.

"I envy you Paris," said Willie, honestly. What he might not learn in Paris!

"I envy you something more than Paris, Willie." Roger smiled down at Sarah, the sad, knowing smile of one who has loved well and lost, but lost only after the loving was finished and he had moved on to better things. Dear old Sarah, his smile was saying, how I hope you'll be happy. I'm really quite fond of you, you know.

And Sarah, to Willie's horror, was blushing, grinning like a little half-wit, nestling into his lapels!

Roger shook Willie's hand one more time. "Good luck, old man . . . the best." He meant it, too, really meant it, and Willie liked him, always had, for at least a full second.

"Oh the wonder of it all!" Willie mumbled inanely, then swung with all his might, smashing Roger Stennis right in the smile, knocking him off his feet and dribbling blood into his costly tie.

Sarah clung petrified to his right arm as he stood with fists clenched, waiting for Stennis to rise so he could knock him down again. But Stennis was in no hurry to rise. His friends dragged him away, heels trailing,

Stennis holding a folded handkerchief to his lips and shaking his head groggily at the madness of Willie McBain, who watched after him ferocious, fists cocked, rigid and trembling in rage.

Willie and Sarah went home weeping and ashamed, and might have been good to one another had it not been for the cops waiting at the door. It seemed that the maniac Lickens had reported the Lickensmobile stolen, and suggested that the police might inquire for the thief in Philadelphia. Was this his idea of a joke? As Willie was led off furious between two brass bellies he thought for a moment of burying his elbows one to a pot and making a break for it. Alone at last! But why die? Life was awful but he was damned if he would give them the satisfaction.

Betrayed twice over, he stewed two hours in a jail cell before the stately Lickens phoned to confirm his identity. He was thinking mostly of Sarah by that time, and his thoughts swung round and round on a well-worn track. He wasn't sorry about Roger Stennis—why should he be? That had been his first clean act in months. No, it was Sarah—there was something wrong, deeper than tears could plumb, and this time he meant to have it out with her.

When he got back she was in her room with the lights out. She was still as stone but he could tell by her breathing she was not asleep. All the better. He snapped on the light and saw her stare back dry-eyed and cold, not moving a muscle.

"You're a coward," he said.

No answer.

"Well? Have anything to say for yourself? Has it been a long day?"

"It's been a miserable day." She was glaring at him as if she'd never seen him before.

"It's always a miserable day when you have to humiliate yourself at every opportunity."

"What do you want from me!" she burst out. "Humiliate! Yes, I was humiliated all right. I've never been so humiliated in my life. I was humiliated by a man who can no more control himself . . . no more . . . who strikes out like a little boy!"

"You mean, who strikes out to protect his so-called woman when she lets herself be turned into a ten-year-old girl, and likes it, revels in it! Is this what I have to expect from you? That every time there's a test you'll snuggle away like a child! Is it? Is it?"

She was crying now and yelling through her tears. "I a child! I a child! Why I felt sorry for that boy, I felt sorry and embarrassed for him! He was trying his hardest to impress you, don't you see, but you thought it was a test. You think everything's a test. You're still back in grade school, taking tests. That's what you want life to be for me, one test after another. Well I can't stand it, you hear? I don't want that kind of life! I want someone I can love and who loves me and who can live with me and be proud of me; yes, and take care of me too. I'm a woman, I'm not your boxing-partner!"

"Boxing-partner?! What does that mean? Shit! What in God's name does that mean? You want someone to be proud? Listen to me! I'll be proud of you when you can be proud of yourself. Take care of you, sure, you telling me I don't take care of you? But as a man takes care of his woman, not as a father his baby girl! I'll respect you when you have something to say for yourself, as one adult to another, when you can stand up and look people in the eye!"

"You mean *punch* people in the eye!"

"I MEAN WHAT I SAY! AND THAT'S ALL! I'M UPSET. I'M UPSET, I'M TERRIFICALLY UPSET AND YOU'RE DISTORTING EVERYTHING I SAY!"

He stepped back. He thought he was through shouting. "It's really very simple," he said. "God, how you upset me . . ."

She sat on the edge of the bed. She had stopped crying, and sat looking at him, eyes narrowed with hate.

"Get out," she said.

He stopped pacing. "What's that?"

"I said get out. I don't love you anymore. I loathe you. You're not a man, you're a bad-tempered little boy. You don't want me as a woman, you want me as a roughneck sidekick to help you bully the other kids on the block."

"Listen," he said. "Some of what you say is right. OK. But what I say is very simple. I want you to be yourself. I want you to be your best. I want you to be proud so I can be proud too, of us. Because I love you. Believe me. I love you."

"You love yourself. You're talking to yourself now, you've got it all worked out. Get out of here. You disgust me." Suddenly she lost control. "I LOATHE YOU I LOATHE YOU I LOATHE YOU," she screamed, and fell weeping hysterically to the floor.

Her hysteria calmed him. He leaned to take her shoulder in his gentle hand and cupping her head smoothe her hair but she screamed GET AWAY FROM ME GET AWAY I LOATHE YOU GET AWAY!

And she twisted from him, squirmed violently, ugly, her face contorted, crawling for the door . . . A red screen came down before his eyes.

"DON'T YOU TALK TO ME THAT WAY!" he yelled. "DON'T YOU DARE, DON'T YOU EVER!" Before he knew he would he hit her, then when he knew hit her again, not out of malice but pure blind rage: clubbed the crawling girl clumsy blows on the head and then to the ribs, knocking her over.

He leaned back against the wall and screamed. She lay on the floor and screamed. She got to her feet, flashed him a look of indomitable hatred, ran to the bathroom and locked herself in.

When next he could speak he bellowed COME OUT OF THERE OR I'LL KNOCK YOUR GODDAM DOOR IN! At which she shouted, vulgar as a whore, FUCK YOU YOU BASTARD GO AWAY I HATE YOU. And he said, choking, "How lovely you are!"

Then, in a little while, he called to her, "Please come out, Sarah. I'm sorry. I do love you, very much. I'm sorry for what I said." He heard no sound but her desperate weeping.

Methodically, in a cold fury, he began to pummel the wall. And even as he smashed one ruined fist after the other weeping and swearing he knew she would love him again, she would forgive him, they would love and be together for the rest of their lives and oh how he would hate her for it.

DATE DUE
